I0824435

The Philosophy of Sherlock Holmes

The Philosophy of SHERLOCK HOLMES

Edited by
Philip Tallon
and
David Baggett

Scholarly publisher for the Commonwealth,
serving Bellarmine University, Berea College, Centre College of Kentucky, Eastern Kentucky University, The Filson Historical Society, Georgetown College, Kentucky Historical Society, Kentucky State University, Morehead State University, Murray State University, Northern Kentucky University, Transylvania University, University of Kentucky, University of Louisville, and Western Kentucky University.

Editorial and Sales Offices: The University Press of Kentucky
663 South Limestone Street, Lexington, Kentucky 40508-4008
www.kentuckypress.com

16 15 14 13 12   5 4 3 2 1

Library of Congress Cataloging-in-Publication Data

The Philosophy of Sherlock Holmes / edited by Philip Tallon and David Baggett.
p. cm.
Includes bibliographical references and index.
ISBN 978-0-8131-3671-4 (hardcover : alk. paper) — ISBN 978-0-8131-3687-5 (pdf) — ISBN 978-0-8131-4056-8 (epub)
1. Doyle, Arthur Conan, Sir, 1859-1930—Characters—Sherlock Holmes. 2. Holmes, Sherlock (Fictitious character) 3. Detective and mystery stories, English—History and criticism. 4. Philosophy in literature. 5. Private investigators in literature. I. Tallon, Philip. II. Baggett, David.
PR4624.P485 2012
823'.8—dc23   2012020842

This book is printed on acid-free paper meeting the requirements of the American National Standard for Permanence in Paper for Printed Library Materials.

Manufactured in the United States of America.

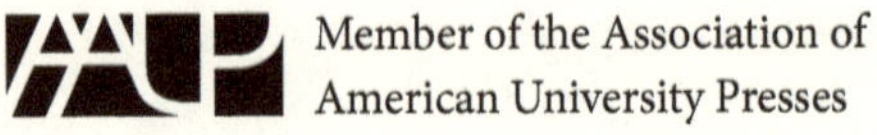

Contents

Introduction

The Case of the Conan Doyle Conference

Philip Tallon and David Baggett

This volume came together at a special Sherlock Holmes colloquium, convened at the University of Bern, near the famous Reichenbach Falls.[1] Despite the fearsome headlines and morbid details popular in the press coverage of the event, it was mostly a delightful and relaxing conference, with many fascinating papers on deep questions raised by Sir Arthur Conan Doyle's famous mysteries.

The location was lovely, with conference rooms that looked out over the falls where Holmes and Moriarty had their famous battle in "The Final Problem." Fourteen esteemed scholars were present, and of the thirteen papers read (Dr. Tallon's not being read for obvious reasons), all were backgrounded by the soft, relaxing whoosh of the cataract as it fell into the pool below—the same pool, of course, where the body of Dr. Tallon was found floating after he failed to appear for his session.

The papers presented are here reprinted in this volume in their original order, accompanied by notes about the conference.

In the first session, Dr. David Baggett's paper, "Sherlock Holmes as Epistemologist," explored the intellectual virtues of Holmes that are conducive to good thinking, whether applied to solving a crime or the mystery of life. Rather than a myopic logic chopper devoid of emotion, as he is often characterized, Baggett argued that Sherlock Holmes exhibits traits that make the most ardent feminist epistemologist proud: passion, instinct, and artistry. These collectively comprise an expansive understanding of reason and rationality that yields not unjustified hubris but hard-won intellectual confidence and courage. Baggett's paper praised the role that intuition plays in understanding the world.

After his paper on the use of abduction, Dr. Baggett fell silent for a long time, as if realizing something.

Next, David Rozema discussed a strange case in the Holmes canon, where Holmes's hatred of a blackmailer seems to send him over the line from hero to the ranks of the criminal class. In "Not the Crime, but the Man: Sherlock Holmes and Charles Augustus Milverton," Rozema argued that though Holmes's behavior is patently illegal, and by many measures immoral, virtue ethics offers a framework for assessing Holmes's actions that casts them in a more promising light.

Kevin Kinghorn's paper proved a fascinating analysis of the nature of deception. Considering and casting to the side insufficient definitions, Kinghorn arrived at a solid definition of deception. Adding considerable interest to Kinghorn's essay was his extensive use of examples drawn from the Conan Doyle stories. Perhaps most interestingly, however, was how Kinghorn's definition of deception illuminated the relationship between Holmes and Moriarty.

Later, Dr. Kinghorn reported to the police hearing Dr. Baggett and Dr. Tallon arguing in the hallway over missing conference funds. The argument ended when Dr. Baggett stormed off.

During the lunchtime keynote speech, Massimo Pigliucci presented a paper titled "Sherlock's Reasoning Toolbox," which examined the powers and problems surrounding deduction and induction. Though Holmes is sometimes chided for being less than precise with his supposedly airtight logic, Pigliucci affirmed Holmes's more inductive, probabilistic method.

At the end of the luncheon, Dr. Tallon suddenly began complaining of stomach pains and quickly left the dining hall. When the conference attendees made their way to hear his paper after lunch, a hastily scrawled note on the door indicated that the paper was moved to the next day. The paper, as printed in the conference schedule, was to be an examination of Aristotle's philosophy of friendship with reference to the friendship of Holmes and Watson, although the amendment to the schedule announced the paper was now called "Watsons, Adlers, Lestrades, and Moriarties: On the Nature of Friends and Enemies." Enemies, it seemed, had been added as a subject for examination as well.

Instead of Tallon's paper, Kyle Blanchette presented his essay, "Eliminating the Impossible," which discussed Holmes's sometime investigation of the supernatural in *The Hound of the Baskervilles* and in a recent Sherlock Holmes film. By using Holmes's investigation of an eerie curse and rumors of a resurrection from the dead, Blanchette asked whether it is ever reasonable to keep open the supernatural as a possible cause of events. This provided a natural way for Blanchette to discuss issues surrounding miracles and other issues in the philosophy of religion.

The only strange event of the session happened when Blanchette sat in the presenter's chair and the chair collapsed, sending him backward and nearly impaling him on a decorative sculpture. If Blanchette had been just an inch taller, the attendees agreed, it could well have punctured his skull.

Andrew Terjesen's paper discussed the controversial death of Sherlock Holmes in Sir Arthur Conan Doyle's "The Final Problem." This was an event that caused so much ire among fans at the time that Conan Doyle received more threats and hate mail than most real-life murderers. Terjesen posed a fascinating question, unique in the ethical literature: "Was it morally wrong to kill off Sherlock Holmes?" Drawing on aesthetics, ethics, and the literature surrounding copyright, Terjesen considered both sides of the equation.

After Terjesen's presentation, the session was briefly interrupted when gunshots were heard outside the hall, although on inspection, the sounds were discovered to have come from firecrackers, probably left by local hooligans. When everyone returned to the hall, however, the projector was no longer functioning, forcing everyone to relocate to the south conference room. Later, police found footprints and a pair of binoculars in the bushes on the south side of the building.

In the same session, D. Q. McInerny, brother of the late well-known philosopher and mystery writer Ralph McInerny (creator of Father Dowling), presented on Holmes as an "Artist of Reason," dispelling notions that Holmes is merely a calculating machine. As evidence, McInerny drew our attention to Holmes's more metaphysical musings about the fundamental intelligibility of the cosmos. McInerny argued that Holmes may just as reasonably be seen to be a philosopher, one looking for the meaning of things—someone passionately dedicated to the truth, not merely facts.

Bridget Costello and Gregory Bassham presented a paper on Holmes's over-mastery of certain subjects and complete ignorance of others, asking whether Holmes's philosophy of mind is sound and whether his obsessive focus on just a few activities is healthy. The paper included discussion of one of the most famous passages in the Holmes canon, wherein Watson records the gaps in Holmes's knowledge of various subjects, including ignorance about the earth's rotation around the sun. Finding Holmes's understanding of memory to be not much more impressive than his understanding of astronomy, the authors offered a helpful critique. They were much easier on Sherlock's narrow interests, perhaps because Holmes is more well rounded than how he presents himself.

In "Passionate Objectivity in Sherlock Holmes," Charles Taliaferro and Michel Le Gall asked which was more important when making an ethical decision: to be analytical, impartial, cool, and dispassionate, or to be passionate and emotionally engaged with and committed to those about whom one cares most. This question is not just relevant to the Conan Doyle mysteries but also to developments in philosophy and literature in the nineteenth century. Despite Holmes's claims to dispassionate objectivity, Taliaferro and Le Gall showed how Holmes is a man with loyalties. Does this make Holmes irrational? Quite the opposite, they argued: "Some passion or acquaintance with passion is essential if one is to be objective and rigorously analytical."

Dr. Tallon had seemingly recovered and was in attendance for the session. Dr. Baggett was likewise present for the reading of the paper. At the end of the session, however, the bearded man everyone took for Dr. Baggett was revealed to be a local drunkard wearing a fake beard. When pressed for an explanation of what he was doing there, the man mumbled some words in French and stumbled away, leaving the beard behind. Dr. Tallon seemed upset by this and rushed out another door.

In another paper, Gregory Bassham considered Holmes's considerable workaholism. As Conan Doyle writes, "[When Holmes] had an unsolved problem upon his mind, [he] would go for days, and even for a week, without rest, turning it over, rearranging his facts, looking at it from every point of view until he had either fathomed it or convinced himself that his data were insufficient." Bassham considered Holmes in light of the psychological signs of being a workaholic, all of which perfectly describe the great detective's lifestyle. Bassham then considered the problems (and pluses) of workaholism, considering why we perhaps should not wish to cure Holmes of his condition.

After this session, Dr. Bassham saw Dr. Tallon complaining to the desk clerk that his room had been burgled and demanding to speak to the cleaning staff. When the hotel clerk offered to call the police, Dr. Tallon refused to let them.

Carrie-Ann Biondi's paper, "The Dog That Did Not Bark," offered lessons in observation: learning to read the book of life. This helps us see not merely when things are present, but when they are notably absent. The question "am I missing something?" can be as useful in philosophy as it was in the famous Conan Doyle story, "Silver Blaze," with its well-known curious incident of the silent dog.

During her presentation, Biondi reported seeing Dr. Tallon out on the lawn, walking toward the falls. Because the window faced away from the falls, however, she was not sure this was where Dr. Tallon was truly heading. This is the last reported sighting of Dr. Tallon. Dr. Baggett was present at the session.

The evening session, a reading of Dorothy L. Sayers's 1935 essay, "Aristotle on Detective Fiction," was held in the grand ballroom. The paper, read by a local actress dressed as Sayers, considered the merits of the detective story against the modern novel, describing how Aristotle's criteria for good drama are satisfied by the well-told whodunit. Witnesses report that Dr. Baggett was present in the session, though some said that they heard him muttering in French under his breath.

Elizabeth Glass-Turner was presenting her paper, "The Grim Reaper on Baker Street," the next morning when she was interrupted by one of the conference staff, who indicated that Dr. Tallon's name badge had been found by the observation pier, along with a solitary shoe. A survey of the attendees revealed his absence. The police were called and Glass-Turner resumed, explaining how the presence of the corpse is a powerful occasion for reflection. "To philosophize is to learn to die," Glass-Turner said, invoking Montaigne. Through examination of the Holmes mysteries, Glass-Turner described how the lifeless body reveals Holmes's and Watson's different senses of the world and the value of human life.

Philip Tallon did not appear at his rescheduled session, and a search party was created. Dr. Tallon's body was found later that day in the falls. The police reported that the railing on the falls overlook had been loosened. Several screws were found on the ground near the scene of the accident, and a screwdriver was found in the pool at the bottom of the falls. Dr. Tallon's head was rather badly smashed, and police could not conclude whether he had sustained head injuries before the fall or after.

Dr. Baggett was held for questioning, then released. The case remains unsolved. However, the local police have recruited an amateur detective, renowned for his ability to solve intractable mysteries. The rumor is that he is close to a solution.

Note

1. This whole account is totally not true.

Sherlock Holmes as Epistemologist

David Baggett

> Discovery is seeing what everyone else saw and thinking what no one thought.
>
> —Albert von Szent-Györgyi

A philosopher friend of mine tends to give his waitresses a hard time, though they never seem to mind. When they ask him if there's anything else he needs, for example, he tends to reply that, now that they ask, he would like to be given the meaning of life. He's a good tipper, but not *that* good.

Beyond containing a skein of mysteries, life itself is a mystery, often an inscrutable one, in need of unraveling. Because omniscience for most of us, unlike Sherlock Holmes's brother Mycroft, isn't our specialization, we could use help in knowing how to go about figuring out life's answers, both big and small. Who better to ask—with Mrs. Hudson's permission, of course—than that paragon of detectives quietly smoking his black pipe in the midst of his chemistry experiments at 221B Baker Street, where tobacco smoke wafts in the air, the fire crackles, fog swirls past the window, and it's always 1892?[1]

Although it's true that the mysteries Holmes set out to solve were a bit smaller in scope than the meaning of life, he wasn't unconcerned about life's broader questions. As a character with feet of clay, Holmes, despite his great powers, was without neither weakness nor susceptibility to temptation. Sometimes saddled with angst and cognitive dissonance enough to put to shame the most ennui-afflicted existentialist, Sherlock Holmes was vulnerable to periods of dark depression and even drug-induced periods of liberation from banal commonplaces and the "insufferable fatigues of idleness."[2] There's evidence to suggest that he thought that if this life is all there is, with no afterlife in which we see ultimate justice effected, then the world is a cruel jest, for "the ways of Fate are hard to understand."[3] At another point he was "in a melancholy and philosophic mood" when he asked, "Is not all life pathetic and futile? Is not [Josiah Amberley's] story a microcosm of the whole? We reach. We grasp. And what is life in our hands at the end? A shadow. Or worse than a shadow—misery."[4]

Yet despite the challenges of life, the darkness of hearts, and ubiquity of suffering, Holmes at one juncture provided a glimpse into his remaining trust in the goodness of reality. In "The Naval Treaty," he held up the drooping stalk of a moss rose, with its dainty blend of crimson and green, before saying, "There is nothing in which deduction is so necessary as in religion. It can be built up as an exact science by the reasoner. Our highest assurance of the goodness of Providence seems to me to rest in the flowers. All other things, our powers, our desires, our food, are really necessary for the existence in the first instance. But this rose is an extra. Its smell and its color are an embellishment of life, not a condition of it. It is only goodness which gives extras, and so I say again that we have much to hope from the flowers."[5]

A remarkable and suggestive passage, even if all too brief, it won't detain us here beyond serving as evidence to suggest that Sherlock saw the power of reasoning that he employed in solving crimes as applicable to life's larger questions. The process of considering questions of what it takes to acquire knowledge, what knowledge ultimately is, and whether or not we have come to possess it is the branch of philosophy called epistemology. Here I explore the topic of Sherlock Holmes as epistemologist. Holmes was no philosopher by trade, of course, but then again, he wasn't an official detective either, despite being unparalleled as a sleuth. Early on we're told that Sherlock's knowledge of philosophy (and politics and literature) was nil although it was encyclopedic in other areas, but in Conan Doyle's second novel about Holmes, he shows knowledge of Goethe and educates Watson on philosopher Winwood Reade. Either Conan Doyle decided to flesh out his character some more, or Watson misjudged Sherlock within the fictional context, but there's a more important point behind those. Watson cast Sherlock, at the end of "The Final Problem," as "the best and the wisest man whom I have ever known."[6] Perhaps we could chalk such accolades up to eulogistic hyperbole, but if Watson's words are taken with any seriousness at all, Holmes was a man of wisdom; and philosophy, etymologically and at its best, is the love of wisdom.[7]

Logic was the forte of Sherlock Holmes, and it's also the language of philosophy. Even though Dr. Watson counted Holmes as having zero knowledge of philosophy, Sherlock's proficiency in the use of logic made him an impeccable candidate to at least *do* philosophy if he were so inclined, however ignorant of the history and concepts of philosophy he may have been. I won't delve inordinately into his use of logic, although I will touch on that topic. Because several other chapters in this volume deal at length with logic, instead, I will broaden the discussion to epistemology in general. Sherlock Holmes, by his own admission, had for his vocation knowing things that other people didn't. I will elucidate some of the reasons why Holmes was able to know what he did—reasons that aren't always, or even typically, associated with the cold calculations of this mental magician. His expansive epistemological method requires an examination of a cluster of interestingly interconnected features of his character and practices if we are to come to understand his effectiveness as a philosophical sleuth. What the study will reveal is that many of the laudable virtues of Sherlock Holmes are generalizable as character and intellectual virtues for us all to emulate to become better thinkers.

Examining the Premises

At the foundation of Sherlock's method was observation. In *The Sign of the Four,* Holmes identified the three qualities necessary for the ideal detective: power of observation, knowledge, and deduction. We will consider each in turn, beginning with observation. Holmes used all of his senses, even augmenting them when he could (as with a magnifying glass), to glean information about the scene of a crime and all the relevant players involved. Each piece of information would get tucked away for later use and timely retrieval, and each datum was considered clay with which to build bricks, or a symptom that a doctor can use to make a diagnosis. Without the data and evidence thus gleaned from a crime scene, he refrained from speculation and conjecture. He recognized the dangers involved in spinning theories too quickly and then, perhaps subtly and unwittingly, twisting facts to suit theories rather than constructing theories to account for the facts. Time and again Watson reports Holmes listening intently to his client's narrative, interjecting questions, his eyes riveted and his full concentration engaged. At the crime scene, Holmes, a genius for minutiae, was like a hound on a scent, darting from place to place taking measurements and collecting samples. Others with Holmes could see, but they didn't observe. Holmes trained himself to see what others would overlook, a talent that didn't merely come naturally, but with intentionality and due diligence. Meticulous attention to detail was axiomatic for Holmes. Not content with general impressions, he concentrated himself on the details, where everything of importance could generally be found. His eyes could see the importance of sleeves, the suggestiveness of thumbnails, and the great issues that may hang from a bootlace.[8]

At the root of the task of epistemology is the challenge posed by the simple fact that appearances don't always correspond with reality. They can be deceiving. Sometimes what seems simple is deceptively complex, and sometimes what appears complicated admits of a simple explanation. The fact that we can be deceived or deluded complicates the epistemic task of finding the truth. Holmes seemed to have an acute recognition of this insight, perhaps accounting for what can be called his aversion to the obvious. Rarely was he content with what may have seemed clear cut and obvious to others. He was interested in what accounted for all the facts, not just those most at the surface. An obvious explanation in "The Beryl Coronet" case was that the son was the guilty perpetrator, appearing to have been caught red-handed. Holmes, searching for an explanation for all the observations he had made and facts in need of an account, remained skeptical. Healthy skepticism about appearances tends to be a salient feature of any credible epistemologist.

Tattoos and Typewriters

Observation gave Holmes the facts of a case. His acquaintance with the annals of crime gave him a vast reservoir of relevant background knowledge from which to draw. Such knowledge was so crucial for detective work that he said of LeVillard, the French detective with quick intuition, that LeVillard remained "deficient in the wide range of exact knowledge which is essential to the higher developments" of his art.[9] Holmes had acquired knowledge of crime not just by his personal experience at solving it, but by the assiduous study he had devoted to learning about its history. He counseled the same. After discovering that a reference of Sherlock's hearkened back to a criminal from the previous century, Inspector MacDonald said, "Then he's no use to me. I'm a practical man." Holmes responded, "Mr. Mac, the most practical thing you ever did in your life would be to shut yourself up for three months and read twelve hours a day at the annals of crime."[10] Sometimes reading, Holmes realized, is the most practical course of action of all, a sentiment likely echoed by anyone who's ever had occasion to teach a philosophy course.

Because of Sherlock's expertise and knowledge, he could instantly recognize the parallels of a new case with its predecessors, detecting not just their parallels and points of similarity, but also their departures and instructive points of disconnect. He was open to their commonalities, but had also acquired a keen sense of what proved new and distinctive. This sensitized him to key points in need of special attention and focus of concentration. He would habitually make reference to analogues from the history of crime, and on occasion be fairly sure of the outcome of his investigation from its outset because of its conspicuous resemblance to its precedents. In almost Wittgensteinian fashion, he was wont to note the family resemblances between crimes that could often furnish the key clues to their resolution. He described his profession to Watson in this way in *A Study in Scarlet:* "They lay all the evidence before me, and I am generally able, by the help of my knowledge of the history of crime, to set them straight. There is a strong family resemblance about misdeeds, and if you have all the details of a thousand at your finger ends, it is odd if you can't unravel the thousand and first."[11] As a rule, once Holmes heard of some slight indication in the course of events, he could guide himself "by the thousands of other similar cases" that would occur to his memory.[12] When necessary, Holmes would consult the index of cases he had compiled, not to mention his record of newsworthy persons he could readily access as needed.

Holmes had also contributed to the available knowledge by writing several monographs cataloging everything from tattoos to cigar ashes, footprints to secret signs. He had considered additional volumes on animals, the influence of trade on the form of the hand, and typewriters. The quality and breadth of his preparation were as impressive as they were effective. Moreover, his knowledge and expertise made him a better and better observer, because it enabled him to develop ever greater proficiency at noticing the right details most likely to provide the strongest clues. Watson's efforts at observation, in contrast, tended to miss the mark for ignorance of knowing where to look.

It's Abduction, Watson!

Other chapters in this book discuss how most of Sherlock's inferences were less deductive than inductive or abductive. Perhaps Conan Doyle was putting "deductive" in Sherlock's mouth but meaning it generically or colloquially. Inductive inferences are less than certain, and they trade on probabilities; Sherlock's occasional reference to something like "the balance of probability" sounds much more inductive than deductive. Abduction, then again, is an inference to the best explanation. Many logicians treat it as a distinctly third kind of inference, neither deductive nor inductive, and it is not uncommonly used in history, science, and philosophy. In a nutshell, it involves identifying a pool of explanation candidates to account for some state of affairs, then narrowing the list down by a principled set of criteria to the single best explanation, then inferring to it as the likely true explanation. The criteria by which the options get reduced include such considerations as explanatory scope, power, and conformity with other beliefs. Sherlock's consistent insistence that all the data be explained is an example of the use of the criterion of explanatory scope. The best explanation has to account not just for some of the data in question, but rather for all the relevant evidence.

In the popular imagination, Holmes's knowledge base is what most likely gets overlooked. His observational skills are legend, but his inferential powers are perhaps best known of all. It's one of the characteristics that make him one of the most memorable of fictional characters. He consistently awed Watson by his demonstrations, the careful explanations of which only mildly tempered the incredulity. Conan Doyle, as is well known, received inspiration for the character of Holmes from his real-life teacher Dr. Bell, who exhibited qualities like those of Holmes. But it's important to emphasize that Sherlock's inferences were only possible because they were predicated on his acute observations and prior knowledge.

Another fictional example of a character who, on the basis of his previous experiences, makes impressive inferences comes from Fyodor Dostoevsky's *The Brothers Karamazov:* "Many said of the elder that, in accepting those who had come throughout the years to entrust their souls to him, to seek his guidance and solace, he had heard so many confessions, secrets, and tales of human despair that he had finally acquired an insight so keen that he could guess, from the very first glance at a newcomer, what he would say, what he would ask him, and even what was really tormenting his conscience. Often the visitor was surprised, confounded, and even frightened on finding that the elder knew his secret before he had even uttered a word."[13]

Sherlock's inferences, though grounded in facts, could be ambitious, and he wasn't always right. Some mysteries remained unsolved. Watson writes that he doesn't chronicle those because they would be stories without endings and readers would lose patience with that. On occasion perhaps there wasn't enough evidence on which to base a conclusion, or perhaps there was and even Holmes missed it. At Norbury, Holmes assumed something more sinister than what was actually there. Irene Adler, of course, was the one woman who beat him, earning his undying respect in the process, and he claimed to be beaten on three other occasions by men. Watson came to expect Holmes to solve well-nigh any mystery he would confront—and for good reason in light of Sherlock's track record. Most typically, Holmes asserted, criminals make mistakes; there tends to be a flaw in the best-laid human plans rendering their discovery more likely.

Here we come to an important point to emphasize. Just as Holmes was slow to weave out a theory to account for the data before he had collected all the evidence he could, he was also careful not to be too slow. This, no doubt, made many of his inferences seem presumptuous or overly ambitious, and no doubt some of them were; his being a fictional character makes this more forgivable. His willingness to give it a shot, though, is both interesting and important. It's instructive because it illustrates, at its best, an epistemic virtue. To get at the idea, consider someone racked with so many doubts about his intellectual abilities that he becomes debilitated and diffident, never or hardly ever willing to risk an inference unless he is completely sure. Some skeptics and strong evidentialists are this way, fearing failure so much they're too hesitant to risk error. The problem with this approach, as William James (1842–1910) noticed, is that it can result in the loss of an important truth. Sometimes risk is the price we have to pay to capture the truth—or to make something true that otherwise wouldn't be. One of the most important lessons of skepticism is that we need to be skeptical even of it. So what appears to be hubris on the part of Sherlock—and numerous times Watson expresses this concern about him—may more charitably be construed as intellectual courage. Perhaps rather than being objectionably presumptuous, Sherlock on at least many occasions struck the right balance between intellectual cowardice on the one side and rashness on the other.

Recall how he chastised Watson on one occasion in "The Blue Carbuncle," where Watson was given the chance to infer whatever he could about the owner of a hat on the basis of a careful observation of the hat itself. Watson claimed to see nothing, to which Sherlock replied, "On the contrary, Watson, you can see everything. You fail, however, to reason from what you see. You are too timid in drawing your inferences."[14] Holmes then went on to make a number of far-reaching inferences about the hat that prove to be accurate. Perhaps Holmes was implicitly suggesting to Watson that a greater measure of inferential confidence was possible. What might seem like Holmes's hubris may actually be intellectual courage.

Numerous times Watson wrote of what he thought to be the character flaws in Holmes of egotism and lack of humility. In their first meeting, Watson could see Holmes was clever, but he also remarked afterward that he was conceited. Indeed, Watson would later claim to be "repelled by the egotism" of Sherlock's insistence that Watson's chronicles should focus more on the logic than the story. Holmes replied by unapologetically insisting it wasn't conceit, but rather justice for his craft that motivated him. "Crime is common. Logic is rare," though later Holmes would come to see the need for narratives to make for compelling reading.[15] Watson would come, though, to see that Holmes stood alone in Europe both in his gifts and experience, which makes the resistance Holmes posed to Watson's analysis understandable: "I cannot agree with those who rank modesty among the virtues. To the logician all things should be seen exactly as they are, and to underestimate one's self is as much a departure from truth as to exaggerate one's own powers."[16] That Sherlock freely admitted that Mycroft's powers exceeded his own seems to bear out his account of matters here. Even if Sherlock was mistaken in thinking that modesty required intellectual dishonesty, he made a good point in stressing that it's not necessarily immodest to acknowledge one's own gifts, any more than it would be to acknowledge those of another. Sherlock was indeed a prodigiously gifted character. If someone were truly to have such powers, objectively acknowledging them would be only honest. Humility is consistent with honesty and intellectual confidence, and epistemic humility is consistent with the intellectual courage it takes to risk being wrong in order to capture the truth.

Holmes knew when his inferences were possibly wrong, and he didn't stop once he came to his tentative conclusions. Like a good scientist, he put his ideas to the test, weighed them on the scales of balancing probabilities, and observed how well they were able to account for new evidence. He was slow to formulate his theories without adequate evidence, but once the evidence arrived, he was willing to move, formulating working hypotheses he would subject to further tests. Knowing he was liable to draw the wrong inferences, he was careful to wait for enough evidence and to await further confirmation even after formulating his account. He was acutely aware that a slight shift in perspective could radically alter the direction of the evidence. If he didn't err on the side of epistemic humility, at least he didn't fall prey to a debilitating sense of intellectual cowardice and diffidence. He cared too much about finding the truth to be silenced by the possibility of error. So he moved ahead, forging and testing each link in the causal chains he envisioned in his head to account for the full range of facts and thus uncover the truth.

Nor did Holmes let the intrinsic unlikelihood of some of his inferences deter him, because he realized that life itself invariably includes wild improbabilities however it plays out. Time and again he affirmed as axiomatic the idea that once the other options are excluded, what remains must be the case. This remains true even if what remains may well be otherwise thought unlikely. Finding the evidence that's actually there has to be accounted for, and on occasion can render as probable an event that, considered by itself, would be an unlikely contingency indeed. He could see, then, that the actual evidence should be followed wherever it leads, even if it's to a conclusion one wouldn't have originally expected. Certain pieces of evidence can render an otherwise unlikely explanation the best and likely true explanation after all. Inference enabled Holmes to move from the foundational facts gleaned from observation and experience to new pieces of knowledge, and he did so with refreshing boldness.

Even if Holmes stands largely absolved of the charge of hubris, there's another charge that we imagine could be leveled against him, to which we now turn.

On Behalf of Irene Adler

What perhaps might strike some people as a bit strange about the phenomenon of Sherlock's unflagging popularity from the late Victorian era to today are certain features of this character that might impress readers and moviegoers alike as off-putting at best or offensive at worst. Sherlock's mistrust of women, immunity from sentiment, and aversion to emotion make him vulnerable to criticism from the ranks of feminist epistemologists—that is, those who bring to bear feminist insights in their epistemic work. Their approaches are wide-ranging and sometimes challenging and brilliant, so it's impossible to do them justice in short compass. For present purposes, it's enough to tip our hat in their direction by identifying a few of their more common concerns.[17] Such concerns arguably find suitable application when we consider the method and mentality of Sherlock Holmes. As a memorable fictional character, he exhibits some of the more extreme traits that occasionally fall within the target of feminist epistemologists. After raising such concerns, we will assess whether and how far Sherlock might be vindicated of such charges. Doing so will give us the chance to discuss additional aspects of his epistemic method that should enable us to see that he wasn't the myopic logic chopper some might think.

Contemporary analytic philosophers tend to write in the analytic spirit, respectful of science, both as a paradigm of reasonable belief and in conformity with its argumentative rigor, its clarity, and its determination to be objective. It's based in the view that knowledge is objective and impersonal, our knowledge is of a world that exists independently of us, and truth is what corresponds with this reality. These traditional features of Western and analytic philosophy represent some assumptions that certain feminist epistemologists call into question.

How do feminists call such seemingly intuitive assumptions about truth and objectivity into question? Their concern is that women have their own perspective on knowledge (or perhaps several perspectives). Whereas the masculinist perspective historically led to a search for impersonal truth and absolute certitude, more feminine perspectives see truth as more personal and absolute certainty as unnecessary. It's often conjectured that the history of men subjugating women means that the experiences of those who are members of a privileged group will differ from those of someone in an underprivileged or subjugated group. The suggestion is often made that such perspectives historically were ignored or disqualified inappropriately just because they weren't the prevailing paradigms. Traditional analytic philosophy privileged impersonal and objective knowledge. So these subjugated perspectives on truth that were more personal (in the sense that the insights came about as a result of a certain kind of personal experience) and subjective (not available to those, say, doing the subjugating) were silenced. Feminist epistemology doesn't treat experience objectively and dispassionately, nor does it hold experience at arm's length. Thus it tends to be more open to the possibility of potentially veridical concrete, felt experiences.

The charge by feminist epistemologists isn't that men ignore experience in epistemology, but rather that they regard experience in a typically male way. Their reasoning about experience has been kept carefully apart from the "interests and emotional involvement" of people generally and women particularly. They have considered themselves justified in doing so because this was thought to be a way to ensure "objectivity," but feminists would say it's but an illusion of objectivity. The quest for complete objectivity itself is misguided because complete objectivity, certain feminists insist, is impossible. What counts as knowledge is too tied up with different kinds of experience, activities, and social relations.

A number of feminist epistemologists hold that there is in every experience an ineffable element—that is, an element no language can adequately describe. Analytic philosophy's reductivist, logic-chopping approach tends to be altogether inadequate to leave room for such important experiences having epistemic significance. This, however, leaves out an important aspect of deeper kinds of knowledge of which we're capable. The claim is that analytic philosophy denies the possibility of nonpropositional knowledge or "merely" intuitive understanding.

In the way that Sherlock Holmes privileged a scientific approach to answering questions, in his quest for complete objectivity, in his claim that reason and emotion are intrinsically and perennially at odds, his discomfort with emotion, and his generally suspicious attitude toward women, he can be thought to fall within the target of feminist epistemologists. A few illustrations should suffice to illustrate these aspects of Sherlock's approach. Take, for example, his penchant for construing mysteries as primarily intellectual puzzles rather than heart-wrenching personal tragedies, which results in his being less empathetic and sympathetic than he ought. In "The Sussex Vampire," Holmes gets chastised in this way: "It may be a mere intellectual puzzle to you, but it is life and death to me!"[18] Detection, he would insist, is an exact science and should be treated in the same cold and unemotional manner; tingeing it with romanticism produces much the same effect as working a love story into the fifth proposition of Euclid.[19] Sherlock's cold reference to the death of Watson's brother stirred Watson's ire, and Sherlock had to apologize: "My dear Watson, pray accept my apologies. Viewing the matter as an abstract problem, I had forgotten how personal and painful a thing it might be for you."[20]

Perhaps the best example of all of the way that Holmes was out of touch with his emotions (an aspect of the character that Jeremy Brett admitted made playing the role oppressive for him) comes in the fascinating exchange between Holmes and Watson after they meet the woman whom Watson would later marry. Holmes denied having noticed her attractiveness after her departure, to which Watson replied, "You really are an automaton—a calculating machine! There is something positively inhuman in you at times." Holmes in reply said, "It is of the first importance not to allow your judgment to be biased by personal qualities. A client is to me a mere unit—a factor in a problem. The emotional qualities are antagonistic to clear reasoning."[21]

After Watson proposed to her, later in the book, Sherlock couldn't congratulate him, despite admitting that she was one of the most charming young ladies he had ever met. "But love is an emotional thing, and whatever is emotional is opposed to that true cold reason which I place above all things. I should never marry myself, lest I bias my judgment."[22] Anything other than dispassionate objectivity purged of the personal was less than what Holmes aspired to. He prided himself on having no prejudices and of following docilely wherever facts may lead. His approach permeated his whole approach to life, and as a result, "women have seldom been an attraction to me, for my brain has always governed my heart."[23]

Vindicating Sherlock Somewhat

Although observation, inference, and experience were crucial for Holmes, they did not exhaust the resources he brought to bear in his detective work, and we run the risk of missing some of his other laudable features if we confine our attention entirely to his cold logic. For his reason, though exacting, was animated by more than logic, or perhaps by a more expansive conception of logic and rationality than one might think. Consider the passion that drove his investigations that would lead him to refrain from eating or sleeping for days on end before solving the puzzle. This is not the way of a cold, calculating machine but of a deeply passionate man who loved his work and yearned to see justice done. His eyes would shine and his cheeks would flush at the exhilarating prospect of doing his work.

Nor was his commitment to justice a legalistic one allowing for no exceptions. More than once, he allowed the guilty perpetrator to go free because of overriding moral extenuating considerations and mitigating factors. His was no impersonal, decontextualized understanding of justice of the type that feminist philosophers rightly critique.

At the risk of epistemic indulgence, he was also willing to accord significance to something like women's intuition, and instinct (and intuition in general) was something of which he seemed fond, predicting that Inspector Baynes, possessing both, would rise high in his profession. His own inferences would come so quickly that Watson characterized them as resembling intuitions; likewise, when Holmes realized that sometimes it's easier to know something than to explain the justification for it, he himself recognized the way knowledge can have features that resemble more immediate apprehendings than just the deliverances of the discursive intellect.

The artistic side of Holmes also revealed more than a logic chopper. His grandmother was the sister of a famous artist, so the idea is that art ran in his blood and happened to take the form of his particular vocation. An enthusiastic musician, he loved art for its own sake, including the art of reason. It would be a worthwhile exploration on another occasion to explore the aesthetic aspects of his epistemic approach and conception of rationality. Ostensibly averse to narrative, Holmes was a dramatist at heart by his own admission. His breadth of view, easy enjoyment of surroundings, and appreciation for the admiration of his work were all characterized by Watson as marks of his artistry.

Holmes also had to a supreme degree imagination, valuing it in others and lamenting its absence, remarking that if Inspector Gregory, a competent police officer, had but imagination he would rise to great heights. Imagination enabled Holmes to put himself into the shoes of others and see things from their perspective, which was a quality at least in tension with the claim that he was entirely lacking in the ability to sympathize. Imagination enabled him to sift evidence and imagine their various possible interconnections until he could come to understand how they all best fit together. He wasn't content just with facts, but with how they interlocked and related to one another. Meeting the challenge of figuring this out, especially in difficult and strange cases, appealed to his imagination and challenged his ingenuity.

Inspector Lestrade, of course, was the paradigmatic example of someone lacking such imagination, and yet he and Holmes were on generally friendly terms. Holmes was moved when Lestrade expressed genuine appreciation and admiration for his work. At the end of "The Six Napoleons," Lestrade said, "We're not jealous of you at Scotland Yard. No, sir, we are very proud of you, and if you come down tomorrow, there's not a man, from the oldest inspector to the youngest constable, who wouldn't be glad to shake you by the hand."

"Thank you!" said Holmes. "Thank you!" and as he turned way, we're told, it seemed to Watson that Sherlock was more nearly moved by the softer human emotions than he had ever seen him.[24] Public notoriety meant nothing to Holmes, but the compliment of a friend meant a great deal. Perhaps this can help make sense of why, after William James finished his magnum opus *The Principles of Psychology,* he lamented not having included a section on the human importance of feeling appreciated.

Almost Human

Why Sherlock Holmes captivates readers is a complex question, but his humanness is likely a big part of it. Despite his almost superhuman powers, he was capable of a quivering lip when he thought his best friend was hurt and of being moved by the admiration of a colleague. Holmes was not the myopic logic chopper some might imagine; he was too human for that. Yet we could, perhaps, suggest in closing that he's not entirely vindicated from the charges of the feminist epistemologists. He was at times overly cold and detached, and the dichotomy in his mind between reason and emotions was likely too artificial, though there's an impressive history of philosophical thinkers who would be inclined to agree with him. But it's likely that the psyche of human beings shouldn't be quite so fragmented—a claim that at this point must stand more as assertion than argument.

Philosophers since Plato have long realized that expertise in an area like crime can result in either a great detective or a horrible criminal. On at least four occasions either Sherlock or Watson mentioned what a great criminal Sherlock could have been, had he chosen to use his gifts in the wrong direction. Although it's hard to imagine, if anything would have tempted him to do so, it might have been the same roots that resulted in his occasional listlessness and torpor, vulnerabilities that show his humanness and perhaps, ironically enough, his need for more humanness. For when Sherlock would on occasion fail to exhibit the right balance of head and heart, or a lamentable lack of empathy, he didn't need to get more in touch with his feminine side—contra the suggestion by certain feminist epistemologists.[25] Rather, he needed to get more in touch with his humanity.[26]

Notes

Thanks to Greg Bassham, Mark Foreman, and Maria Owen for helpful comments on an earlier draft. Any remaining difficulties in this chapter owe entirely to their patent irresponsibility.

Epigraph from I. Good, ed., *The Scientist Speculates* (New York: Basic Books, 1962), 15.

1. Thanks to Christopher and Barbara Roden for the inspiration for such a description, which I paraphrased. All Holmes references in this chapter come from their edited volume of Sir Arthur Conan Doyle, *The Complete Sherlock Holmes* (New York: Barnes & Noble, 2009).

2. "Wisteria Lodge," 838.

3. "Veiled Lodger," 1056.

4. "Retired Colourman," 1068.

5. "Naval Treaty," 425–26.

6. *Sign of the Four,* 449.

7. Conan Doyle does characterize Moriarty as a philosopher: "He is the Napoleon of crime, Watson. He is the organizer of half that is evil and of nearly all that is undetected in this great city. He is a genius, a philosopher, an abstract thinker. He has a brain of the first order" ("Final Problem," 440.) Some of Conan Doyle's other references to philosophy are less explicable, from "philosophical instruments" in the scientific laboratory to the "brow of a philosopher above and the jaw of a sensualist below" in describing Colonel Sebastian Moran in "The Empty House" (461). Holmes would also assume a half comic and "wholly philosophical" view when his affairs were going awry ("Missing Three-Quarter," 597).

8. "Case of Identity," 47.

9. *Sign of the Four,* 76.

10. *Valley of Fear,* 741.

11. *Study in Scarlet,* 11.

12. "Red-Headed League," 160.

13. Fyodor Dostoevsky, *The Brothers Karamazov* (1880; New York: Bantam Books, 1981), 33.

14. "Blue Carbuncle," 227.

15. "Copper Beeches," 295.

16. "Greek Interpreter," 406.

17. Helen Longino's "Feminist Epistemology as a Local Epistemology" is a powerful example of this literature. It can be found here: *Aristotelian Society Supplementary Volume* 71, no. 1 (1997): 19–36.

18. "Sussex Vampire," 997.

19. *Sign of the Four,* 76.

20. Ibid., 79.

21. Ibid., 82.

22. Ibid., 140. Interestingly enough, he was more concerned about the deleterious effect of love on his analytical abilities than drugs.

23. "Lion's Mane," 1044.

24. "Six Napoleons," 563.

25. I resonate with Susan Haack on this score; see her "Knowledge and Propaganda: Reflections of an Old Feminist," *Partisan Review* 60 (1993): 556–65.

26. Linda Patrik, the sister-in-law of Theodore Kaczynski, the Unabomber, was once asked what she had learned as a philosopher from the experience, to which she responded, "Based on this whole experience, I have lost respect for tremendous intellect. I have discovered that genius needs to be coupled with heart and loving relationships with people to have a positive impact on society. I now know that intellectual brilliance alone has great dangers" (http://www.union.edu/N/DS/s.php?s=1622).

Not the Crime, but the Man

Sherlock Holmes and Charles Augustus Milverton

David Rozema

"As Cunning as the Evil One"

"The Adventure of Charles Augustus Milverton" is, in many respects, unique among Sherlock Holmes's adventures.[1] In the first place, Holmes does not investigate any crime, nor is he asked to. Rather, he becomes a criminal himself, burgling a man's house and witnessing his murder without trying to prevent it or report it. Second, his antagonist, Charles Augustus Milverton, is described by Holmes as "the worst man in London"; he likens Milverton to the venomous serpents at the zoo, "with their deadly eyes and their wicked, flattened faces," and tells Watson, "I've had to do with fifty murderers in my career, but the worst of them never gave me the repulsion which I have for this fellow."[2] This intensity of feeling is strikingly unusual for Holmes, who nearly always has at least some understanding of—sometimes even respect for—the criminals he is tracking.

What sort of a man could induce such revulsion in Holmes, noted for his emotionally detached, logical attitude toward the criminals he tracks down? Charles Augustus Milverton, we learn, is "the king of all blackmailers."[3] He has made a fortune by paying high sums for secret letters that would compromise people of wealth and reputation, then demanding much higher sums to keep the letters a secret. He waits for just the right moment—an impending wedding, political appointment, or public honor—and then springs his trap. Most of the time his victims pay what he demands, but even in the cases where they do not, Milverton profits, for the public humiliation and loss that results from exposure makes him even more feared and enables him to demand even higher sums. "With a smiling face and a heart of marble, he will squeeze and squeeze until he has drained [his victims] dry."[4] Because he is already wealthy, Milverton can afford to pay the highest prices for any damaging letters, and he can also afford to bide his time until the most profitable opportunity presents itself. As Holmes says, "He is far too rich and far too cunning to work from hand to mouth." This cold, calculating cruelty and greed especially incenses Holmes and causes him to call Milverton the worst man in London: "I would ask you how could one compare the ruffian, who in hot blood bludgeons his mate, with this man, who methodically and at his leisure tortures the soul and wrings the nerves in order to add to his already swollen money-bags?"[5] And if that is not enough, it seems that Milverton's victims are more often women than men—less able to defend themselves against blackmail and more likely to comply with his demands. This, of course, is as ungentlemanly as a man could be. Despite appearances, Milverton is no gentleman.

The law is no deterrent to Milverton's blackmailing either. As Holmes points out, "What would it profit a woman, for example, to get him a few months' imprisonment if her own ruin must immediately follow? His victims dare not hit back." Holmes's encounter with Milverton proves that the comparison with a venomous serpent is apt: the man is cold-blooded, cunning, slippery, deceptive, and deadly—"as cunning as the Evil One."[6] Holmes has been commissioned by Lady Eva Blackwell ("the most beautiful debutante of last season") to negotiate an agreement with Milverton that would prevent the revelation of some imprudent letters that Lady Eva had written to a young country squire years ago. These letters would suffice to break off the match between Lady Blackwell and her fiancé, the earl of Dovercourt. Milverton has all the airs of an aristocrat, including "a perpetual frozen smile" that Watson says is "insufferable."[7] Though Lady Eva cannot afford to pay more than £2,000 for the letters—a fact Milverton is aware of—he will take no less than £7,000, insisting that "the occasion of a lady's marriage is a very suitable time for her friends and relatives to make some little effort upon her behalf."[8] It is clear that Milverton has very finely estimated the maximum amount he can make from this blackmail attempt and is ruthless in his pursuit of it. He is even prepared for Holmes's sudden attempt to wrest the letters from him by force: he is as quick as a rat and armed to the teeth, and in any case, he is not so foolish as to have the letters with him when he visits Holmes's apartment.

Holmes Crosses the Line

Then the game is afoot. But it is a very different game Holmes plays this time. He proceeds to spy out Milverton's house by posing as a plumber and becoming engaged to Milverton's housemaid, though he never intends to actually marry her. When he learns his way around Milverton's house, discovers the location of his safe, and knows what his nightly habits are, Holmes proceeds to burglarize the house—with an insistent Watson in tow, of course—in the attempt to steal the letters that Milverton is using for blackmailing Lady Blackwell. Both Holmes and Watson feel the exhilaration that comes with the robbery—the masks, the disguises, the secrecy. Holmes has even gotten ahold of a "first-class, up-to-date burgling kit, with nickel-plated jemmy, diamond-tipped glass cutter, adaptable keys, and every modern improvement which the march of civilization demands."[9]

Holmes's careful research and planning is thwarted, however, by an unusual late-night visit between Milverton and a prospective seller. Just after Holmes has opened the safe where the black mail is kept, and just as he is about to burn them all in the fireplace, Milverton enters the room. Holmes and Watson quickly hide behind the heavy curtains and clandestinely watch as Milverton, reading some legal documents, awaits his visitor. The visitor is a woman, with a veil over her face and a mantle around her chin. Referring to a letter she had sent him, Milverton prepares to negotiate the purchase of some compromising letters she had apparently told him she was ready to sell. However, when she lifts her veil and drops the mantle, Milverton recognizes her as one of his recent victims, whose marriage and reputation he had ruined when she was unwilling to pay him off, and whose husband had subsequently died of sorrow. Before any of them can act—Milverton, Holmes, or Watson—the lady shoots Milverton repeatedly in the chest. With a grip on the wrist, Holmes stops Watson's instinctive move to go after the woman and to help Milverton (who is beyond help anyway). "I understood the whole argument of that firm, restraining grip—that it was no affair of ours, that justice had overtaken the villain, that we had our own duties and our own objects, which were not to be lost sight of."[10]

As soon as the lady is gone, Holmes crosses to the open safe and proceeds to pour all the letters—all the black mail—into the fire, including the letter the secret lady had written to arrange the fatal visit with Milverton. He has to hurry, as the shots have aroused the household, and he and Watson have to outrace the servants to escape. The slower Watson is very nearly caught as the two of them scale the garden wall of the estate.

In a nice ironical twist, Inspector Lestrade calls on Holmes the following morning to request his help in solving the murder. It is clear that Lestrade, going by the report of the household staff, thinks the murder was committed by two men and is completely unaware of the woman's presence there that night. Holmes refuses to help with the case, telling Lestrade, "The fact is that I knew this Milverton, that I considered him one of the most dangerous men in London, and that I think there are certain crimes which the law cannot touch, and which therefore, to some extent, justify private revenge."[11]

Investigating Holmes's Ethics

This unique adventure of Holmes's is not just an intriguing story, it also raises some important moral and ethical questions. Are Holmes's actions justifiable? He becomes engaged to a woman with no intention of marrying her, feigning affection merely in order to get information; he is guilty of unlawful entry and burglary; he destroys private property; he witnesses a murder and does nothing to apprehend the murderer; he flees the scene of a crime. These are not the actions of a virtuous man but those we'd expect of a vicious one. So is Holmes a vicious man? Is he motivated by an extreme hatred of Milverton—a hatred that goes beyond what is reasonable? Does he, in this case, allow his emotions to get the better of him? Or are his passions not only understandable, but also justified? Is it ever right for a private citizen to go above the law, as Holmes says? And if so, when and why is it right? Is Holmes right in saying that private revenge was justified in this case?

Let's begin to tackle these questions by stating the obvious: Milverton is a criminal. Blackmail is against the law. And the law against it is not unjust. For if justice is the fair distribution of common goods, as Aristotle reminds us,[12] and one of those goods is privacy in personal affairs that do not threaten public safety, then the exposure of these private affairs against the will of those involved is unjust. Furthermore, there is nothing in the story itself that would lead us to question the ethical validity of this law. It's a law common to many societies and governments. The problem, as already mentioned, is that this law, practically speaking, is unenforceable in Milverton's case. He is far too cunning to get caught. Holmes says, "If ever he blackmailed an innocent person, then we should have him."[13] His victims are indeed guilty of something—of indiscretion or imprudence in their private correspondence—but these are not crimes themselves. In fact, it's not clear that they are even vices in the general sense. As we learn from the particular case Holmes is involved in, the imprudence revealed in Lady Blackwell's letters to the young squire was a function of her youth and the passion everyone expects to find between a young man and a young woman. Prudence and discretion, like all virtues, have to be acquired, and it is unreasonable to expect too much too soon. Besides this, there is the matter of privacy, which we've already noted as a citizen's right.

Some moral philosophers would say that moral judgments should not take into consideration the circumstances or the stages of personal development when making a judgment of a person's actions. Kant's moral philosophy, for example, excludes temporal or hypothetical conditions from the determination of moral principles. Moral imperatives are categorical, transcending the factors of the particular situation and the particular moment. To use one of his examples, a false promise is a violation of moral law, regardless of who does it, regardless of the circumstances, and regardless of the individual's level of intellectual development or character formation. Under this framework, Holmes would indeed be acting immorally when he becomes engaged with Milverton's housemaid, and also when he breaks into Milverton's house, cracks his safe, destroys his property, and then fails to report the murder. Of course Milverton's actions, too, would have to be condemned under Kant's framework. What Kant's moral philosophy fails to address are the practical questions of what a person of good will would or should do in cases where it's a question of how to respond to the immoral acts of others, and how to judge these responses. This criticism, however, is somewhat off the mark, for Kant doesn't claim to be addressing these questions. In his best-known work on moral philosophy, *The Fundamental Principles of the Metaphysics of Morals,* he is unconcerned with the practical application of his principles to particular cases.[14] He leaves it to each of us to use our reason to discover the practical application of the moral law for ourselves. He is simply giving us the metaphysical foundation for the moral law: it is found in the ideal of a good will. Kant does not say whether there are (or have been) any actual persons with a perfectly good will—perhaps he would agree that Jesus and/or the angels do. Rather, he presents the conception of a perfectly good will—one that always and only wills the categorical imperative to treat other rational beings as ends in themselves, having absolute, intrinsic value, seeing them as fellow citizens in a kingdom of ends. The conception of a good will, then, serves as a regulative ideal for us in moral matters. This is what Kant thinks of as practical philosophy, but it is not very helpful when it comes to what we would ordinarily call practical, for it doesn't address questions of rectification: what is required of a person of good will when a morally corrupt person is unchanged and unchecked by either moral or civic law. It is somewhat inappropriate, then, to apply this sort of moral framework to this case involving Milverton and Holmes. It can easily be granted that Holmes does not possess a perfectly good will, but even if he did, the Kantian framework cannot provide us with an answer to the question of whether or not Holmes's actions are morally justified.

On the other hand, as Kant's critique shows, a consequentialist framework (which holds that the moral worth of an action is dependent on the outcomes of that action) fares no better in such a situation. Because a consequentialist approach requires some degree of predictability about the outcomes of an action in order to make a moral judgment, there is no surety about the justifiability of the action until after the fact. The higher the unpredictability of the outcome, the lower the reliability of the judgment. It is true, for example, that Holmes's planning and preparation made it highly likely that he would succeed. Let's assume that Holmes's planned actions were designed to produce the most beneficial outcome for the most people, based on the prediction that things would most likely go as planned. Yet the way that things went was very different from what he had predicted. If we use the consequentialist approach, it seems that we would have to say that the actual result of the affair—Milverton being murdered and the murderer getting away with it—was less just than if things had gone the way Holmes expected. Yet the implication of Holmes's remarks at the end of the story (that some crimes—the ones the law cannot touch—justify private revenge) is that the actual outcome was perfectly just. That's the problem with the future: it can't be predicted with any accuracy, which presents a problem for a consequentialist approach. Furthermore, there is no agreement among consequentialists as to what counts as the most beneficial, or how to measure this so-called beneficence in an objective manner.

The point is that neither of these frameworks provides an adequate means to judge the moral merit (or demerit) of Holmes's actions in the Milverton case—or, indeed, for any similar case. The Kantian approach is too general and idealized to provide criteria for a judgment, and the consequentialist approach, along with its other faults, fails to take into account the motives behind a person's action. The most comprehensive approach—and the one that fits best with our natural intuitions—is that laid out by Plato and Aristotle: the approach that makes use of both a regulative ideal and also takes into consideration the circumstances, motives, and possibilities of particular cases. This approach, commonly known as virtue ethics, recognizes both the universality of moral principles and the possible differences in how those principles ought to be applied, depending on the particular situation. In this framework, the locus of morality is the character of the individual person. It is persons who are either virtuous or vicious, either good or evil; the rightness or wrongness of actions is judged in relation to what a fully virtuous person would do in a given situation. This approach also allows for degrees of goodness and evil: a person could be more or less virtuous or vicious in relation to the two extremes of complete virtue and complete vice. Because both virtues and vices must be acquired, there are also different levels of expectation with regard to virtuous action. In other words, learning virtue (or vice) is part of growing up, part of learning to become fully human. Under this framework, a person cannot be judged to be either good or evil on the basis of actions alone, or on the basis of an unattainable ideal. An act may be out of character; involuntary acts that may unwittingly result in some harm do not count against a person of good character, and involuntary acts that unwittingly produce some good do not count in favor of a person of bad character. Thus, it is not unreasonable to sympathize with young Lady Eva—or any number of other young, passionate men and women—in their sometimes indiscreet or imprudent communications. It is also under this framework that we have the best chance of making an accurate evaluation of the moral questions and arguments found in this story. So let us now apply this approach to various aspects of the story.

Aristotle, Plato, Holmes, and Milverton

It is true that Milverton's schemes would fail if the exposure of the secrets found in the letters he collects were taken less seriously by those he threatens to give them to. If, for example, the earl of Dovercourt were more forgiving and understanding of his fiancée's youthful ways (after all, he was most likely guilty of the same thing), and if the attitudes of both the members of London's high society and the members of the paparazzi whose report on them were less predatory, then the exposure of these letters would not cause much of a stir, and certainly would not prevent the marriage. Holmes tells Milverton, "I shall advise [Lady Blackwell] to tell her future husband the whole story and to trust to his generosity." Milverton chuckles at this, saying, "You evidently do not know the Earl."[15] Holmes knows, too, that this will not work. Holmes could, of course, try to talk Lady Eva out of marrying a man who is so ungenerous, but that's not what she has hired him to do. The earl is indeed less generous than he ought to be, and probably more concerned with public acceptance than he ought to be. Perhaps Lady Blackwell is guilty of the same. No doubt there is plenty of blame to go around; we see the same faults in our own institutions. In fact, it is probably worse: just witness the depths of depravity many people will go to in order to dig up dirt, and the exorbitant costs they can demand to keep it quiet. Politics, as usual. This is not to deny that there are many things we should know about each other, especially if we are being asked to decide who will serve us in public office, but there is an obvious lack of judgment when it comes to determining what pieces of personal information are relevant to the decisions we must make.

However, Milverton does not and cannot make an ethical case for what he is doing. He doesn't pretend that his exposures might do anybody any good; he freely admits that his aim is his own selfish personal gain. The people he blackmails are not necessarily (and probably not even usually) public servants. He targets the rich and aristocrats, whether they be in public service or not. This alone reveals Milverton's malice and is reason enough for condemning him. But the malice goes much deeper. As Holmes points out, Milverton's selfish motives are augmented by his genius, his intellectual facility. Holmes says, "The fellow is a genius in his way, and would have made his mark in some more savoury trade"[16]—such as private investigation. The comparison to Holmes himself is irresistible, and appropriate.

It is the misuse of Milverton's intellectual virtues that make him so morally vicious. Milverton uses his genius for the sole end of making his fortune—bad enough, one might say—by circumventing the law and inflicting suffering on his victims. Holmes, on the other hand, uses his genius in service to the law and his fellow citizens. Granted, his motives are not purely altruistic (he has his vices, and he enjoys his reputation and his earnings too), but by comparison with Milverton, Holmes is closer to moral virtue than vice. It is precisely because Milverton resembles Holmes in his genius that Holmes becomes so incensed by Milverton's abuse of that genius. Holmes, like Milverton, is usually calm and detached in his dealings with others, giving the impression of cold calculation. Yet it is just this attitude in Milverton's dealings with his victims that causes Holmes to despise him so much. Holmes knows that this attitude is often needed in investigating crimes: strong emotions might blind an investigator to the best interpretation of the evidence and lead to incorrect deductions. However, the immediate aim of investigating crimes is to catch the criminal and bring him to justice: Milverton's aim is just the opposite: to catch the unsuspecting, helpless victim and bring her to ruin.

Moreover, it is precisely Milverton's genius, his intellectual cunning, that makes him effectively untouchable by the law. How beautifully ironic, then, that Holmes uses his own genius to do exactly what Milverton has done in order to bring him to justice! In order to stop this man from operating outside the reach of the law, Holmes devises a plan that requires him—Holmes—to operate beyond the reach of the law.

So is Holmes acting virtuously in this case?

The first important thing to realize in evaluating the moral worth of Holmes's actions is that the only reason the law is, practically speaking, ineffective in this instance is because of Milverton himself: his soul is a combination of high intelligence and low moral character, with the latter directing the former. If he were not the sort of man he is, the law might find a way to stop him. But it has not, and it cannot. This is why Holmes says that "there are certain crimes the law cannot touch"[17]—not because the law is not circumspect, but because there are people like Milverton who will misuse their intellect to find a way to nullify its force. A law that cannot be enforced is no better than no law at all. Recognizing this possibility, what is to be done in such a case? If there were no moral obligation or principle to prevent these sorts of criminals, then there would be nothing to stop the Milvertons of the world from ruling it, and nothing wrong in letting them do so. So who—what kind of soul—could stop him, and should stop him? It would have to be one of similar intelligence but with a better character. If such a man were virtuous, he would see that it was his obligation to stop the unjust actions of such a vicious man. It may even be his pleasure to do so, because, as Aristotle states, a truly virtuous man would find his greatest pleasure in doing what is noble and would be pained to do otherwise. Now Holmes may not be truly virtuous—he may have mixed motives—but if he is doing what a virtuous man would do, then his actions accord with virtue and are therefore ethically justifiable.

A second important realization is that this is an unusual case, with extenuating circumstances. Holmes does not ordinarily engage in criminal activity, and he would not do so if he could acquire his object otherwise. Of his pretended engagement to the housemaid, Holmes says to Watson, "It was a most necessary step. . . . You must play your cards as best you can when such a stake is on the table." Of his burglary attempt he says:

> I have given it every consideration. I am never precipitate in my actions, nor would I adopt so energetic, indeed, so dangerous a course, if any other were possible. Let us look at the matter clearly

> and fairly. I suppose you will admit that the action is morally justifiable, though technically criminal. To burgle his house is no more than to forcibly take his pocketbook—an action in which you were prepared to aid me.[18]

Watson agrees, "so long as our object is to take no articles save those which are used for an illegal purpose." Furthermore, he points out, the circumstances are such that no alternative course of action is possible, if they are to prevent the letters from being revealed: "The unfortunate lady has not the money, and there are none of her people in whom she could confide. Tomorrow is the last day of grace, and unless we can get the letters tonight, this villain will be as good as his word and will bring about her ruin. I must, therefore, abandon my client to her fate or I must play this last card."[19]

Both Plato and Aristotle recognize that there are times when either dire circumstances or the malevolent actions of others make it incumbent upon a virtuous man that he perform acts that he would ordinarily not do—acts that he otherwise would condemn. In *Republic,* for example, Socrates indicates that it would be wrong to return a borrowed weapon if the owner of the weapon is mad with rage when he asks for it back, and intends to do harm with it.[20] Again, at the end of book 2 of *Republic,* Socrates recognizes the valid (and maybe even the noble) use of falsehoods—against enemies, when our friends are out of their minds, or when educating the youth into a love of goodness through stories and song.[21]

This latter passage is of particular importance because Socrates is discussing the distinction between what he calls a "true falsehood" and a "falsehood in words." It is this latter kind of falsehood—a falsehood in words—that he says can be usefully used by a decent person in the cases mentioned above. A true falsehood, by contrast, is a false belief held in "the most important part of ourselves about the most important things."[22] The most important part of ourselves, Socrates indicates, is our soul—our character—and the most important things are the ideas we hold about what is good, just, and beautiful. A belief of this sort guides and shapes a person's whole way of life. If the belief is false, then the life will be a false one as well—that is, the life of a vicious soul. And if the belief is true—if it's a "true truth" as opposed to a "true falsehood"—then the life will be a true life, the life of virtue. In other words, a true falsehood is what one will always find in the heart of every person who voluntarily commits wicked acts. The distinction between these two kinds of falsehoods is important because Socrates is saying that a falsehood in words is useful to a virtuous person only as a weapon against a true falsehood held by someone who is vicious or acting as a vicious person would. Look at the times he says a falsehood in words is useful:

1. Against an enemy—a true enemy, someone who holds a true falsehood in his soul and thereby harms himself and others by his vicious character and way of life.
2. To treat a friend who has lost his mind and is acting as a vicious person would, thereby harming himself and others by his actions. Socrates says that in this case the falsehood in words is like giving a drug to someone who is sick.
3. In stories and songs used to teach young people the ideals of virtue and evoke a passion for the virtuous life. From the context of this part of *Republic,* it is clear that Socrates thinks the only reason these songs and stories have to be falsified at all is because it is so difficult (if not impossible) to find actual human beings that are completely virtuous. Such heroes are extremely rare. Thus, when we tell their stories in order to teach and inspire the young, we will have to alter those stories in such a way that we do not give the wrong message. In short, even the best of men sometimes succumb to true falsehoods.

The point, then, is that there are occasions—though they would be rare—in which it is actually the part of a virtuous person to do what would ordinarily be unethical or unreasonable. Aristotle makes a similar point in his discussion on voluntary and involuntary acts at the beginning of book 3 of the *Nicomachean Ethics.* An involuntary act is one that is either due to constraint—an outside or uncontrollable force—or due to ignorance of particular facts—excusable ignorance of who is affected, or of the particular consequences of the action, or of the proper method or manner of carrying out the action, or of the appropriate use of the tool used in carrying out the action. By contrast, a voluntary act is one where a person knows all the relevant facts and has the power to decide and will her course of action. In short, a voluntary act is one for which the person can be held accountable, and an involuntary act is one for which the person cannot be held to account. However, after giving these primary criteria for distinguishing between a voluntary and an involuntary (or nonvoluntary) act, Aristotle discusses exceptional cases—cases when the circumstances dictate that a reasonable person must act unusually. For example, in the midst of a storm at sea, a ship's captain might decide to jettison his cargo in order to save the crew. This is definitely a voluntary act and would, under normal circumstances, be condemned. However, under the unusual circumstances described, it is a right decision and exactly what a wise, virtuous person would do.[23] This example shows that even though we can have a universal conception of a virtuous person, this person's acts cannot be judged apart from knowing the character of the people he is dealing with and the conditions under which he must decide his course of action.

Closing the Case

Now we can return to Holmes, Watson, and Milverton. If what Holmes says is true—that there are crimes that the law cannot touch, and that the blackmail carried out by Milverton is just such a crime—and if it is true that a virtuous person is obligated to rectify such injustices to the extent that his or her abilities allow, then certainly Holmes and Watson (and maybe even Milverton's murderess) are justified in carrying out Holmes's plan. If we wonder whether it is a sign of viciousness in Holmes that he takes pleasure in carrying out his plan—well, not even this is certain, for a virtuous person will indeed take pleasure in doing what he can to rectify injustices.

Does this show that Holmes is a virtuous man? Yes—to a degree. Because he voluntarily does what a virtuous man would do, to that extent he follows virtue. His revulsion at the vileness of Milverton's character shows that he has the right reaction to someone who is a cold, calculating criminal, who preys on the most vulnerable as his victims, and who abuses his gift of genius. Crimes of passion, though voluntary, are more excusable and understandable. All those who know Holmes—Watson, Arthur Conan Doyle, his avid readers—know that he has his vices. He would not be nearly so interesting without them, because without them, he would not be at all like the rest of us. He is, after all, a man.

So is Milverton—the kind of man whose character is truly wicked. Next to him, Holmes is clearly on the side of virtue. This, then, is the basis of Holmes's judgments and decisions: not the crime, but the man. In the end, our moral judgments and decisions are based not on each other's actions, but on the kind of persons we are.

"The Adventure of Charles Augustus Milverton" has a nice tag. At the end of the story, Holmes recalls seeing a photograph of the woman who shot Milverton in a shop window. Without a word, he takes Watson to the shop, where they both look at the photograph of the woman with her famous husband. "Then I caught my breath," writes Watson, "as I read the time-honoured title of the great nobleman and statesman whose wife she had been. My eyes met those of Holmes, and he put his finger to his lips as we turned away from the window."[24] Never do we learn who she was.

Fitting, don't you think?

Notes

1. Sir Arthur Conan Doyle, "The Adventure of Charles Augustus Milverton," in *The Complete Sherlock Holmes* (New York: Barnes & Noble Classics, 2003), 2:113–25. All quotations from this story are cited by page number from this edition.
2. Ibid., 2:113.
3. Ibid.
4. Ibid., 2:114.
5. Ibid.
6. Ibid.
7. Ibid., 2:115.
8. Ibid., 2:116.
9. Ibid., 2:118.
10. Ibid., 2:123.
11. Ibid., 2:125.
12. See Aristotle, *Nicomachean Ethics* (New York: Macmillan, 1962), book 5, 1130b:30–35.
13. "Charles Augustus Milverton," 2:114.
14. Immanuel Kant, *The Fundamental Principles of the Metaphysics of Morals* (New York: Macmillan, 1985).
15. "Charles Augustus Milverton," 2:115.
16. Ibid., 2:113.
17. Ibid., 2:125.
18. Ibid., 2:118.
19. Ibid.
20. Plato, *Republic* (Indianapolis: Hackett, 1993), 6 (331c).
21. Ibid., 58 (382c–d).
22. Ibid., 58 (382a).
23. For the complete discussion, see Aristotle, *Nicomachean Ethics*, 1109b:30–111b:4.
24. "Charles Augustus Milverton," 2:125.

A Case of Insincerity

What Does It Mean to Deceive Someone?

Kevin Kinghorn

Whether disguising himself as an Italian priest in "The Final Problem" or leaving false evidence of his own death in "The Adventure of the Empty House," Sherlock Holmes always seems to be one step ahead of friends and adversaries alike. Holmes's ultimate goal, of course, is to thwart the maneuvers of criminals throughout London. As we watch him do so time and again, we notice that he often relies on trickery of some sort. He hides his true intentions when speaking to suspects, he misdirects them as to his whereabouts, he lulls them into a false sense of security. In short, Holmes regularly relies on deception to getter the better of others.

One way of exploring Holmes's use of deception would be to investigate when deception is and isn't morally acceptable. Clearly, deception is sometimes deplorable, as when James Windibank cruelly impersonates a suitor to his daughter-in-law in "A Case of Identity," or when Moriarty in "The Final Problem" draws Watson away from Holmes with a fake note about a patient as part of a plan to isolate and kill Holmes. At other times, though, deception seems entirely appropriate, as when we note that Holmes's reason for masquerading as a priest in the previously mentioned story is to escape Moriarty's murderous pursuit. Admittedly there have been a few philosophers, such as Immanuel Kant (1724–1804), who have argued that deceptive lying is always wrong. But most philosophers hold the view, which is surely correct, that deception is sometimes morally permissible and sometimes not.

Although the line between appropriate and inappropriate deception is an interesting question (and one discussed at length in Chapter 2 of this volume), I want to explore the prior question of what deception is. That is, I want to look at the nature of deception itself and what conditions would need to be met for us rightly to conclude that an act of deception has taken place. In what follows, we'll explore various definitions of *deceive,* identifying the shortcomings of these definitions until we finally arrive at a satisfactory explanation of the concept. Once we arrive at this final definition, we will see that it implies something rather surprising about Holmes's relationship with his nemesis, Professor Moriarty.

Going beyond the Dictionary

One of the jobs of a philosopher is to bring clarity and precision to the terms we use in everyday language. Often dictionary definitions lack the nuance needed to distinguish one concept from similar—though importantly different—other concepts. The Merriam-Webster dictionary defines *deceive* as "to cause to accept as true or valid what is false or invalid."

This definition, though, is far from adequate. In "A Scandal in Bohemia," Holmes takes elaborate steps to discover that Irene Adler has hidden a certain photograph behind a sliding panel in her sitting room. Holmes informs Watson during an evening conversation at Baker Street that they will call on "the woman" the next day and recover the photograph while they are waiting for her to receive them. Holmes tells Watson that they will go at "eight in the morning. She will not be up, so that we shall have a clear field."[1] In point of fact, however, when they arrive the next morning they are told by the maid: "My mistress told me that you were likely to call. She left this morning with her husband by the 5:15 train from Charing Cross for the Continent."[2] In one of the few times in which Holmes is outfoxed, "the woman" has been a step ahead of him.

Holmes had announced to Watson that Irene Adler would not be up at eight in the morning and that they would have an opportunity to recover the photograph. But Holmes was mistaken. All the same, Holmes did cause Watson to accept as true something that was actually false. His action thus meets our dictionary definition of *deceive.* Surely, though, it isn't right to say that Holmes deceived Watson. Holmes made an honest mistake. Perhaps we'd want to say that he unintentionally misled Watson. But genuine deception seems to be a different concept from an honest mistake, even if both can cause someone else to end up with a false belief. We must thus amend our initial definition to exclude those times when we honestly offer other people information that happens to be false.

Double Bluffing about an Empty House

An easy way to exclude honest mistakes from qualifying as deception is to propose the following definition for *deceive:* "To communicate something one believes to be false, with the intention that another person comes to believe it."

In our example from "A Scandal in Bohemia," Holmes intended to convey a true statement to Watson. It's just that the statement, unbeknownst to Holmes, was false. This new definition gets to the important point that deception involves an intention to get someone else to believe what we ourselves don't believe. Is our latest definition, then, an acceptable one? Not yet.

To see why, consider the plot line from "The Adventure of the Empty House." Holmes is on the run from adversaries who are plotting to kill him. He places a wax bust bearing his likeness in a chair in a room at Baker Street. Holmes then pulls the shades, and he lights the room so that at evening, a silhouette of the bust is clearly visible to those on the street below. He subsequently has the following exchange with Watson, in which he explains his plan to catch an enemy in the act of attempted assassination:

> "My dear Watson, I had the strongest possible reason for wishing certain people to think that I was there when I was really elsewhere."
>
> "And you thought the rooms were watched?"
>
> "I *knew* that they were watched."
>
> "By whom?"
>
> "By my old enemies, Watson. . . . Sooner or later they believed that I should come back to my rooms. They watched them continuously, and this morning they saw me arrive."
>
> "How do you know?"
>
> "Because I recognized their sentinel when I glanced out of my window. He is a harmless enough fellow. . . . I cared nothing for him. But I cared a great deal for the much more formidable person who was behind him . . . the most cunning and dangerous criminal in London. That is the man who is after me to-night, Watson, and that is the man who is quite unaware that we are after him."[3]

Holmes hides in an empty house across the street, having also alerted the police to be on watch. Holmes and the police eventually capture the man in question, Colonel Sebastian Moran, after Moran shoots a sniper bullet through the wax bust.

In the story line, we are told that Moran's sentinel spotted Holmes back at Baker Street early in the day. For the sake of discussion, we might imagine Holmes making several loud, public statements that day that he will not be returning home that evening. We imagine here that Holmes is actually engaged in an effort to make the sentinel think that Holmes really is going to be at home that evening. That is, we imagine Holmes as envisaging that the sentinel will take Holmes's own public proclamations as an attempt to throw any would-be assassins off his trail. Holmes here would be engaged in double bluffing. He would be saying something that is actually true—namely, that he won't be at home that evening. Yet Holmes would foresee that a suspicious assassin would interpret his true statement as an attempt to say something false and misleading to any eavesdropping enemies.

If we now look back at our working definition of *deceive,* we can see why it is inadequate. In our case of double bluffing, Holmes would indeed be trying to deceive his would-be assassin. Yet he wouldn't actually be saying anything he believes to be false. So on our current definition his actions wouldn't count as deception (even though clearly he would be trying to deceive). What this shows is that we need to revise our definition so as to account for cases of double bluffing. We can do this by removing the requirement that the content of what the deceiver communicates be something that he or she "believes to be false." What remains important in the concept of deception is that the deceiver intends that the deceived person end up believing something that the deceiver believes to be false. As the case of double bluffing shows, a deceiver could have this intention even while uttering a true statement.

Deceptions about That, not This

Taking into account the conclusions of the previous section, we are now left with the following working definition of *deceive:* "To communicate something with the intention that another person comes to hold a false belief about it."

Yet this definition still needs refining. In "A Case of Identity," the scoundrel James Windibank cruelly disguises himself and pretends to be a suitor of his stepdaughter, Miss Sutherland. His invented character, Hosmer Angel, then abruptly disappears, leaving the stepdaughter distraught. Holmes investigates the case of Hosmer Angel's disappearance and comes to suspect strongly that James Windibank and Hosmer Angel are one and the same. He then invites Windibank to his residence at Baker Street, and the following exchange takes place:

> "Good-evening, Mr. James Windibank," said Holmes. "I think that this typewritten letter is from you, in which you made an appointment with me for six o'clock?"
>
> "Yes, sir. I am afraid that I am a little late, but I am not quite my own master, you know. I am sorry that Miss Sutherland has troubled you about this little matter. . . . Of course, I did not mind you so much, as you are not connected with the official police, but it is not pleasant to have a family misfortune like this noised abroad. Besides, it is a useless expense, for how could you possibly find this Hosmer Angel?"
>
> "On the contrary," said Holmes quietly; "I have every reason to believe that I will succeed in discovering Mr. Hosmer Angel."
>
> Mr. Windibank gave a violent start and dropped his gloves. "I am delighted to hear it," he said.[4]

When Holmes states that there is reason to believe that Hosmer Angel will be discovered, he does not intend that Windibank actually come to believe this to be true. That is, Holmes doesn't intend that Windibank come to think that there really is someone named Hosmer Angel whose whereabouts can be discovered. Rather Holmes merely wants to plant the idea in Windibank's head that he, Holmes, thinks there is some actual person named Hosmer Angel. Holmes is temporarily throwing Windibank off the scent so that he will be off guard when Holmes finally levels the accusation that Windibank has been masquerading under the pseudonym Hosmer Angel.

For our larger discussion of deception, what is important from this example is that the statement Holmes communicates (namely, that there is reason to believe that Hosmer Angel will be discovered) is not actually the matter on which Holmes is attempting to mislead Windibank. Holmes intends to mislead Windibank about his (Holmes's) own beliefs about Hosmer Angel, even though his actual statement to Windibank is that actual reasons exist for thinking that Hosmer Angel might yet be discovered.

The definition we've been considering is this: "To communicate something one believes to be false, with the intention that another person comes to believe it." However, we have now seen that we can communicate one thing to someone, with the intention that they be deceived about another thing.

We thus need to revise again our definition of *deceive* so that Holmes's communication to Windibank counts as an act of deception (which it clearly is). We can do this by removing the stipulation that the content of a deceiver's statement must be the same as the content of the false belief the deceived person comes to hold. We might thus be led to the following definition of *deceive:* "To communicate something with the intention that another person comes to hold some false belief."

By stipulating only that the deceiver comes to hold some false belief, we remove the condition that this false belief must mirror exactly the content of what the deceiver communicates. This latest definition of *deceive* allows us, rightly, to say that Holmes's statement to Windibank is an act of deception.

Langurs and Pharmaceutical Manipulation

There is still some work to be done, though, if we are to arrive at an adequate meaning of *deceive.* What our latest definition lacks is a reference to why the deceived person comes to hold a false belief. Consider the case of Professor Presbury in "The Adventure of the Creeping Man." Presbury becomes infatuated with a much younger woman, and to allay her concerns about their age difference, he seeks a bizarre kind of help from a scientist named Lowenstein. Watson informs us that Lowenstein was "tabooed by the profession" and "was striving in some unknown way for the secret of rejuvenescence and the elixir of life."[5]

Lowenstein provided Professor Presbury with a serum to be taken every nine days. The serum did provide remarkable strength and vitality to Presbury, particularly the day the serum was taken. Unfortunately, there were serious side effects. The serum had somehow been extracted in part from a langur, an animal described as "the great black-faced monkey of the Himalayan slopes."[6] After each dose of serum, Presbury would behave much like a monkey, climbing vines, harassing the family dog, and sometimes even walking on all fours. During the intense period following each dose, we're told by the professor's daughter that "there are times when he has no recollection of what he does."[7]

As the inventor of the serum, Lowenstein is well aware of its general side effects. Although the actual story gives us no reason to think that he intends Presbury to lose his memory or believe he is a monkey, we might suppose for sake of an example that he does intend it. That is, we might imagine that Lowenstein has the sinister goal of making Presbury believe he is a monkey. After administering a dose of the serum to Presbury, Lowenstein might then whisper in his ear, "You are a monkey." In this example, Lowenstein would be communicating something to Presbury with the intention that Presbury come to hold a false belief. This example would thus be an instance of deception according to our latest definition of *deceive.* Yet causing someone to hold a false belief by such manipulative means as drugs, hypnotism, or brainwashing is surely not the same as deceiving someone. To distinguish deception from mere manipulation we will need to specify the reason that the deceived person comes to hold a false belief. What seems key to the concept of deception is that the deceived person's reasoning process includes an assumption about the sincerity of the person communicating the information.

In our everyday conversations with others, we assume that—all things being equal—others are being forthright in what they tell us. Unless we have some reason to think that someone isn't telling us the truth as best they understand it, we assume that they are in fact being truthful. This universal assumption we make about others can be demonstrated in the fact that we all learn language. As the philosopher Ludwig Wittgenstein (1889–1951) emphasized, language is never something we ourselves invent privately. It is a public construct and thus something we must learn by exposure to it.

How does anyone learn a language? Perhaps as children we witness a parent pointing to objects and saying "chair" or "cat" or "dog." If we did not accept at face value that these objects are indeed associated with the terms uttered by the adults in our lives, we would never learn a language. Even if we did suspect that our parents—or, if we are adults, our foreign language teachers—might be misleading us, how could we ever check their forthrightness? We would have to take some other person's word for it that we were being misled. In the end, there really is no way to learn a language but to take other people's testimony to us at face value.

Once again, if we have no specific reason to think that a person isn't being forthright, the fallback position is that he or she is indeed being forthright. Only hardened cynics, disillusioned about humanity on account of the lies told by those they trust, fail to make this assumption about the sincerity of others in everyday life.

This assumption about others' sincerity seems to be the key point in distinguishing deception from other forms of manipulation. In cases of deception, the deceived person's evidence or line of reasoning relies in some way on the (false) belief that others are being truthful. So let us consider the following definition of *deceive:* "To communicate something with the intention that another person comes to hold some false belief, where the reasons the deceiver manufactures rely on an incorrect assumption that he is sincere."

Is this definition finally adequate to capture all cases of deception? Almost. We still have one slight (and final) amendment to make.

Double Agent Watson

Our last amendment focuses on the question of whether it must be my own insincerity on which the person I deceive mistakenly relies. An elaborate example from Glen Newey[8] (b. 1961) demonstrates that my deception of another person can be accomplished by making use of someone else's insincerity. Let me illustrate the kind of example Newey has in mind by referencing an imagined, collaborative plan devised by Holmes and Watson.

Let us suppose that one of Sherlock's adversaries, Major Baddie, visits Watson at his medical practice and tries to convince him to betray Holmes. Watson, of course, would never do such a thing. However, let us suppose that Watson tells Holmes of the visit beforehand, and they devise a plan for Watson to be a double agent. Watson will pretend to be in cahoots with Major Baddie and will feed him misinformation.

We suppose that Watson then earns the trust of Major Baddie. Watson and Holmes decide to use their advantage to keep Major Baddie from moving some stolen jewels he has hidden. The police, Holmes and Watson have learned, have received a tip and are closing in on the location of the jewels. Holmes and Watson want to allay Major Baddie's fears about the police investigation by convincing him that the police really aren't making any progress. Toward this end, Watson tells Major Baddie something that is false—namely, that the police are pursuing false leads and aren't actually making any headway in the case. Watson also tells him that Holmes misguidedly believes that the police *are* making progress.

As a final ploy to convince Major Baddie that he is safe from the police and has no reason to move the jewels, Holmes himself visits Major Baddie and announces, "You know, the police really don't have a clue in the case; so I suppose the jewels must really be safe." This statement is of course false, and Holmes knows it to be false. But Major Baddie thinks that Holmes thinks it's true. Because Major Baddie mistrusts Holmes's intentions, he interprets Holmes's statement as an attempt to pull off a double bluff. That is, here's what Major Baddie thinks: "Holmes mistakenly believes that the police are closing in. The reason he's telling me that they're *not* closing in is that he knows I'll naturally believe the opposite of what he says. He's trying to bluff his way into making me move the jewels and thereby reveal their whereabouts." This is what Major Baddie is thinking, and the reality is that Holmes knows this is what he's thinking.

In this elaborate example, Holmes is indeed trying to deceive Major Baddie. However, what he actually tells Major Baddie is, in reality, both true and believed to be true by Holmes. So in deceiving Major Baddie, Holmes has said nothing other than the straightforward truth. His deception does not rely on any mistaken assumption on Major Baddie's part that he, Holmes, is sincere. Indeed, he's relying on the idea that Major Baddie will assume he's not sincere! The deception is pulled off by Watson's insincerity in Watson's earlier statement to Major Baddie that Holmes wrongly believes that the police are making progress.

So instead of requiring that my deception of another person hinge on an assumption about my sincerity, our definition of *deceive* should merely reference someone's believed sincerity. Admittedly the insincerity through which deception is pulled off will typically involve the deceiver's own insincerity. But as our last elaborate example showed, this is not always the case.

We arrive now at our final definition of *deceive:* "To communicate something with the intention that another person comes to hold some false belief, where the reasons the deceiver manufactures rely on an incorrect assumption of someone's insincerity." This, I think, gets to the heart of what deception is. It also leads us to a conclusion about Holmes's interactions with Moriarty that may come as quite a surprise.

The Games People Play

The big surprise is that Holmes never actually deceives Moriarty. Aside from elaborate examples like the one involving Major Baddie, deception relies on an assumption by the deceived person about the deceiver's own sincerity. However, Moriarty doesn't make this assumption about Holmes.

Moriarty is of course the criminal mastermind whom Holmes regards as uniquely his intellectual equal. In "The Final Problem" he says of Moriarty: "He is the Napoleon of crime, Watson. He is the organizer of half that is evil and of nearly all that is undetected in this great city. He is a genius, a philosopher, an abstract thinker."[9] Holmes then relays to Watson the nature of his ongoing efforts to ensnare Moriarty: "He saw every step which I took to draw my toils round him. Again and again he strove to break away, but I as often headed him off. I tell you, my friend, that if a detailed account of that silent contest could be written, it would take its place as the most brilliant bit of thrust-and-parry work in the history of detection. Never have I risen to such a height, and never have I been so hard pressed by an opponent. He cut deep, and yet I just undercut him."[10]

Having gained the upper hand over Moriarty such that Moriarty's criminal network was days away from being exposed, Holmes is confronted by Moriarty at his Baker Street residence. Moriarty acknowledges that, owing to Holmes's continued "persecution," "I am in positive danger of losing my liberty."[11] Moriarty demands that Holmes withdraw from his pursuit, warning of an "extreme measure" (the implication being future physical harm) if he does not. Holmes refuses, leading to Moriarty's final summation of their relationship: "It seems a pity, but I have done what I could. I know every move of your game. . . . It has been a duel between you and me, Mr. Holmes. You hope to place me in the dock. I tell you that I will never stand in the dock. You hope to beat me. I tell you that you will never beat me. If you are clever enough to bring destruction upon me, rest assured that I shall do as much to you."[12]

Moriarty's reference to a game between himself and Holmes is instructive. There is a mutual understanding of the stakes of their engagement and of the mutual goal of trying to outwit the other. It will be a contest of intellect and cunning. Each move from the other person will be analyzed in an attempt to understand the strategy behind it and to counter it. Clearly there is no assumption that the other person will be well-meaning or sincere in anything that is said or done.

The game of cat and mouse between Holmes and Moriarty continues throughout the European countryside until they meet, dramatically, at Reichenbach Falls in Switzerland, ending in Moriarty plunging to his death. In attempting to outfox the other person at every turn in their journey, their contest is akin to a game of cards. When playing poker or some other card game, players do not try to deceive others. Their bluffing could only count as genuine deception if others assumed they were sincere in their communication. Clearly this is not the case in a game of cards. Instead, a card player seeks to manipulate the thinking of others at the table even while others know full well that this is what the player is trying to do. The contest among players is one of trying to pick up the right kind of information, even though only some of the information coming from each player, it is mutually recognized, will be true. This kind of contest is similar to one in which magicians might engage as they perform tricks for one another in a game of one-upmanship, with each magician trying to uncover how each magic trick on display is really done. That kind of contest is the one in which Holmes and Moriarty engage.

Because they have a mutual understanding of the nature of their contest, Holmes and Moriarty can gain no advantage over the other by relying on the general assumptions people make in everyday contexts about the sincerity of others. Holmes thus never actually deceives Moriarty, just as Moriarty never deceives Holmes. With his elaborate disguises and strategic misdirection, Holmes indeed deserves to be ranked as a master deceiver. Watson, perhaps the person most commonly fooled by Holmes's disguises, could attest to that! Our discussion has clarified what it truly means to deceive someone. However, our conclusion, showing the link between deception and sincerity, also means that, strictly speaking, deception is not one of the tools available to Holmes as he engages with Moriarty. Perhaps if Holmes gave Moriarty a serum made from a langur so that Moriarty forgot he was engaged in a contest. . . . Well, that would be one elaborate example too many.

Notes

1. Sir Arthur Conan Doyle, "A Scandal in Bohemia," in *The Complete Sherlock Holmes* (New York: Doubleday, 1960), 173. All further citations are to this edition.
2. Ibid., 174.
3. "Empty House," 490.
4. "Case of Identity," 199.
5. "Creeping Man," 1082.
6. Ibid., 1082.
7. Ibid., 1075.
8. Glen Newey, "Political Lying: A Defense," *Public Affairs Quarterly* 11 (1997): 93–116.
9. "Final Problem," 471.
10. Ibid.
11. Ibid., 472.
12. Ibid., 473.

Sherlock's Reasoning Toolbox

Massimo Pigliucci

"It is simplicity itself. . . . My eyes tell me that on the inside of your left shoe, just where the firelight strikes it, the leather is scored by six almost parallel cuts. Obviously they have been caused by someone who has very carelessly scraped round the edges of the sole in order to remove crusted mud from it. Hence, you see, my double deduction that you had been out in vile weather, and that you had a particularly malignant boot-slitting specimen of the London slavey." So says Sherlock Holmes to a befuddled Dr. Watson in "A Scandal in Bohemia"[1] while explaining how he deduced that his old friend had gotten wet and that his servant had been careless—except that this was not an instance of deduction, in the philosophical sense of the term, but rather a form of induction. Understanding the difference between these two basic types of reasoning is fundamental to appreciate how Holmes operates, and it will lead us through a brief tour of logic, science, and the art of fine reasoning.

Conan Doyle tells us that Holmes doesn't know anything about philosophy, which perhaps accounts for why he refers to his logical method as deduction, while it is in fact a complex and highly effective mixture of different kinds of reasoning. Of course, Holmes does not always succeed in his endeavors, as for instance in the case of the scandal in the (now defunct kingdom of) Bohemia mentioned above. In that adventure, he is outfoxed by a woman from New Jersey, Irene Adler, whom he will subsequently always refer to as "the woman."[2]

How to Guarantee Truth

Let us start our tour with deduction, the foundation of logic and mathematics. Deduction is what philosophers call a truth-guaranteeing type of reasoning, meaning that if the premises of a deductive argument are correct, then the conclusion must inescapably be true. Of course, the trick is in that all-important "if" clause. It was Aristotle (384–322 BCE) who first explored deductive reasoning, particularly as exemplified in the form of syllogism, arguably the most famous of which is a variant on the following:

> PREMISE 1: All men are mortal.
> PREMISE 2: Sherlock Holmes is a man.
> CONCLUSION: Sherlock Holmes is mortal.

The above can be read as follows: If P1 is true, and if P2 is true, then C must necessarily be true—nice and elegant, exactly the sort of reasoning that would appeal to Holmes. In fact, the famous detective often displays a preference for simple and elegant reasoning, particularly if it leads to inescapable conclusions. In several stories, he tells Watson something along the lines of, "How often have I said to you that when you have eliminated the impossible, whatever remains, however improbable, must be the truth?"[3] In "The Priory School," he says that "it is impossible as I state it, and therefore I must in some respect have stated it wrong."[4] In both cases, the implication seems to be that a strict logical analysis of the facts leads to one and only one inescapable conclusion—a guarantee of truth.

The dream of developing a system of thought on the basis of which one can deduce facts about the world with absolute certainty goes back to Aristotle's mentor, Plato (428/427–348/347 BCE), and resulted in a long tradition of philosophical thought appropriately known as rationalism. That school arguably had for its last strong champion René Descartes (1596–1650). Descartes was a bold philosopher, most famous for his (ultimately failed) thought experiment known as radical doubt. He acknowledged that both our senses and our faculty of reasoning can be deceived, which means that we can never be sure of anything we say about the world. However, Descartes argued, we can be absolutely sure of at least one thing: I think, therefore I exist (the famous maxim *cogito, ergo sum*). There is absolutely no possibility of my being mistaken about this very simple but crucial fact. The idea is that even if I am systemically deceived, I have to exist in order to be deceived, so my very thinking that I may well be deceived is incontrovertible evidence of my existence—as a thinking being. I can't run this same thought experiment about you, nor you me, but you can run it for yourself. Having found this solid anchor, he then tried to logically deduce other facts about the world, to reconstruct natural philosophy from scratch, as it were. That's where the trouble started: it turns out that the only way Descartes could move past the *cogito* was by invoking God as guarantor of truth, for which he lacked a noncircular argument. His attempt to establish God's existence appealed to the same rational faculties that he had earlier called into question. The attempt to appeal to God to guarantee the clear and distinct deliverances of reason while assuming that those same deliverances could be used to argue for God's existence led to what some commentators have dubbed the Cartesian circle. Descartes's approach using deduction to move from the certitude of some beliefs about oneself to certitude about beliefs concerning the external world and God failed. It was a remarkable enterprise and a seminal moment in the history of philosophy, and the failure of his effort was instructive.

None of the above implies that we should abandon the use of deduction, but it does mean that there are strict limits on what it can accomplish. In fact, although deduction is the essential tool in formal logic and mathematics, it won't do for science, everyday life, and of course criminal investigations. Why not? The answer becomes clear if we go back for a moment to our syllogism above and think about it more carefully. In particular, look at the two premises: "All men are mortal" (P1) and "Sherlock Holmes is a man" (P2). How do we know that these are, in fact, true? P2 is the result of direct observation (well, not exactly in Holmes's case, because he is in fact a fictional character and not a man, but you get the gist). We can examine any particular being and determine that because of his anatomy, physiology, or even DNA structure, he is indeed a member of the species *Homo sapiens*, and more particularly belongs to the male sex. Of course, observations are fallible, as Descartes painfully realized, so we cannot be 100 percent sure that Holmes is a man, regardless of how many tests we run on his biology. This is important because it introduces an element of probability (as opposed to certainty) into the whole affair, already undermining the idea that deductive reasoning is truth preserving. Holmes himself is aware of this problem, as is evident, for instance, from a comment he makes in *The Hound of the Baskervilles*: "We balance probabilities and choose the most likely. It is the scientific use of the imagination."[5]

But it gets worse—much worse. Let us turn again to P1, the premise that all men are mortal. It is necessary to state it in such absolute terms because if we were to say that most men are mortal, then the conclusion would not follow: Holmes may turn out to be one of the few exceptions and may never die. But how do we know that all men—without exception—are mortal? The long and the short of it is that we don't. What we can say instead is that we have never observed a man who was immortal (leaving aside for a moment the not necessarily trivial problem of how, exactly, we would recognize an immortal in a crowd of mortals). That is, we are generalizing from a series of observations, what philosophers call induction. An induction, therefore, is at best as good as the data that we have available. In "The Copper Beeches," Holmes endeavors to help Miss Violet Hunter, who has been employed under most unusual circumstances by a fellow named Jephro Rucastle. It turns out that Rucastle was using Miss Hunter in an attempt to dissuade a man who was courting his own daughter (who resembled Hunter) from pursuing her. Rucastle wished to force his daughter to sign over her inheritance to him—a project that would have floundered had the lover kept up his romantic interests. (At the end of the story, Rucastle is attacked and maimed for life by his own starved mastiff dog.) Holmes cannot initially make sense of what is going on in the case, and in a rather uncharacteristic outburst of temper, he cries to Watson, "Data! Data! Data! . . . I can't make bricks without clay."[6]

The Problem of Induction

More data, in and of itself, is still not going to be enough, according to philosopher David Hume (1711–76). Hume articulated one of the most difficult problems in epistemology—a problem that still haunts philosophers and scientists, and that would much bother Holmes, had he devoted more time to the study of philosophy during his retirement: the problem of induction. Remember that induction is a method of generalizing from a set of observations (Holmes's "Data! Data! Data!"). For instance, I can be highly confident that the sun will rise tomorrow even in the absence of any understanding of astronomy and planetary orbits, the reason being that there is a long record of observations of the sun doing just that. Because there have been no exceptions so far, it is reasonable—the inductivist would say—to assume that tomorrow is not going to be an exception either.

The famous logician Bertrand Russell (1872–1970), however, spoke of an example that should make the inductivist pause.[7] It is known as Russell's inductivist chicken, and it goes like this: when the chicken is brought into the farm, he may notice that he is being fed every day at the same time by the farmer. Being a cautious inductivist, though, the chicken doesn't jump to any conclusion and instead awaits for more data to come in. After a long time, he feels that his data sheet is detailed enough and he can confidently make the prediction that the following day, at the usual time, he will be fed. That happened to be the day, sadly, when the farmer wrings his neck. This little story illustrates the point that induction, unlike deduction, is not truth preserving, because it only produces probabilistic conclusions, which may very well turn out to be wrong in any particular instance—sometimes fatally so, as in the case of the philosophically naive chicken.

Hume's problem with induction, however, went much deeper. He noted that not only does induction not guarantee truth, but also that we do not really have any good justification for assuming that induction works as a way of reasoning about the world. The problem can be appreciated most starkly by simply asking the question, why do we think induction works? Pretty much the best answer we can give is, because it has worked in the past. However, a moment of reflection will show that the latter is itself an example of inductive reasoning. In other words, we are trying to justify induction by induction, thereby falling into another instance of the classical logical fallacy of begging the question or circular reasoning. This ought to be deeply troubling not only to philosophers but to criminal investigators because it potentially undermines Sherlock's cherished trust in logic and reason. (Hume, incidentally, was far too pragmatic a man to actually suggest that we should give up reasoning altogether; his point is that perhaps we should be a bit more humble about our much-vaunted powers of rationality.)

If all of the above isn't problematic enough, here is another bombshell dropped by Hume: even the otherwise truth-preserving method of deduction must, at some point, be based on inductive reasoning, which means that it falls prey to the same problem of induction articulated by Hume, and which has remained pretty much unsolved to this day. To see this, let us go again back to our simple syllogism about Holmes's demise: we have already noticed that P1, "All men are mortal," is not something deduced from first principles. It is not a logical necessity that men be mortal; it just happens to be the case.[8] This means that our premise that all men are mortal is in fact the result of generalizing from a set of observations—in other words, it is the result of induction! It turns out that this is a general situation: the premises of a deductive argument often are the result of preexisting induction, which means that even the truth-preserving character of deduction is in fact built on shaky foundations.[9]

In *A Study in Scarlet,* our hero manages to solve a complex case involving two murders that had baffled the police and that require the reader to go through a lengthy excursion into a side story involving Brigham Young, the founder of the Mormon church. In one of his characteristic minilessons to Dr. Watson about the art of detecting, Holmes boldly states, "From a drop of water a logician could infer the possibility of an Atlantic or a Niagara without having seen or heard of one or the other."[10] We now know enough about logic to recognize that such aspirations, even for an ideal reasoner, are unfounded: the problem of induction and the failure of the rationalist program in philosophy pretty much guarantee that not even a mind as great as Holmes's own brother, Mycroft, could possibly achieve such a feat.

It is rather peculiar that Conan Doyle—who was well read and sensitive to the cultural debates of his time—did not pay more attention to the difference between deduction and induction in developing the character of Holmes. This is particularly so because he wrote his stories shortly after the great induction debate, which involved major figures of Victorian England, including John Stuart Mill (1806–73) and none other than Charles Darwin (1809–82). The great induction debate unfolded between two of the major British philosophers of Darwin's time, Mill and William Whewell (1794–1866), and was an early attempt to solve the problem posed by Hume.

Mill thought that scientists could use two kinds of induction, which would mutually reinforce each other. Enumerative induction is a process of generalization from observations to generalities supported by the principle of universal causation, the idea that all phenomena have causes and that it is logical to attribute similar causes to similar phenomena. Eliminative induction is an operation by which the causes of natural phenomena are discovered by successive elimination of unsuitable alternatives on the basis of tests as stringent as can be devised. Indeed, it is easy to see that Mill's approach has much in common with what Holmes does in many of his adventures.

Whewell, however, would have none of it because he thought that scientific investigation had to start with hypotheses, not observations, because hypotheses have the value of guiding one's inquiry, telling us where and how to observe. When a hypothesis is confronted with the data, one knows if it is true, according to Whewell, because of what he called consilience: "The cases in which inductions from classes of facts altogether different have thus jumped together, belong only to the best established theories which the history of science contains. And as I shall have occasion to refer to this peculiar feature of their evidence, I will take the liberty of describing it by a particular phrase; and will term it the Consilience of Induction."[11] Consilience is often referred to as abduction, or inference to the best explanation, and chapters 1 and 12 in this book will argue that this is what Holmes really did. Yet the case is far from settled; it is easy to find instances where the detective refuses to speculate in generating hypotheses á la Whewell. For instance, in two of the already mentioned adventures, *A Study in Scarlet* and "A Scandal in Bohemia," Holmes says that "it is a capital mistake to theorize before you have all the evidence. It biases the judgment."[12] Mill would have wholeheartedly agreed.

The great induction debate has to do with Darwin because Mill and Whewell, despite their differences, concurred that Darwin's work in *On the Origin of Species* was based on deduction and was therefore bad science. In the end, it became obvious that Darwin was correct: the theory of evolution is not a mass of conjectures but—ironically—an inductive argument along the very same lines proposed by Whewell. As Darwin himself put it (and pace Holmes): "How odd it is that anyone should not see that all observation must be for or against some view if it is to be of any service!"[13]

How to Falsify Hypotheses

Be that as it may, we are still stuck with Hume's problem of induction. There are hints that Holmes himself foresaw one possible solution and made it part of his practice. In *The Sign of Four,* our hero is jolted out of a drug-induced stupor by the visit of Lady Mary Morstan. In the midst of the complex action that develops, Holmes at one point remarks, "I never make exceptions. An exception disproves the rule."[14]

This idea that exceptions disprove rules, and that therefore a single exceptional case demolishes a cherished hypothesis, is at the foundation of the boldest attempt yet to solve the problem of induction: Karl Popper's (1902–94) theory of falsificationism. Popper was interested in the distinction between science and pseudoscience, what he called the demarcation problem.[15] He was convinced, for instance, that Freudian psychoanalysis is not scientific (despite Freud's protestations to the contrary) for the simple reason that pretty much any observation about human behavior can be accommodated by the theory. If every possible new data can only confirm the theory and nothing can conceivably disconfirm or falsify it, then the theory is not a scientific one, according to Popper.

To see the contrast, consider a real scientific theory, like Einstein's general relativity. It makes specific predictions about the behavior of light (for instance, that it should bend by a certain degree around massive objects, because the presence of mass makes space-time curve). Not only is it the case that such a prediction was not made by rival theories (like Newtonian mechanics, which predicted less bending), but it has withstood many experimental tests. Had the theory of relativity failed one such test, according to Popper, we should have abandoned it. Holmes, apparently, would agree. For instance, in "The Adventure of Black Peter," in which he is faced with a gruesome murder by harpoon, Holmes says that "one should always look for a possible alternative, and provide against it. It is the first rule of criminal investigation."[16] It is that "provide against it" that captures the essence of Popper's falsificationism.

Still, even falsificationism—despite Popper's high hopes—does not get us out of the trouble that started with Hume's problem of induction. To see why, let us consider how astronomers reacted to an apparent failure of Newton's laws of mechanics. In 1821, the astronomer Alexis Bouvard had calculated a series of tables predicting the position of what was then thought to be the outermost planet in the solar system, Uranus. The problem, as Bouvard soon recognized, was that there was a significant discrepancy between the predictions and the actual positions of the planet in the sky. According to a strict interpretation of falsificationism, Bouvard and his colleagues should have at that point rejected Newton's theory, as it was manifestly and systematically incompatible with a large set of data. But they didn't. Instead, Bouvard immediately intuited the obvious answer: there must have been another planet that was influencing Uranus's orbit, thus accounting for the anomaly. A few years later, on September 23, 1846, Neptune was discovered within one degree from the position calculated by the astronomer Urbain Le Verrier. Newtonian theory was safe, and the solar system had acquired a new member.

The episode illustrates that the actual practice of science is very different from what Popper at first proposed, and in particular that scientists do not throw out a hypothesis for which there is a lot of confirmatory evidence, even in the face of some disconfirming evidence, until they absolutely have to, and probably not until they have a better alternative handy. How do they do that? In a way that Holmes himself explained in "The Reigate Puzzle": "It is of the highest importance in the art of detection to be able to recognize, out of a number of facts, which are incidental and which vital. Otherwise your energy and attention must be dissipated instead of being concentrated."[17] What is "of extreme importance in the art of detection" happens to be also of extreme importance in the practice of science, which in fact is one reason why intuition and practice account for a lot more in science than a purely rationalistic interpretation of it might allow. Science may not be an art, but it surely isn't a mechanical method that could be automatically performed by a mindless piece of computer software—just like crime detection.

Holmes the Pragmatic Scientist

So what, exactly, was the method used by Holmes so brilliantly in the four novels and fifty-six short stories of the original canon written by Conan Doyle between 1887 and 1927? We have seen that it is certainly not deduction, as so often maintained by Dr. Watson or by Holmes himself. For instance, in *A Study in Scarlet,* the great detective explains that "when a fact appears to be opposed to a long train of deductions, it invariably proves to be capable of bearing some other interpretation."[18] However, interpretation is not something that is particularly appropriate for deductive reasoning. Deduction is the sort of argument that mathematicians use to prove theorems, and facts cannot be opposed to deductive inference—unless those facts happen to be both part of one of the premises and empirically wrong.

It is one form or another of inductive reasoning that Holmes deploys throughout his adventures, but even so, his method is complex, sometimes even contradictory, which may help explain why Watson is so often dumbfounded by how his companion arrives at a given conclusion. In *The Sign of Four,* Holmes says, "I never guess. It is a shocking habit—destructive to the logical faculty,"[19] but as we have seen earlier, in *The Hound of the Baskervilles,* he claims that "we balance probabilities and choose the most likely. It is the scientific use of the imagination."[20] Yet probabilistic assessments, and even more so imagination, are quite incompatible with the rigid logical approach implied by the first quote.

Other stories give us additional clues to Holmes's modus operandi. In "The Problem of Thor Bridge" the detective is faced with an apparently open-and-shut case: the wife of a prominent senator is found murdered by a single shot of a Webley .455 revolver while clutching in her hand an incriminating note from the senator's lover. Moreover, the revolver is found, with just one shot fired, in the lover's wardrobe. Not convinced by what to everyone else seems obvious, Holmes declares that "we must look for consistency. Where there is a want of it we must suspect deception."[21] In this case, for instance, it seems odd that the lover should be so calculating in her plan, and yet so careless as to leave both the note and the revolver to incriminate her. Rather, Holmes surmises, the whole affair smells much more clearly of framing. Sure enough, the solution lies in the conclusion that it was the scorned wife, not the lover, who had planned the whole thing, including her suicide and the planting of the incriminating evidence against her rival. Holmes even manages to find an identical pistol in the river near the bridge where the alleged murder had taken place—the pistol that had actually been used by the wife to kill herself and that had ended up in the river through an ingenious mechanism involving a stone and a string. The second pistol had been fired in advance to convince the police that it was the lover who killed the wife. None of this has much to do with deduction, and in fact not even with induction per se, but it is a splendid example of the combination of intuition and rigorous thinking that are truly Holmes's hallmark.

In "The Adventure of the Three Students," Holmes is faced with an unusual case when he uncovers which of three students at a prestigious college attempted to cheat on an important examination. If the plan had been successful, it would have embarrassed the college because of a large amount of money to be awarded through the examination in the form of a scholarship. Our detective at one point exclaims, "Let us hear the suspicions. I will look after the proofs,"[22] which seems an uncharacteristic case of Holmes being open to entertain hypotheses before searching for facts—the precise opposite of what he states in other stories.

Is Sherlock Holmes simply an inconsistent practitioner who is far less rational than he would like to make his companion believe? Not at all. In fact, Holmes is doing just what any reasonable scientist would do: using all the tools available to the investigative profession to aid logical thinking, and picking the right set of tools from a broad toolbox, depending on the characteristics of the problem at hand. Looked at it this way, it is not surprising that Holmes deploys different methods on different occasions, and that he even seems to be inconsistent about his approach. As philosophers like to say, just because you have a hammer it doesn't mean that every problem is a nail. It pays to have more than just a hammer in your logical toolbox.

The analogous conclusion—that there is no such thing as the scientific method—seems to be a consensus now among philosophers of science. The discipline went through a period in which philosophers were attempting to come up with a relatively simple criterion for telling science apart from other human intellectual activities. During the latter part of the twentieth century, the emphasis shifted to a more historically informed study of how science actually works, as opposed to how it should work. Over the last twenty years or so, philosophers have joined forces with social scientists to situate science in the complex social web of human activities, meaning that—for instance—decisions about funding priorities and what counts as important science are not made only according to strictly logical procedures, but rather are a reflection of societal preferences and priorities, as well as, to some extent, the outcome of the very human quirks of individual scientists.

None of the above should be interpreted as saying that either science or rational reasoning is arbitrary, just like our analysis of how Holmes actually proceeds does not detract from the brilliance of his reasoning powers. Holmes, like modern scientists, is a pragmatic thinker, one who combines the intuition that comes from long practice with time-tested procedures and shortcuts for arriving at the truth. As the great detective himself put it in *A Study in Scarlet:* "The theories which I have expressed there, and which appear to you to be so chimerical, are really extremely practical—so practical that I depend upon them for my bread and cheese."[23] And this is as it should be.

Notes

1. Sir Arthur Conan Doyle, "A Scandal in Bohemia," in *The Complete Sherlock Holmes* (New York: Doubleday, 1960), 161. All quotations are from this edition.

2. Holmes has a notoriously low opinion of women and never seems to have been involved romantically. Irene Adler is the classic exception to the rule, although his draw to her, not surprisingly, seems to be more intellectual than emotional.

3. I found this or an equivalent phrase in the following stories: *The Sign of Four,* "The Adventure of the Beryl Coronet," "Silver Blaze," "The Adventure of the Priory School," "The Adventure of the Bruce-Partington Plans," and "The Adventure of the Blanched Soldier."

4. "Priory School," 550.

5. *Hound of the Baskervilles,* 687.

6. "Copper Beeches," 322.

7. The reference to Russell's inductivist chicken is found in chapter 6 of his *Problems of Philosophy* (San Mateo, Calif.: Plain Label Books, 1936).

8. On the question of whether it really would be desirable to be immortal—as so many assume—see, for instance, Bernard Williams, "The Makropulos Case: Reflections on the Tedium of Immortality," in *Philosophy: Basic Readings,* ed. Nigel Warburton, 118–34 (London: Routledge, 2004).

9. In some cases, the premises of a deductive argument are axioms that are not derived from observation, as in the case of mathematical or geometrical theorems. It

would then seem that, at least in the case of mathematics, deduction really does deliver truth. It is on the basis of such assumption that Bertrand Russell and others during the early part of the twentieth century attempted to establish mathematics on entirely logical, self-consistent foundations, as recounted with humor and great imagery in Apostolos Doxiadis and Christos Papadimitriou's graphic novel *Logicomix* (New York: Bloomsbury, 2009). However, even mathematics is not safe after all: logician Kurt Gödel famously proved his incompleteness theorem in 1931, which demonstrates that it is not possible to find a complete and consistent set of axioms in mathematics. Logicians and mathematicians have not slept well since then.

10. *Study in Scarlet,* 23.

11. William Whewell, *The Philosophy of the Inductive Sciences* (J. W. Parker, 1840), 230, italic in the original.

12. *Study in Scarlet,* 27.

13. Charles Darwin, *More Letters of Charles Darwin: A Record of His Work in a Series of Hitherto Unpublished Letters,* vol. 1, ed. Francis Darwin and A. C. Seward (London: John Murray, 2003), 240.

14. *Sign of Four,* 96.

15. For more on the demarcation problem, see Massimo Pigliucci, *Nonsense on Stilts: How to Tell Science from Bunk* (Chicago: University of Chicago Press, 2010).

16. "Black Peter," 567.

17. "Reigate Puzzle," 407.

18. *Study in Scarlet,* 49.

19. *Sign of Four,* 93.

20. *Hound of the Baskervilles,* 687.

21. "Problem of Thor Bridge," 1065.

22. "Three Students," 600.

23. *Study in Scarlet,* 23.

Watsons, Adlers, Lestrades, and Moriarties

On the Nature of Friends and Enemies

Philip Tallon

In his *Nicomachean Ethics,* Aristotle praises friendship with powerful words. "For without friends no one would choose to live," he asserts, "though he had all other goods."[1] Friendship is helpful in nearly every stage and station in life (though Aristotle does pause to mention that bitter people and the elderly have a hard time making friends). Friendship comforts, protects, and corrects, and perhaps most beneficially, Aristotle writes, "those in the prime of life it stimulates to noble actions—'two going together'—for with friends men are more able both to think and to act."[2] Friendship can bring the best out of us.

Given the importance of friendship in Aristotle's mind, it makes sense that he would discuss it in his main treatise on ethics. It's still a bit of a surprise, however, that two out of the ten chapters in *Nicomachean Ethics* are devoted to friendship. For Aristotle (and others in the ancient world), friendship was a big deal. C. S. Lewis, writing in *The Four Loves,* notes that for the ancients "friendship seemed the happiest and most human of all the loves; the crown of life and the school of virtue."[3]

Yet in Lewis's estimation, the modern world ignores friendship and what is most unique about it: "Very few modern people think Friendship a love of comparable value or even a love at all."[4] As Lewis suggests, we often understand friendship as a kind of watered-down romantic love or perhaps displaced family affection. Lewis uses literature to make his point. Whereas romantic and parental love have been star players in the literature of the last few centuries (especially romantic love), friendship is lucky to get a part in the chorus. He writes, "I cannot remember that any poem since *In*

Memoriam, or any novel, has celebrated it. Tristan and Isolde, Antony and Cleopatra, Romeo and Juliet, have innumerable counterparts in modern literature: David and Jonathan, Pylades and Orestes, Roland and Oliver, Amis and Amile, have not."[5] Lewis's observation was astute fifty years ago and is still relevant today: since Lewis's death, the lovers' stories mentioned have all been portrayed in major Hollywood movies. The friendships have not.

Although Lewis is fundamentally correct here—friendship is often overlooked—I must strain to point out one pairing in modern literature that bucks the trend: Holmes and Watson. In fact, with the exception of Romeo and Juliet, the friendship of Holmes and Watson is surely better known now than the rest of the great romances of the Elizabethan stage. Furthermore, the names Holmes and Watson are so deeply connected with friendship that they have come to be synonymous with the idea. To be a Sherlock means to be a detective. But to be someone's Watson means being a supportive and loyal friend—the kind who cares enough about you to tolerate your annoying quirks and yet also refuses to tolerate your drug habit. If friendship is as important as Aristotle suggests, then we might want to investigate it, learning about its philosophical dimension and also seeing some examples of true friendship. In this chapter we will examine the friends and enemies of Sherlock Holmes as a way of recovering this ancient virtue, which is underpraised and often misunderstood.

As a bonus, Holmes's relationships can teach us more than just about friendship. Holmes is a man known for his enemies as well. Though perhaps slightly less of a household word than Watson, to be someone's Moriarty means to be an archenemy. The figure of Moriarty, though introduced and killed within the span of a single story ("The Final Problem"), looms large in our memories. To imagine Holmes without Moriarty is almost as difficult as imagining Holmes without Watson. I will thus conclude with an examination of the nature of enemies.

The Baker Street Irregulars and the Diogenes Club: Two Preliminary Kinds of Friendship

The word *friend* is much vaguer than *son, daughter, husband, wife,* or *lover.* We sometimes call someone a friend when we really mean an acquaintance. We probably have online friends whom we have never met. It's likely that we have work friends we see all the time, but we would not attend their funeral. In the age of Facebook, the word *friend* has been watered down to such a point that it implies little more than you know someone's name and don't actively hate him.

What defines a friend? How and how much do you have to like someone for him to count? Even in Aristotle's day, there were different levels of friends, and friendship could encompass drinking buddies, coworkers, teammates, and close intimates. All friendship is a form of knowing "reciprocated goodwill," Aristotle indicates in the *Nicomachean Ethics*, but he quickly moves on to distinguish between three kinds of friends: friends of use, friends of pleasure, and friends of virtue.[6]

The first is based in mere usefulness, like needing a ride to school or someone to help you with precalculus. Friends of use are essentially people you get on with for some benefit that comes from an amiable relationship. This might be your office mate, the guy who cuts your lawn, or your nutritionist. You chitchat when you see them but never think of them when they aren't around. Many work relationships are friendships of utility.

Holmes certainly has friends of use. In fact, most of his lasting relationships were of this type. One notable example is Holmes's working relationship with the Baker Street Irregulars, the street urchins who perform surveillance and run legally questionable errands on behalf of Holmes. He pays them for this, of course, but their relationship is amiable. They treat Holmes with respect, calling him "sir" and "guv'nor," and Holmes is likewise polite and generous with his pay.[7]

Mrs. Hudson, Holmes and Watson's landlady, also seems to be this kind of friend. For Holmes at least, their relationship is always defined by business (he pays a goodly rent, she puts up with his nonsense). Once Holmes moves out, we can hardly imagine him bothering to send Mrs. Hudson a Christmas card (if he did so for anyone, that is)—though it's worth noting that according to Watson, Mrs. Hudson is far fonder of Holmes than he apparently is of her.[8]

The second type of friendship Aristotle describes is based on the pleasure of each other's company. Aristotle notes that this is closer to real friendship because it is less about some extrinsic benefit and more about mutual enjoyment. This friendship is based in emotional, social, or perhaps sexual pleasure (that is, friends with benefits, as young people say). This could involve hanging out with the class clown just to laugh at his jokes, spending time with a popular person because of the whirl of excitement that surrounds her, or hooking up with someone at band camp just because you are bored. But this kind of friendship can be fleeting as well because it is only based on witty conversation or some other pleasurable activity. If the class clown becomes depressed and therefore less funny, a friend of pleasure will stop hanging out with him. Likewise, if the popular girl or boy suddenly becomes a pariah, the friend of pleasure moves on. When the pleasure stops, the friendship stops.

It is hard to say that Holmes had many friendships of this sort. Describing his university days, Holmes describes himself like this: "I was never a very sociable fellow, Watson, always rather fond of moping in my rooms . . . so that I never mixed much with the men of my year."[9] Holmes does mention one friend, Victor Trevor, a classmate with whom he bonded, mostly over their mutual friendlessness.

Despite this one blip on the radar, it is still clear that Holmes did not value socializing for conversation for its own sake, and apparently he never sought out mere chums—though he didn't go as far as his brother Mycroft did, founding a special establishment, the Diogenes Club, where conversation was forbidden. In "The Greek Interpreter," Holmes describes this club to Watson:

> There are many men in London, you know, who, some from shyness, some from misanthropy, have no wish for the company of their fellows. Yet they are not averse to comfortable chairs and the latest periodicals. It is for the convenience of these that the Diogenes Club was started, and it now contains the most unsociable and unclubable men in town. No member is permitted to take the least notice of any other one. Save in the Stranger's Room, no talking is, under any circumstances, allowed, and three offences, if brought to the notice of the committee, render the talker liable to expulsion. My brother was one of the founders, and I have myself found it a very soothing atmosphere.[10]

Given that Holmes enjoyed this atmosphere, and given the scarcity of other friends besides Watson in his life, it is easy to assume that Holmes had little use for friends of pleasure. Though not shy, Holmes was clearly not a clubable man.

Watson: Friend of Virtue

This brings us to the third kind of friendship, which is the truest for Aristotle. This friendship is based on mutual appreciation and respect for the friend's good character:

> Perfect friendship is the friendship of men who are good, and alike in virtue; for these wish well alike to each other [as] good, and they are good themselves. Now those who wish well to their friends for their sake are most truly friends; for they do this by reason of own nature and not incidentally; therefore their friendship lasts as long as they are good—and goodness is an enduring thing.[11]

Two criteria jump out immediately from Aristotle's description of perfect friendship: being "alike in virtue" and "wish[ing] well of one another." Translating this a bit, we might call these two criteria shared virtue and shared support. True friends, then, are equals in terms of character and wish the good of each other. This is fine and sensible.

But are Holmes and Watson friends of this sort? It might seem on the surface that Watson and Holmes are not alike in virtue, but rather are quite unlike in a certain sense. Watson is the marrying type (being married either once or twice, depending on whom you ask), whereas Holmes has a more monkish temperament. Moreover, Watson is less inquisitive and slower-witted than Holmes. Holmes can be snappish and rude, while Watson behaves like the well-bred British subject that he is. These latter two differences show themselves in nearly every Conan Doyle mystery when Holmes stingingly criticizes his friend's poor detective skills. Do these differences prevent their friendship from being perfect?

As an eminently sensible philosopher, Aristotle of course does not imply that the likeness that friendship needs should be confused with sameness. Nor does occasional conflict rule out working for the good of the other. In the next section, we will see how a deeper examination of Aristotle's criteria (and Holmes and Watson's relationship) reveals how exemplary their friendship was.

Shared Virtue

Watson and Holmes are alike in virtue in that they are both matched in having a high level of character. They're both educated and thoughtful, and they care deeply about justice. Further, they both have highly developed skills. Watson is a crack shot and a medical man. Holmes is a skilled boxer and the greatest detective in the history of the world. Perhaps most importantly, they both have a taste for setting off on adventures and they have the courage (another virtue of Aristotle's) to carry them through to the end.

Though Holmes seems the greater of the two men because of his skill in detection (and in many senses he is, though he's also prone to some darker vices than Watson), it is worth noting that Watson's greatest skill is apparent on virtually every page of the Holmes stories. Because of Conan Doyle's fictional framing device, we hear of Holmes's greatness through the excellent prose of Dr. Watson. Though Holmes dismisses Watson's stories as melodramatic, a true fan likes them just the way they are. In this sense, Watson, together with Holmes, cocreates the greatest detective stories ever written.

As indicated above, together with a matched level of excellence, friends must also recognize and acknowledge each other's virtue. Friends know they appreciate the virtue in the other, or else they could not be true friends. Mutual admiration is crucial for friends of virtue. Watson clearly admires Holmes, saying Holmes was "the best and wisest man whom I have ever known."[12] Here, though, more than any other area, Holmes nearly fails at friendship. Perhaps because Holmes so often chides Watson's purple prose style and slowness of detection, or because of Holmes's cold manner, it seems that Watson is sometimes unsure of the mutuality of appreciation. However, when Watson is shot, this reveals to him, once and for all, that even to this most calculating of men, Watson is not a mere friend of use:

> It was worth a wound; it was worth many wounds; to know the depth of loyalty and love which lay behind that cold mask. The clear, hard eyes were dimmed for a moment, and the firm lips were shaking. For the one and only time I caught a glimpse of a great heart as well as of a great brain. All my years of humble but single-minded service culminated in that moment of revelation.[13]

Shared Support

A certain level of equality is necessary for the highest form of friendship. Yet it is possible for two people to have equal virtue and not be friends. Friendship is about more than similarity in character. As Aristotle indicates, friends also actively support one another, doing good for the other. This element is also picked up by Thomas Aquinas (whose philosophy sometimes has a Watsonish quality in relation to Aristotle, whom he calls simply "*The* Philosopher"). Aquinas states that living a happy human life requires friends, because friends help each other to flourish:

> If we speak of the happiness of this life, the happy man needs friends, as the Philosopher says (Ethic. ix, 9), not, indeed, to make use of them . . . [but] that he may do good to them; that he may delight in seeing them do good; and again that he may be helped by them in his good work. For in order that man may do well, whether in the works of the active life, or in those of the contemplative life, he needs the fellowship of friends.[14]

Watson's eventual success at getting Holmes off cocaine is one shining example of this kind of helping.[15] Plus, in nearly every story Watson supports Holmes by acting as a sounding board for Holmes's theories. As Watson recounts in one of the later stories, "The Creeping Man":

> [Holmes] was a man of habits, narrow and concentrated habits, and I had become one of them. As an institution I was like the violin, the shag tobacco, the old black pipe, the index books, and others perhaps less excusable. When it was a case of active work and a comrade was needed upon whose nerve he could place some reliance, my role was obvious. But apart from this I had uses. I was a whetstone for his mind. I stimulated him. He liked to think aloud in my presence.[16]

A former military man, Watson's cool head and military-issue revolver serve Holmes well many times. To be sure, friendship with Holmes provides Watson with much-desired excitement, satisfaction in helping to right wrongs, and fodder for his stories.

In "The Adventure of the Illustrious Client," Holmes is severely beaten by thugs hired by Baron Gruner. Rushing to Holmes's bedside, Watson is concerned. Having ascertained that Holmes will survive, he immediately asks, "What can I do, Holmes? Of course it was that damned fellow who set them on. I'll go and thrash the hide off him if you give the word."[17] Like a true friend, Watson wants something to do for Holmes. Like a man of action, his first thought is of thrashing the wicked baron.

As alike in virtue, friends share many good qualities. As mutually supportive, friends work to bring those qualities out of each other. These two qualities combine to create a relationship where two persons almost combine into one. Because of how like you a friend is, and because you stand on equal footing, you can share things with a friend more easily than a parent or a lover. For Aristotle, a friend is "another self."[18] Though it is hard to say what Aristotle explicitly means here, the phrase makes intuitive sense. Michael Chabon, the author of *The Final Solution,* a work of Holmesian fan fiction, backs this up when he writes that Holmes and Watson are "an archetypical pair who have only Quixote and Sancho as rivals in the hearts of readers and in the annals of imaginary friendship, that record of wildly limited men who find in each other, and only in each other, the stuff, sense, and passion of one whole man."[19]

Shared Activity

The character of this mutual support, however, must be clarified. The support of friends is not a servile waiting at the elbow, but more often a silent encouragement by working alongside. A friend encourages your love of sports trivia not by explicitly praising your knowledge, but by arguing with you about who the best NFL team is.

The desire of friends is for each other's company, but not in the sense of lovers. Lovers are focused on their love for one another, but friends rarely talk about their friendship. As C. S. Lewis phrases it, "We picture lovers face to face but Friends side by side; their eyes look ahead."[20] Friends want to be together so that they can enjoy some activity. This is why groups of friends are not limited to just two, as romantic pairings are; more friends together amplifies the shared pursuit. Friends join together to do something. At the end of his discussion of friendship, Aristotle makes this clear: "Whatever it is for whose sake they value life, in that they wish to occupy themselves with their friends; and so some drink together, others dice together, others join in athletic exercises and hunting, or in the study of philosophy, each class spending their days together in whatever they love most in life; for since they wish to live with their friends."[21] True friends, then, need to meet often and share their lives together. Watson is a true friend to Holmes because he enjoys living with Holmes and is always game for an adventure. His appreciation and support for Holmes is not found in his voluble praise for Holmes's brilliance as much as his willingness to sit in a hedge on a cold night.[22]

On Enemies

Aristotle, Holmes, and Watson help us to understand what it means to have friends. However, in the process, they also help us to understand what it means to have enemies. To gain a rough understanding of what it means to have an enemy, we can simply invert Aristotle's general definition of friendship and call it "reciprocated ill will." For whatever reason, practical or moral, enemies wish each other ill (at least in the specific sphere in which there is antagonism).

Like friends, enemies can take all shapes and sizes. As a citizen of any country, it is likely that we have some political enemies somewhere. Likewise, as sports fans or members of a political party, there are those within the country that wish us (or our team or party) ill. These are less philosophically interesting for our present concern. Personal enemies are far more illuminating to study because these relationships defined by antagonism can be clear indicators of the kinds of people we are.

Holmes, as a good heroic character, has many enemies; in nearly every case, he's striving against someone. Let's look at three different types of personal enemies Holmes has and show how each of these can be understood as an instance of opposition in one or more of the key areas of true friendship.

Irene Adler, Competitor

I will start with the most innocuous form of enemy, which I will dub a competitor. Having a competitor means having a relationship defined by opposition in some shared sphere of activity. Instead of sharing in the activity in a friendly way, however, your opposition to one another defines your relationship and will likely threaten your mutual goodwill. This kind of competition is different from a friendly game of basketball, where the competition is desired and even necessary. All too many businesses wish not only to win the market, but also to put their competitors out of operation. Likewise, political parties do not desire competition from their opposite and would prefer to be able to consistently set policies that reflect their ideology. Serious sports fans can get into this mode if they take things too far, but a rational sports fan knows that ultimately, without real competition, the game would be boring. Competitors, as I am using the term, are enemies because they offer *unwanted* competition. Competitors do not support each other, which is a key element in friendship. Quite the opposite is true. One competitor's success depends on the other's failure.

Irene Adler is the infamous woman from "A Scandal in Bohemia" and a true competitor with Holmes. Hired by the future king of Bohemia to retrieve an embarrassing picture of the nobleman and Adler, Holmes lays clever plans to retrieve the portrait. Adler, however, who has no intention of using the portrait to embarrass the future king, is annoyed by the plans to steal her property and so stays one step ahead of Holmes, foiling his plans. Holmes and Adler here are not merely engaged in a game of sport. Neither desires the other to succeed. Holmes has his reputation on the line, and Adler has her own honor at stake. Because Irene Adler and Sherlock Holmes are alike in their virtues of cleverness, however, the competition is fierce.

Adler's brilliance in this case trumps Holmes's, and she even taunts the detective by greeting him on the street after having escaped his clutches (though Holmes is not aware that it is Adler, who is in disguise). When Holmes does manage to gain entrance to Adler's house to steal the incriminating picture, she has already fled the country, leaving behind only a picture of herself, which Holmes keeps. Interestingly, Holmes's admiration for Irene Adler (and hers for him) grows through the process, creating a form of reciprocal goodwill that Sherlock retains for the rest of his days, as Watson attests.

Inspector Lestrade, Rival

The second kind of enemy, the rival, is similar to a competitor, except that in the case of rivalries, reciprocal goodwill is not nullified by overt competition in some common activity, as is the case with the competitor. With rivals, antagonism is generated in a group because of some tension that arises from shared activity, anxiety about inequality of excellence, or simply the wavering of reciprocal goodwill. Rivals are often friends of some kind, or at least seem to be friends. Or, perhaps, two people may have a relationship that oscillates between friendship and enemy-ship. Hence, the more colloquial term for a rival would be *frenemy.*[23]

Humans being fallible, friendships may falter and turn toward antagonism simply out of weakness or moral failure. Little irritants might turn friends slightly against each other. This is the most common case of "frenemy relationships" (friends failing to consistently support each other) but not the most significant. Here the failure of mutual support is mostly due to weakness of the will.

More significantly, rivalry may arise when a new addition to a group of friends has the same set of skills—for instance, when the class clown is suddenly matched by an equally funny classmate. Here the rivals share the same goal (to make the students in the class laugh), but the presence of both may well reduce the ability of each to express his talent. Likewise, two skilled leaders may fall into rivalry in a company, sports team, or group of friends. As Aristotle and Aquinas saw, part of the activity of friendship is giving and supporting one another. However, a rival takes away one's ability (or one's perceived ability) to contribute fully. This is because the rival has the same skills and abilities. Most of the time, people who are alike can learn to work together. What harm is there in being one of the two funny people? But until very similarly gifted people learn to share the role, there will be tension.

Interestingly, this kind of enemy relationship suggests something about friendship. Equality of every kind may not always benefit friendship because friends may have a difficult time establishing their separate excellences. Holmes and Watson are unlikely to become rivals because in areas of medicine and prose writing, Watson is superior, and in areas of reasoning and criminology, Holmes is superior. Because of their different skill sets, Holmes and Watson can each contribute fully without stepping on each other's toes.

Most significantly, another version of rivalry occurs when two persons would seem to be equally matched but one is actually the superior. This threatens the ability of one or the other to offer his talents, but it also causes the inferior person to become insecure about his level of excellence. In *A Study in Scarlet,* we can see that Holmes and several inspectors on the police force have this kind of rivalry.

Called out to investigate a murder in their first case together, Holmes gives Watson the rundown on the London detectives:

> "Gregson is the smartest of the Scotland Yarders," my friend remarked; "he and Lestrade are the pick of a bad lot. They are both quick and energetic, but conventional—shockingly so. They have their knives into one another, too. They are as jealous as a pair of professional beauties. There will be some fun over this case if they are both put upon the scent."
>
> I was amazed at the calm way in which he rippled on. "Surely there is not a moment to be lost," I cried, "shall I go and order you a cab?"
>
> "I'm not sure about whether I shall go. I am the most incurably lazy devil that ever stood in shoe leather—that is, when the fit is on me, for I can be spry enough at times."
>
> "Why, it is just such a chance as you have been longing for."

> "My dear fellow, what does it matter to me. Supposing I unravel the whole matter, you may be sure that Gregson, Lestrade, and Co. will pocket all the credit. That comes of being an unofficial personage."
>
> "But he begs you to help him."
>
> "Yes. He knows that I am his superior, and acknowledges it to me; but he would cut his tongue out before he would own it to any third person. However, we may as well go and have a look. I shall work it out on my own hook. I may have a laugh at them if I have nothing else. Come on!"[24]

This gives us a good sense of why rivalries arise. Here Holmes notes that although Lestrade and Gregson are the best of Scotland Yard, they are not up to his level of skill. Because of the realities of the police force, however, Gregson and Lestrade are falsely seen to be Holmes's superiors (or at least equals). So when they work together, tension over who is the superior detective arises between the Inspectors and Holmes (and apparently among the detectives as well). The following scene drives this point home.

When Holmes arrives at the scene of the murder, he's presented with a dead body and some writing: RACHE. Gregson and Lestrade make a few bad guesses about the meaning of the word (guessing it to be the unfinished name RACHEL) and can guess little about the nature of the crime. Holmes blows both of them out of the water with his skills in observation and reasoning:

> "I'll tell you one thing which may help you in the case," he continued, turning to the two detectives. "There has been murder done, and the murderer was a man. He was more than six feet high, was in the prime of life, had small feet for his height, wore coarse, square-toed boots and smoked a Trichinopoly cigar. He came here with his victim in a four-wheeled cab, which was drawn by a horse with three old shoes and one new one on his off fore leg. In all probability the murderer had a florid face, and the finger-nails of his right hand were remarkably long. These are only a few indications, but they may assist you."
>
> Lestrade and Gregson glanced at each other with an incredulous smile.
>
> "Poison," said Sherlock Holmes curtly, and strode off. "One other thing, Lestrade," he added, turning round at the door: "'Rache'

> is the German for 'revenge'; so don't lose your time looking for Miss Rachel."
>
> With which Parthian shot he walked away, leaving the two rivals open-mouthed behind him.[25]

As befits the behavior of rivals, Holmes intentionally embarrasses Gregson and Lestrade as retaliation for their lack of recognition of his superior skills.

It is worth mentioning that in later stories, Holmes and the other inspectors get along better. In "The Empty House," Holmes refers to the inspector as "my friend Lestrade."[26] But this is undoubtedly because Lestrade and the rest of the police have adjusted to the inequality between them and Holmes in detection. This suggests that rivalries that arise from oversimilarity can easily fade away if those involved come to a better understanding of their equality (or inequality).

Professor Moriarty, Foe

The third kind of enemy is the worst, and one that is nearly impossible to turn to friendship. If a true friend is another self, a true foe is the antiself, with whom you have no shared feeling of goodwill at all. Although competitors may incite anger and rivals may incite insecurity, a foe arouses loathing. This is not because foes oppose your actions (though they will do that), or because they do not wish the good for you (though they do not wish it), but because your natures are fundamentally at odds with one another.

The existence of a foe explains why, though Holmes often approached solving crimes like a game, occasionally he would take an exceptional personal disliking to a criminal. One example is Charles Augustus Milverton, a sly London blackmailer nearly as cunning as Holmes himself.[27] Another is Grimesby Roylott, a terrible man whom Holmes accidentally kills in "The Adventure of the Speckled Band," although he admits that it will not "weigh very heavily upon [his] conscience."[28]

Among the ranks of foes, none is more famous than Professor Moriarty, who is perhaps the most famous villain in all of modern literature, despite appearing in only one Holmes story as a living threat. Nevertheless, his ghost looms over the Holmes stories in our memory, and subsequent adaptations have expanded Moriarty's fictional longevity. Why is this so?

As Aristotle would have quickly seen, Holmes and Moriarty are true enemies because they are well matched in terms of their virtues, except that Moriarty's virtues are applied to an evil end. Hear Holmes's description of Moriarty in "The Final Problem," and note how much his brilliance sounds like Holmes's:

> His career has been an extraordinary one. He is a man of good birth and excellent education, endowed by nature with a phenomenal mathematical faculty. At the age of twenty-one he wrote a treatise upon the Binomial Theorem, which has had a European vogue. On the strength of it he won the Mathematical Chair at one of our smaller universities, and had, to all appearances, a most brilliant career before him. But the man had hereditary tendencies of the most diabolical kind. A criminal strain ran in his blood, which, instead of being modified, was increased and rendered infinitely more dangerous by his extraordinary mental powers. Dark rumors gathered round him in the university town, and eventually he was compelled to resign his chair and to come down to London, where he set up as an army coach. So much is known to the world, but what I am telling you now is what I have myself discovered. . . . He is the Napoleon of crime, Watson. He is the organizer of half that is evil and of nearly all that is undetected in this great city. He is a genius, a philosopher, an abstract thinker. He has a brain of the first order.[29]

Holmes and Moriarty are the greatest of enemies, but they perhaps could have been great friends—had Moriarty not been bent toward evil.

After this vivid introduction, we see Holmes and Watson fleeing England to escape death at the hands of Moriarty and his henchmen. They go to Switzerland, where Moriarty alone encounters Holmes at the Reichenbach Falls; they grapple and both tumble (Watson thinks) over the cliff into the deadly pool below.

Had this been the death of Holmes, it would have been a sad day for the fans but a fitting end for the great detective. Holmes's hatred of Moriarty was no moral failing on his part but rather a proper perception of Moriarty's masterful criminality. Holmes had met his match and was even willing to die in order to remove him from the world. We hear this from Holmes's own mouth when he first encounters Moriarty in London:

> "It has been a duel between you and me, Mr. Holmes. You hope to place me in the dock. I tell you that I will never stand in the dock. You hope to beat me. I tell you that you will never beat me. If you

> are clever enough to bring destruction upon me, rest assured that I shall do as much to you."
>
> "You have paid me several compliments, Mr. Moriarty," said I. "Let me pay you one in return when I say that if I were assured of the former eventuality I would, in the interests of the public, cheerfully accept the latter."[30]

That Holmes was willing to die to rid the world of its greatest criminal reveals two significant things. First, although enemies want to harm us, they may also unknowingly bring the best out of us. As when Watson was shot, we see in this moment of crisis the substance of Holmes's character. Here is a man for whom criminal detection was not just an intellectual problem. It was a moral crusade. In facing Moriarty, Holmes is at his finest—and, one might also say, at his most fulfilled. Holmes is ridding the world of his opposite number, a shadow version of his own genius.

Second, that Holmes must be willing to die to rid the world of Moriarty shows us that, unlike other forms of enemies, a foe cannot be turned into a friend. Holmes comes to admire Adler and befriend Lestrade, but he and Moriarty remain locked in combat to the end. If we keep our wits about us, a rival or a competitor can be transformed into a friend of use, pleasure, or even of virtue. But a foe cannot. Foes must be avoided or thrown off the falls.

May we all be lucky enough to find our own Watsons or Holmeses and to turn our Adlers and Lestrades into friends—and may we never find a Moriarty.

Notes

1. Aristotle, *Nicomachean Ethics,* ed. Lesley Brown and trans. David Ross (London: Oxford World Classics, 2009), 8.1.

2. Ibid.

3. C. S. Lewis, *The Four Loves* (New York: Harvest/HBJ, 1960), 87.

4. Ibid.

5. Ibid.

6. Aristotle, *Nicomachean Ethics,* 8.3.

7. Sir Arthur Conan Doyle, *The Sign of Four,* in *The Complete Sherlock Holmes* (New York: Doubleday, 1960), 126–27. All further citations are to this edition.

8. "Mrs. Hudson, the landlady of Sherlock Holmes, was a long-suffering woman. Not only was her first-floor flat invaded at all hours by throngs of singular and often undesirable characters but her remarkable lodger showed an eccentricity and irregularity in his life which must have sorely tried her patience. His incredible untidiness, his

addiction to music at strange hours, his occasional revolver practice within doors, his weird and often malodorous scientific experiments, and the atmosphere of violence and danger which hung around him made him the very worst tenant in London. On the other hand, his payments were princely. I have no doubt that the house might have been purchased at the price which Holmes paid for his rooms during the years that I was with him. The landlady stood in the deepest awe of him and never dared to interfere with him, however outrageous his proceedings might seem. She was fond of him, too, for he had a remarkable gentleness and courtesy in his dealings with women." "Dying Detective," 932.

9. "The *Gloria Scott,*" 374.

10. "Greek Interpreter," 436.

11. Aristotle, *Nicomachean Ethics,* 8.3.

12. "Final Problem," 480.

13. "Three Garridebs," 1052.

14. Thomas Aquinas, *Summa Theologica* (Raleigh, N.C.: Hayes Barton Press, 1925), 1–2, Q4, A8.

15. "Missing Three-Quarter," passim.

16. "Creeping Man," 1071.

17. "Illustrious Client," 984.

18. Aristotle, *Nicomachean Ethics,* 9.9.

19. Michael Chabon, *Maps and Legends: Reading and Writing along the Borderlands* (San Francisco: Harper Perennial, 2008), 27.

20. Lewis, *Four Loves,* 98.

21. Aristotle, *Nicomachean Ethics,* 9.12.

22. Though understandable for literary reasons, it was unfortunate for Holmes that he was not able to make more friends of virtue. Because of his medical work and his marriage (or marriages), Watson could not always be around. If Holmes had expanded his coterie of friends, he might have been able to accomplish even more, and he might have been less prone to boredom and drug use.

23. Chuck Klosterman dubs the kind of enemy I am calling a rival a *nemesis,* and what I'm calling a foe an *archenemy.* Though Klosterman isn't interested in getting into why these relationships occur, I think he pretty accurately describes the nature of these two sorts of enemies. I owe a debt to Klosterman for suggesting that the subject of enemies was worth exploring, and sparking the inspiration for the second part of this essay. Chuck Klosterman. "Nemesis," in *IV: A Decade of Curious People and Dangerous Ideas* (New York: Scribner, 2006), 243–48.

24. *Study in Scarlet,* 26–27.

25. Ibid., 32.

26. "Empty House," 492.

27. For more on this, see David Rozema, "Not the Crime, but the Man: Sherlock Holmes and Charles Augustus Milverton" (chap. 2, this volume).

28. "Speckled Band," 273.

29. "Final Problem," 470–71.

30. Ibid., 473.

Eliminating the Impossible

Sherlock Holmes and the Supernatural

Kyle Blanchette

Two Tales of Holmes and Haunting

In the opening scene of Guy Ritchie's first movie adaptation of Sir Arthur Conan Doyle's beloved and enduring literary franchise, *Sherlock Holmes* (2009), the audience promptly makes the acquaintance of a most sinister character by the name of Lord Blackwood. Looming over a young woman as she lies flat in a trance, dagger in hand, ready to take her own life, Blackwood is engaged in what appears to be a form of black arts. In a move that typifies the clash between Holmes and Blackwood throughout the movie, Holmes and Watson manage to save the young woman in the nick of time through sheer ingenuity and brute force. We soon find out that five other women have already been successfully sacrificed at Blackwood's hand in the service of his greater purpose, during which time he has eluded the grasp of the shrewd detective. Blackwood is finally tried, condemned, and hanged for his crimes, but as he ominously points out just before his execution, "Death is only the beginning."[1] Indeed, starting with his alleged resurrection, the rest of the movie follows Blackwood as he performs a series of what appear to be dark miracles, simultaneously arousing the fears of his countrymen and piquing the insatiable curiosity of Sherlock Holmes. But things might not be as they seem.

Guy Ritchie's recasting of both the character of Holmes and the style of Holmesian storytelling was destined to garner its detractors, considering the directorial liberties Ritchie takes with Conan Doyle's eminently familiar creation. Despite some clear differences and elaborations, there is significant overlap between Ritchie's treatment of Holmes and the classic one. One salient point of continuity is the motif of the supernatural as a possible explanation for the events of a particular case, a theme that can be found throughout Conan Doyle's Sherlock corpus, including within the pages of *The Hound of the Baskervilles.* In this novel, a case of potentially supernatural proportions is brought to the attention of Holmes and Watson by Dr. James Mortimer. Through a mutual interest in science, Mortimer was a close friend of the recently deceased Sir Charles Baskerville, owner and resident of Baskerville Hall and keeper of the Baskerville fortune and legacy. Sir Charles was walking on the moor one night outside his estate when he suddenly died of a heart attack. Though he was known to have a heart condition, one curious piece of evidence at the scene of his demise suggested that his death was likely the result of something more than a simple heart attack: near the body were the paw prints of a gigantic hound!

Although this odd fact would be interesting in and of itself, it is made all the more provocative by the legend that haunts the Baskerville family line—that of the hound of the Baskervilles. According to family legend, a demonic hound with characteristics fantastically beyond those of ordinary earthly hounds has been the cause of several violent deaths in the Baskerville line. The first appearance of this horrifying hound was at the lethal expense of Hugo Baskerville, a man of godless repute who held the manor of Baskerville long ago, at the time of the Great Rebellion. Hugo was smitten with a local daughter of a yeoman, and as she was insistent on avoiding Hugo, he and several of his companions resolved to kidnap her and tie her up in the upper chamber of his manor. The young lady managed to escape from the estate, though not before overhearing the debauched carousing and fiendish affairs of Hugo and his dark cohorts in the rooms below. Immediately upon discovering her absence, Hugo set out with his horse after the unhappy maiden in hopes of overtaking her, but regrettably both met their grisly end through the agency of the hellish hound, "a foul thing, a great black beast, shaped like a hound, yet larger than any hound that ever mortal eye has rested upon . . . [with] blazing eyes and dripping jaws."[2]

Appealing to supernatural explanations for various phenomena in human experience, whether we have in mind answers to prayer, the purported macabre happenings of haunted houses, or the existence of the universe itself, is as fascinating as it is pervasive. In the world of fiction, all sorts of narratives, particularly Gothic, mystery, and detective stories, allude to the supernatural as a possible explanation that looms eerily over the events in question, even if the true explanation of the facts often turns out to be far more—well, natural. One might be tempted to think that reflection on the supernatural belongs solely within the realm of theology, but this would be far too hasty. Not only was there a time in Western intellectual history in which the disciplines of theology and philosophy were virtually indistinguishable (for example, the Middle Ages), but more importantly, contemporary philosophers of religion have as their principal goal the rigorous exploration and resolution of questions about the supernatural. According to these philosophers, be they atheists, theists, or something in between, there is objective truth to be discovered about the supernatural through reason and the disciplined examination of evidence, which belies the conviction of many that beliefs about the supernatural are a matter of whimsical opinion at best or downright superstition at worst. So, in good Holmesian fashion, let us flex our powers of objective deduction and practice some good old-fashioned ratiocination as we take up the subject of the supernatural and its relationship to these two key cases in Sherlock Holmes lore.

"Immaterial, My Dear Watson!"

Clarity is power in the twin arts of rigorous thought and winsome persuasion, and Holmes would no doubt concur. A good way to begin our discussion is thus with a precise determination of what we mean when we call something supernatural. To develop a working definition of the supernatural, we first need to put our finger on what we mean by natural. Although the definition of the natural, or nature, is a matter of some controversy among philosophers, with different thinkers advocating broader or narrower conceptions of its scope, the definition of nature developed by Paul Draper suits entirely for our purposes. It runs as follows: Nature consists of the "spatiotemporal universe of physical entities together with any entities that are ontologically or causally reducible to those entities."[3]

Let us unpack this helpful definition. By "physical" here, Draper is referring to those fundamental entities studied by physicists and chemists, including things like atoms, molecules, and gravitational fields. To say that some complex or composite entity is ontologically reducible to physical entities is to say that it is made up of nothing more than physical ingredients. Its being is composed completely of physical entities. Similarly, to assert that some complex or composite entity is causally reducible to physical entities is to say that that thing is explainable in terms of the causal powers of lower-level physical entities. If one or the other or both of these conditions hold, it is reasonable to call something natural. Philosophers sometimes use the words *natural* and *material* interchangeably, but on Draper's definition, *natural* is the broader term. It includes things like electromagnetic fields and other physical forces, whereas *material* would refer more narrowly to things such as atoms and quarks.[4] When speaking about the physical footprints found near the body of Sir Charles, Holmes notes that at least the footprints themselves are "material."[5]

As one would expect, Draper defines the supernatural in terms of this understanding of nature. We will adopt his view that "x is supernatural if x is not a part of nature and x can affect nature."[6] Notice that nonnatural entities do not necessarily qualify as supernatural entities. One interesting example of a group of things that are nonnatural and yet also nonsupernatural would be numbers. Numbers are not ontologically or causally reducible to physical entities, and yet on most conceptions of numbers, they are unable to affect nature. Some classic examples of things from the history of Western philosophy that are supernatural would be God and Cartesian souls. More esoteric examples include psychic energy, spirits, and perhaps even ghoulish, giant hounds.

Metaphysical Musings

Now that we have gotten working definitions of *nature* and *supernatural* on the table, we are prepared to explore a couple of fundamentally opposed philosophical positions that are based on these concepts. Metaphysical naturalism is usually the conviction that supernatural entities do not exist. When philosophers speak of metaphysics, they are referring to beliefs and questions about the nature of ultimate reality. Metaphysics is the business of characterizing and categorizing reality into an overarching ontology—that is to say, into a catalog of existing things that carves reality at its joints, as it were. Accordingly, those who hold to metaphysical naturalism hold that there is simply no such thing as the supernatural. Note that one can be a metaphysical naturalist while still holding to the existence of various nonnatural, though not supernatural, entities. As one would expect, this is a view commonly found among atheists, although it is by no means limited to their number. Alternatively, theists of various stripes must logically reject this view, believing as they do in the reality of supernatural entities such as God.

Likewise, metaphysical supernaturalism is the view that supernatural entities do, in fact, exist. Typically a supernaturalist holds that both supernatural and natural things exist. Indeed, traditional theists believe that the supernatural realm is the explanation or the productive cause of the natural realm; that is to say, God, a supernatural and necessary Being, is the explanation for all nonnecessary, contingent beings, which includes (but is not necessarily limited to) the entire natural realm. Many theists further hold that many necessary truths also depend on God for their existence by being thoughts in God's mind, such as the truths of logic, morality, and mathematics. Although it is no doubt true that in Western philosophy the supernatural and supernaturalism are concepts usually found in the context of traditional theism or something close to it, one need not be a theist to be a supernaturalist. In other words, it is entirely possible for one to believe in the existence of the supernatural without believing in God, let alone the Judeo-Christian God. New Age religion as well as some forms of philosophical idealism would fall into the category of nontheistic, supernaturalist philosophies.

At this point, we have laid out working definitions of nature, the supernatural, metaphysical naturalism, and metaphysical supernaturalism, all toward the end of setting the philosophical table for the upcoming meat and potatoes of our discussion. Our positions—or, we might say, our theories—are coming into focus. However, before we can admit a theory into the pool of live options as a plausible explanation of the facts, the theory has to be at least possible. Most people would readily affirm that natural explanations and causes for phenomena in the world are not only possible, but also extremely common. Our focus will thus be on the possibility or impossibility of supernatural explanations for certain happenings. The discerning reader will notice that this is essentially the perennially engaging subject of miracles.

Preposterous Possibilities

In the feature film, after having investigated Lord Blackwood's alleged resurrection from the dead, Watson and Holmes have a short but highly provocative exchange as they walk along an alleyway of nineteenth-century London. Signaling a slightly more serious tone than is usually present between the two characters throughout the movie, Watson avers, "You know, Holmes, I've seen things in war I don't understand. In India, I once met a man who predicted his own death, right down to the number and placement of the bullets that killed him. You have to admit, Holmes, that a supernatural explanation to this case is theoretically possible." Sherlock's illuminating response is important:

"Agreed. But it is a huge mistake to theorize before one has data. Inevitably, one begins to twist facts to suit theories, instead of theories to suit facts."[7] Watson and Holmes may not realize it, but in this small exchange, they are skirting deep philosophical waters regarding the supernatural.

At this point, the Holmesian detective in some of us might be getting frustrated with all of this conceptual analysis. At what point, it might be asked, are we going to get our fingers dirty examining the actual evidence? However, we must take care not to underestimate the power of our presuppositions. Indeed, the more unaware and uncritical we are of our philosophical precommitments, the more likely they are to govern our thinking in a whole host of irrational ways. Our presuppositions will invariably affect the way we assess evidence for competing hypotheses. In the present case, if we believe miraculous explanations are impossible, we will not even consider them, so it is important for us to think critically about our theoretical beliefs and judgments before conducting empirical investigations. We can take heart that our theoretical analysis will spill over into the empirical world of the detective soon enough.

Eliminating the Impossible

In common parlance, the word *miracle* is used to refer to a wide variety of occurrences, not all of which are supernatural. In both the Blackwood and the Baskerville cases, however, the sense of the word *miracle* in view is clearly that of an unusual event that seems to conflict with natural or scientific laws.[8] Modern skepticism toward the possibility of miracles taken in this narrow sense originated at the time of the Enlightenment, or the Age of Reason, a period in which thinkers aimed to throw off the shackles of traditional religion in order to pursue knowledge through the unfettered application of reason. Although most of the arguments against miracles take place in the context of theism, particularly Judeo-Christian theism, we may safely abstract them from that religious context and obtain some essential elements that pertain to supernatural events brought about by lesser supernatural beings (such as demonic hounds) or natural beings ostensibly endowed with supernatural powers (such as our friend, Lord Blackwood).

The Deists of the seventeenth and eighteenth centuries were fond of arguing that God had created the world with a set of unalterable natural laws, never to intervene in the world again. God was conceived as a grand watchmaker who created the watch of the universe, wound it up, and let it tick without any further tinkering or special intervention beyond sustaining it in being. The main motivation for this understanding of God's relationship to the world was the universally deterministic understanding of nature that was thought to follow from Newtonian physics—the Newtonian world machine. Everything was believed to be governed by inexorable cause and effect: if sufficient conditions are in place, the effect will certainly be produced. Because miracles could only be conceived as violations of these immutable laws of nature, they were quite naturally judged to be impossible.

Of course the rise of quantum theory in modern science has demonstrated that there is an irreducible element of indeterminacy in certain systems in nature. If this indeterminacy is ontological rather than epistemic—that is, if the randomness we observe is not merely a result of our limited (and influencing) observation, but is rather an actual feature of the natural world in itself—then the natural world is not analogous to a deterministic machine after all. This does not really solve the problem of miracles, however, because there are still quantum physical laws governing such systems; the difference is that these laws are probabilistic in nature.[9] We still have to face the possibility of a miraculous event breaking the probabilistic laws of quantum physics.

Avoiding Cosmic Transgression

In *The Hound of the Baskervilles,* after Dr. Mortimer finishes relating to Holmes and Watson the Baskerville legend of the hound and the events surrounding Sir Henry Baskerville's curious demise, he begins to discuss several people. One of them is a "hardheaded" (read "level-headed") countryman who has independently reported seeing a hound that meets the same description as the ghoulish hound of the legend. Dr. Mortimer describes these sightings as "several incidents which are hard to reconcile to the settled order of Nature."[10] But what exactly is the "settled order of Nature"? To be a significant obstacle to the miraculous, the settledness of nature must be something more than nature's mere regularity. An exception to the overall regularity of nature would hardly be problematic in and of itself, unless that regularity is in some sense absolute. In other words, in order to be a physical and logical challenge to miracles, the settledness of nature spoken of by Dr. Mortimer must be something like a structure of causal relations that entails a kind of necessity in the way nature operates.[11]

Here we must make a critical distinction between two different types of necessity: natural and logical. To see the difference, consider the following jocular proposition offered by Alvin Plantinga in the service of explaining this very distinction: "Voltaire once swam the Atlantic." Clearly, he notes, there is a sense in which this proposition is not only implausible but impossible. It is not so much a logical sense of impossible as a natural one. As he puts it, "Eighteenth-century intellectuals (as distinguished from dolphins) simply lacked the physical equipment for this kind of feat."[12] So the above proposition is impossible or necessarily false in a natural or causal sense. The properties and laws of nature make it such that certain things cannot possibly happen in the course of natural events. Indeed, Deists seem to have conceived of natural laws as known principles that enable us to make certain conditional judgments about what can and cannot happen given a certain causal condition in the natural world. An example of such a conditional would be, "If water is at or below thirty-two degrees Fahrenheit, it freezes." In a real sense, then, miracles are naturally impossible.

But are natural laws also necessary in a logical sense? In other words, is there something internally inconsistent in or essentially wrong about the concept of a miracle? One way of arguing that miracles are logically impossible is to posit that natural laws are defined by, or at least entail, certain universal generalizations about the way events happen in the world given certain natural conditions. On this view, of course, a violation of such a law would be incoherent and thus impossible because a universal generalization cannot logically coexist with an exception.[13] This understanding of natural law assumes, however, that the world of nature is a closed system of natural cause and effect that can never be subject to any other causal influence, including supernatural agency. The mere fact that nature operates in a lawful fashion is not enough to sustain the burden of proof that would be necessary to establish that the natural world is a closed system. More argumentation would be required to secure this conclusion.

Let us suppose that the objector to the possibility of miracles is up to the task. How might she go about proving the closedness of nature? Nature would be a thoroughly closed system in the relevant sense if either the existence of supernatural entities were impossible, or if it were impossible for supernatural entities ever to interfere with the natural world. Notice that it is not enough here simply to establish that supernatural entities do not now exist, or cannot now interfere with nature. This is because, for all we know, it is possible for supernatural entities to emerge out of natural entities in such a way that they can exert causal force on nature. Some philosophers believe the human soul is an instance of such emergentism.[14] Moreover, for all we know, it is possible that currently existing supernatural beings who now lack the ability to interfere with nature may later acquire that ability. All of this logic chopping may seem rather abstruse to the nonphilosopher, but it only goes to show that it often takes quite a bit of work to show that a concept is logically impossible. If one tries and fails to demonstrate that supernatural entities cannot exist or that supernatural entities can never interfere with nature, it becomes plausible that nature is open and that miracles are at least possible. When it comes to supernaturalism, most skeptical thinkers, from David Hume to Antony Flew, would agree that miracles are at least logically possible.[15]

If nature is an open system, then it is entirely possible for God, or some other sufficiently powerful supernatural agent, to interfere with nature in such a way that is beyond its causal capacity.[16] Had the supernatural agent in question not interfered, natural law would have been operative, so its integrity remains intact. In other words, natural laws only tell us what would happen in the absence of interference from outside of the natural order. Thus, despite eighteenth-century skeptic David Hume's widely popular characterization of miracles as violations of natural law, miracles need not be characterized in such a way. In the above instance, natural law would not be violated but rather suspended—a characterization that makes it clear that the genuineness of natural laws has not been brought into question.[17]

We have seen that the reality of natural law hardly renders miracles impossible. A miracle is certainly, by definition, a naturally or physically impossible event, but it is not a logically impossible event if there exists a supernatural agent with sufficient power to impede natural law. It is also important to note that it is perfectly coherent for one to be agnostic, or even reasonably skeptical, about the reality of the supernatural while also believing that miracles are at least possible. Even if miraculous events are rather implausible or improbable, it does not follow that they are impossible. If the reasoning of this section is sound, and in the absence of any other reason to doubt the possibility of the miraculous, Watson and Holmes are absolutely correct that we simply cannot rule out the theoretical possibility of a miraculous explanation for a given phenomenon.

Overcoming Sinister Obstacles

Even if the miraculous intervention of the supernatural is possible, how can we reasonably conclude that a miracle is the best explanation for some given phenomenon? Is appealing to the supernatural to explain some event in nature even legitimate in the first place? An interesting theme shows up more than once in *The Hound of the Baskervilles* that would short-circuit appeals to the supernatural right from the start. According to Dr. Mortimer, "There is a realm in which the most acute and the most experienced of detectives is helpless"—namely, the supernatural.[18] Holmes is even more to the point when he explains to Watson, "If Dr. Mortimer's surmise should be correct and we are dealing with forces outside the ordinary laws of Nature, there is an end of our investigation."[19] The basic sentiment here seems to be that the supernatural realm is inscrutable or perhaps inaccessible, beyond the reach of human investigation. Even if some supernatural force or agent is the veritable explanation of some occurrence, detectives have no means of assessing the truth or falsity of this explanation. Sherlock's implicit claim here seems to assume that the supernatural, if it exists, would never enter our sphere of cognition in such a way that we could detect it or identify it as supernatural.[20] However, what evidence could be procured for such an assumption? At the very least, this seems nearly as hard to prove as metaphysical naturalism, which would seem to require us to scan all of reality to disprove the existence of the supernatural. So let us proceed on the reasonable assumption that it is at least epistemically possible—that is, possible as far as we know—for the supernatural to act in the world in such a way that we can detect it.[21]

The position that the supernatural realm is inscrutable is similar to the claim of many scientists that the discipline of science simply cannot speak to the supernatural, although it is broader if we think of science as a discipline solely concerned with physical realities and natural processes. The assumption here seems to be that when it comes to explaining why things happen in our world, we ought to adopt a kind of methodological naturalism. However, if we are defining science broadly as rigorous, evidence-based reasoning about the events that happen in the world, there seems to be no good reason for an unbending methodological naturalism in a scientific approach to investigation and knowledge. A little reflection reveals that the notion that a scientific worldview leaves no room for the supernatural is just a thinly veiled affirmation of metaphysical naturalism. Unless we have conclusive evidence for this viewpoint, we must remain open to evidence for the supernatural. Our methodology should be aimed at truth, and if a supernatural explanation is the best one among a pool of live explanations, so be it. We must be careful not to assume that the logical explanation will always be a natural one.

Yet there is another way one might interpret these opaque comments from Holmes about investigating the supernatural. In the course of his conversation with Dr. Mortimer about the hound of Baskervilles, Holmes confesses, "I have hitherto confined my investigation to this world. . . . In a modest way I have combated evil, but to take on the Father of Evil himself would, perhaps, be too ambitious a task."[22] Maybe Holmes means to say that a detective cannot reasonably hope to catch a demonic criminal. Presumably, in order to do that, we need an old priest and a young priest, or something of that sort. True enough, but cannot the scientific detective follow the evidence and reasonably conclude that something supernatural is afoot? At the very least, this modest endeavor does not seem too ambitious a task.

Of course, if supernatural explanations are admitted into science, broadly speaking, one must take care to avoid what is famously known as the "God of the gaps" fallacy, a specious form of reasoning sometimes employed by supernaturalists that postulates God, or some other supernatural agent, as an explanation when faced with scientific ignorance about natural processes or events in the world. It is surely fallacious to make unwarranted appeals to the supernatural in order to explain current gaps in scientific knowledge because further investigation could very well plug up a given gap in the future with a perfectly adequate naturalistic explanation. We need much more than mere ignorance if we are to make a justified inference to the supernatural. We therefore come face to face with the problem of evidential criteria.

Clues and Criteria

After commenting on the inability of the detective to investigate the supernatural, Holmes makes this interesting assertion: "But we are bound to exhaust all other hypotheses before falling back upon this one."[23] Indeed, for an event to be considered a miracle in the relevant sense, it needs to be beyond not only known natural laws, but also unknown natural laws. The event has to be such that we can conclude that no naturalistic explanation will likely ever be forthcoming. In other words, we need to have reasonable certainty that the event in question will remain permanently unexplainable in naturalistic terms. Otherwise, further investigation could reveal a hidden natural law, and we have fallen headlong into "God of the gaps" reasoning. As Draper astutely puts it, "The search for natural causes should continue until the best explanation of the failure to find one is that there is none."[24]

Some philosophers dispute that there actually exists such a point of no return as far as naturalistic explanations go. They argue that it is always possible that new information will prompt a revision of current understandings of natural law in relation to any seemingly unexplainable events such that the event will become explainable in naturalistic terms. Although it may be true that there is always a possibility, however remote, of finding a natural explanation for a seemingly supernatural event, this does not prevent us from reasonably concluding that the supernatural is the most probable explanation of some event on the basis of the evidence we do have. Theistic philosopher Richard Swinburne argues that if a natural law is sufficiently well entrenched, any attempt to modify the law in order to accommodate a certain counterexample would be clumsy and would upset the whole structure of science. Similarly, Margaret Boden argues that such ad hoc, or contrived, revision would severely weaken the predictive power of science.[25]

Swinburne freely admits that just as all claims about what constitute natural laws are subject to further revision, all claims about miracles that contradict those laws are also subject to revision. However, he still maintains that when confronted with a genuine counterinstance to highly confirmed natural laws, it is more reasonable to uphold the adequacy of the laws and declare the counterinstance permanently unexplainable than to modify the laws and undermine the structure of science. Others argue that it is better to suspend judgment until we have repeatable counterinstances, and the debate continues.[26] When it all shakes out, there does seem to come a point when it would be unreasonable to bank on a possible, though wildly unlikely and entirely unknown, natural explanation for a seeming miracle when far more likely supernatural explanations are available. After sufficient investigation, the best explanation for our not finding a naturalistic explanation is that one does not exist.

Thus Saith the Evidence

How, then, does our favorite detective fare in the two cases at hand? Holmes is surely right that we must be careful not to twist facts to fit theories, rather than the other way around. As we have noted, however, one must be careful not to rule out an explanatory possibility simply because of one's unexamined presuppositions. How do we move from a supernatural explanation being a bare theoretical possibility to its being a viable option, and then how do we move from its being one of many plausible explanations to the best explanation? We have shown that the most rational course for the scientific detective to take in these cases is to pursue naturalistic explanations as far as reasonably possible until the best explanation for an unexplained event is that there is no naturalistic explanation. Surely Holmes's methodology in both cases before us is a picture-perfect example of this valid and penetrating method of reasoning. It would be woefully premature for him to jump to a supernatural conclusion before significant investigation into potential natural causes has been conducted. The more improbable it is that a naturalistic explanation exists, the more probable it is that a supernatural explanation is the right one.

Take, for example, the most noteworthy alleged miracle in the *Sherlock Holmes* movie: Lord Blackwood's resurrection. To determine that Blackwood truly died by hanging, Watson takes his pulse for a few seconds. Ordinarily this would be sufficient to determine whether a man is dead, especially after he has been hanged right before your eyes. In this case, however, Blackwood has ingested a special toxin known to produce an "apparently mortal paralysis enough to mislead a medical mind even as well-trained" as Watson's.[27] In addition to this, Blackwood uses a hidden harness that distributes the weight around his waist to keep his neck from breaking. Upon discovering that Blackwood is back from beyond the grave, Holmes does the rational thing by pursuing natural explanations first, both for Blackwood's alleged resurrection as well as for his subsequent feats of supposed black magic. As it turns out, Blackwood is not endowed with supernatural powers after all. As Holmes eventually discovers, "There was never any magic, only conjuring tricks."[28] Indeed, in as early as the opening scene, and precisely because he is looking for it, Holmes finds and disables an odd mechanism that was likely intended to produce an apparently supernatural effect. Holmes knew to look for all too natural magical tricks first.

The same basic methodology is employed by Holmes in the case of the supposedly supernatural hound of the Baskervilles. The evidence at the beginning of the investigation relevant to the supernatural hypothesis consists of a family legend, footprints of a giant hound near the site of Sir Charles's demise, and scattered sightings, mostly by uneducated peasants, of the hound around the moor.[29] The only further evidence suggesting that the hound in question could be supernatural is the firsthand sighting of the hound by Holmes, Watson, and Sir Henry Baskerville near the end of the novel, which reveals that the hound indeed has "blazing eyes" and "dripping jaws." Still, all of this evidence taken together is far from sufficient to underwrite a supernatural explanation. Too many other perfectly plausible naturalistic explanations remain, especially when evidence for all-too-human foul play begins to be discovered. Indeed the fact that the heir to the legacy, Sir Henry Baskerville, has his boot stolen is positive evidence that the hound in question is ordinary after all, because it needs a scent in order to know whom to attack. Finally, the family legend surely is more likely to be the product of human imagination and superstition than reliable evidence for a supernatural hound. Indeed, the hound ends up being a huge, though quite material, hound with phosphorous applied to the jaw to mimic the family legend.

Fiction within Fiction

Because philosophers love thought experiments, let us indulge in a few modifications of these two cases to make things more interesting, supernaturally speaking. In the former case, suppose Holmes could discern that Lord Blackwood was without a pulse and a heartbeat for a full day. Suppose further that he is hanged right before Sherlock's eyes, with Holmes having full knowledge that there is no hidden harness to keep Blackwood's neck from breaking. Finally, suppose that he is buried in an airtight coffin underneath six feet of dirt for the course of the day, during which time Sherlock Holmes is guarding the burial site. Yet despite all of this, Blackwood climbs out of the ground after twenty-four hours. What then? Similarly, consider the following reconstruction of the evidence surrounding the case of the hound of the Baskervilles: imagine that Holmes comes face to face with the hound of the Baskervilles in the middle of the unpopulated moor. He pulls out his revolver and unloads an entire round into the creature at point-blank range, but the bullets pass right through it, leaving the ghoulish hound utterly unaffected and unharmed. Imagine that the hound then levitates, pushes Holmes instantly to the ground with a mysterious force, and finally disappears. Last, imagine that this happens multiple times, and Holmes comprehensively searches the section of the moor each time to ensure that no person and no technology is in the vicinity. What now?

It seems clear enough that if these two thought experiments were to become actual, a supernatural explanation would be far more probable than some unknown naturalistic explanation. At some point, given what we know about well-established natural laws, the detective's relentless desire to find a nonsupernatural explanation turns into a naturalistic version of blind faith that flies in the face of the evidence. This would especially be the case if we have independent evidence that the supernatural realm exists. So long as these two thought experiments represent genuine supernatural possibilities, the Holmesian detective in all of us must hold fast to the elementary principles of supernaturalist reasoning that have been shrewdly deduced before your very eyes.

Notes

1. *Sherlock Holmes,* DVD, dir. Guy Ritchie (2009; Burbank, Calif.: Warner Home Video, 2010).

2. Sir Arthur Conan Doyle, *The Hound of the Baskervilles,* in *The Complete Sherlock Holmes* (New York: Doubleday, 1960), 675. Subsequent citations to Conan Doyle's work are from this text.

3. Paul Draper, "God, Science, and Naturalism," in *Oxford Handbook of Philosophy of Religion* (New York: Oxford University Press, 2005), 278.

4. Ibid., 277–78.

5. *Hound of the Baskervilles,* 681.

6. Draper, "God, Science, and Naturalism," 277.

7. *Sherlock Holmes* DVD.

8. Michael Peterson et al., *Reason and Religious Belief: An Introduction to the Philosophy of Religion* (New York: Oxford University Press, 2003), 173–74.

9. William Lane Craig, *Reasonable Faith* (Wheaton, Ill.: Crossway Books, 2008), 248–49.

10. *Hound of the Baskervilles,* 681.

11. George I. Mavrodes, "Miracles," in *Oxford Handbook of Philosophy of Religion* (New York: Oxford University Press, 2005), 306–7.

12. Alvin Plantinga, *The Nature of Necessity* (New York: Oxford University Press, 2007), 1–2.

13. Mavrodes, "Miracles," 308–9.

14. Draper, "God, Science, and Naturalism," 279.

15. Mavrodes, "Miracles," 306.

16. Draper, "God, Science, and Naturalism," 283. In fact, God, or a supernatural being with power comparable to God, could simply alter natural law.

17. Mavrodes, "Miracles," 309–10.

18. *Hound of the Baskervilles,* 680.

19. Ibid., 684.

20. The same basic sentiment can be found on Sherlock's lips in two other Holmes tales: "Neither of us is prepared to admit diabolical intrusions into the affairs of men" ("Devil's Foot," 960), and "The agency stands flat-footed upon the ground, and there

it must remain. The world is big enough for us. No ghosts need apply" ("Sussex Vampire," 1034).

21. Indeed, if someone has independent reason to believe a variegated realm of supernatural entities exists, this will raise the antecedent probability that a purportedly miraculous event is truly miraculous, so long as the event in question lines up with our understanding of the kinds of things contained in the supernatural realm.

22. *Hound of the Baskervilles,* 681.

23. Ibid., 684.

24. Draper, "God, Science, and Naturalism," 297. This should be our methodology if we are investigating a purportedly miraculous event without any prior reason to believe (perhaps via divine revelation or some other source of knowledge about the supernatural) that a miracle would occur in the specific instance in question, which seems to be the situation in both Holmes cases before us. Even theists should be skeptical of individual claims to the miraculous because most theists would concede that miracles are rare occurrences. We need enough evidence to overcome such antecedent improbability in order to render a supernatural explanation the best one. However, if the theist has good reasons to believe God has revealed His intentions to act in certain miraculous ways, she may very well be within her epistemic rights to infer that a purportedly miraculous event truly is a miracle without driving all reasonably live naturalistic explanations into the ground, so long as that event lines up with the revealed pattern of action. In short, our evaluation of the evidence for a particular miraculous claim should not be conducted in isolation from other relevant evidence. See Peterson, *Reason and Religious Belief,* 184–86.

25. Peterson et al., *Reason and Religious Belief,* 181–82.

26. Ibid., 182.

27. *Sherlock Holmes* DVD.

28. Ibid.

29. Both Watson and David Hume allude to the tendency of uneducated persons to be superstitious, and both have a point. If we are to trust testimony of miracles as true, we must be discerning as to whose testimony we are trusting. Hume also levels other objections to testimonies of the miraculous, and the debate over Hume's views on testimony and probability still rages in contemporary philosophy of religion. For Hume's objections, see Michael Peterson et al., *Philosophy of Religion: Selected Readings* (New York: Oxford University Press, 2007), 473–80.

Was It Morally Wrong to Kill Off Sherlock Holmes?

Andrew Terjesen

The "Great Hiatus" is the term used by Holmes scholars to refer to the period of time between Holmes's tumble off of Reichenbach Falls in the "Adventure of the Final Problem" and his resurfacing three years later (in the chronology of Doyle's stories) in "The Adventure of the Empty House." During those three years, Holmes was presumed dead and had gone deep undercover to trap all of Moriarty's lieutenants. By the end of that story, he had succeeded in arresting the last member of Moriarty's criminal organization who posed a threat. Holmes's activities during those three years are never portrayed in detail in any of the Holmes stories written by Conan Doyle.[1] We do get occasional references to what happened during the Great Hiatus in later stories, but there is a great deal of mystery surrounding them that other writers have tried to shed light on (such as in Nicholas Meyer's *The Seven-Percent Solution*) without reaching any consensus.

In reality, Holmes had been absent from the pages of the *Strand* magazine for much longer than three years. Holmes and Watson returned to the *Strand* in *The Hound of the Baskervilles* in 1901, but that serial seems to be set in 1889, before the events of "The Final Problem." By his own admission, Conan Doyle had intended to kill off Holmes in "The Final Problem," as he had grown tired of the character. Why Conan Doyle returned to writing Sherlock Holmes stories after so many years has never been satisfactorily settled, although we have some clues.

According to Conan Doyle, he received many letters condemning his decision to kill off Sherlock, including one from an old woman which began, "You brute."[2] Supposing the woman meant her words, did Conan Doyle deserve this morally loaded condemnation of his actions as an author?

Did he act immorally in killing off this beloved character simply because he was tired of writing about him? Clearly, many fans of Sherlock Holmes thought that Conan Doyle owed them more adventures featuring Holmes. Had Sherlock Holmes gone from being the work of Sir Arthur Conan Doyle to a public good?

Authorship and Ownership

Sherlock Holmes was the intellectual property of Conan Doyle, but what does that mean? The philosopher John Locke (1632–1704) set forth a theory of property that has become the foundation of modern liberal theory. According to Locke, something becomes our property once we put our labor into it.[3] Take, for example, a blue garnet stone. For a long time it sits in the earth and does not belong to anybody. The first person who finds it is now said to own the gemstone. From the example so far, one might be tempted to think that property is simply a matter of first possession, but this theory fails to explain what it is about first possession that gives one the rights over property. It seems too arbitrary because it seems to boil down to "finders keepers, losers weepers." Locke's labor theory has gotten far more attention because it offers an account as to why the first person to take possession has a right to continued possession.

If someone were to take away the gem from the person who dug it up after he had gone to all that trouble, then the thief has also taken the labor that belonged to the person. To Locke, this seemed like a violation of a basic natural right to our bodies. To prevent this from happening, laws have been created that govern the disposition of property and enable people to enforce their property rights. The person who dug up the blue garnet now has the right to it and can only surrender that right by making the choice to do so. No amount of labor put into the gem after the initial discovery will transfer the property rights without the owner's say-so. If the gem's owner gives it to a jeweler to cut the stone into a more pleasing shape, the jeweler does not become the co-owner of the garnet through this process. Instead, the owner only parts with it if he or she decides to give it to someone, and that usually happens only after being offered a significant amount of money in exchange. That's how the blue garnet at the heart of the mystery in "The Adventure of the Blue Carbuncle" was claimed by the person who originally found it; it then passed from owner to owner by legal means until it ended up in the possession of the countess of Morcar. When James Ryder took it from the countess, he did so without her permission. Even though he made a great effort to hide it in a black-tailed goose, he was never the rightful owner of the gem. Nor did the gem become the possession of Mr. Peterson when he found it in the goose. As long as the chain of possession could be traced back to its legitimate owner, it could not become anyone else's property. If the gem had been abandoned, however, that would be a different story. Mr. Peterson came into possession of the goose because Mr. Baker left it behind after his scuffle. If someone chooses to neglect his property, then after a certain period of time, it is possible for others to claim it because of the labor they put into it—in this case, picking the goose up and cooking it.

The story I've just told is at the core of most theories of property in Western legal systems (though some of the specific details and rights might differ). However, not everyone agrees that this presentation of private property is legitimate. Pierre-Joseph Proudhon is famous for his slogan "Property is theft."[4] Proudhon was taking issue with the way property rights are defined by the legal system. For example, the blue garnet might have been dug up by someone who was hired to do so, but it is legally regarded as the property of the employer. Or the countess may have bought the gem using money she obtained from renting out her land to the people who actually farmed those lands—land she probably inherited from her family (who had claimed it a long time ago, and who may not have actually farmed it themselves for centuries). Viewed in this manner, property seems to involve stealing from the people who actually put labor into it. Karl Marx was initially sympathetic to Proudhon's idea, but he eventually criticized it as self-contradictory. After all, theft implies that what is taken is someone's rightful property. Marx instead argued that the notion of property changes depending on the socioeconomic structure of society.[5] From Marx's perspective, Locke and those who followed him seemed to be in the grip of a capitalist system that continues to dominate today and were perpetuating it through their particular notion of private property. Proudhon and Marx raise some important questions about whether *property* has an essential definition. It is true that property rights have been modified by legal systems (and not always in the same way) so that they can be transferred by the will of the original property holder. However, if property were entirely a social construction, then those who are unaware of society's rules would have no sense of property. The behavior of children at a very young age seems to indicate that notions of ownership come long before we have a sophisticated understanding of society. It's not conclusive proof, but it's a good enough reason to take Locke's notion seriously for the time being.

Even if property isn't a natural right as Locke envisioned, there are strong moral arguments as to why we need to recognize such rights. When offering reasons for a moral principle, most philosophers rely on one of two kinds of argument. The first kind is the consequentialist argument, so called because it appeals to the consequences of our actions to determine their right or wrongness. From a consequentialist point of view, property rights are good because they help organize society, keep it stable, and reward our labors. A society without property rights would be confusing because no one would know which fields to plow or where they would be able to sleep each night. If property rights are not recognized, then we would live in an uncertain world because anyone could try and take our food or shelter from us. If we cannot keep the product of our labors, why should we labor beyond what we could immediately consume?

The other kind of moral argument is a Kantian argument, which is named after the philosopher Immanuel Kant (1724–1804). Kant was a proponent of a moral philosophy in which the consequences did not matter. What mattered for Kant was that our actions be inspired by the right intentions, which he understood to be a respect for persons. We show respect for persons when we treat them as equals and rational agents capable of making their own choices. To paraphrase his words, respect means treating people as ends in themselves and not merely as means to our own enjoyment.[6] Kant gives an example of someone who needs to borrow money and will only be able to do so if he promises to repay it, but he knows that he cannot repay the loan.[7] In that case, the lender is being used as a mere means because the false promise is the reason why the loan is made. If the lender knew the borrower couldn't pay it back, then he wouldn't have made the loan in the first place. Treating the lender with respect would entail being honest about one's financial situation and hoping that the lender will be moved and choose to give you the money without requiring repayment. A false promise removes the lender's choice and as a result his dignity as a free agent.

In Kant's view, property is a necessary condition of agency. If we are going to be able to make plans and take actions, then we have to be secure in the belief that our efforts will not be frustrated by theft. When Ryder and the maid conspire to take the blue carbuncle from the countess, they treat her as if she existed merely to provide them with wealth. On a grander scale, if no one respected property, there would be no point in having things. Ryder's theft only makes sense if he believes that the things he buys with the gem will not be taken from him.[8] Human actions depend on the assumption that we can enjoy the products of our labors. No one wants to be used as a tool to acquire things for someone else. According to Kant, people recognize the need for property rights and agree to create a system in society for enforcing them so that we can act as free human beings.

Both consequentialist and Kantian arguments arrive at the same conclusion: we need to enforce property rights. The arguments used to justify these property rights, however, are different, which has implications for how exactly we understand these rights in particular cases. Intellectual property rights, like Conan Doyle's rights to his stories, have proven particularly difficult to achieve consensus on. The consequentialist argument is the one most often cited in defense of intellectual property rights. If Conan Doyle were not guaranteed the rights to Sherlock Holmes, then he would not have had much incentive to create such a character. All the effort he put into the initial stories would have been for naught if someone else could write their own Sherlock Holmes stories and sell them to a different magazine.[9] Realizing that there is no advantage to creating a new character, he could have instead spent his time writing stories about the adventures of Edgar Allan Poe's detective C. Auguste Dupin. Of course Poe would have had no reason to create Dupin if Conan Doyle and others were just going to produce knock-offs. The lack of intellectual property rights would be deleterious to cultural development. New stories, ideas, or inventions would still develop as long as the effort of creation requires significant compensation. The consequentialist argument relies on the claim that the absence of copyright would create a world that possessed far less good than a world with copyright. Unfortunately for that form of argument, there are reasons to think that the loss of copyright (or placing more severe limits on it than exist today) would not have much of an adverse effect on society overall. Moreover, there are ways in which extensive copyright can have other damaging effects to society. For example, it could prevent any scholarly discussion of Sherlock Holmes stories without express permission.

The Kantian argument concerning intellectual property is not concerned with working out the benefits or costs of copyright. Instead, the question is whether intellectual property is necessary for our free agency. Indeed it is. Much like with tangible property like gemstones, intellectual property helps guarantee that people make choices freely. For example, authors choose to put effort into their creations in the belief that they will benefit in some way from the process. Most often this is in the form of money. Developing a new character like Sherlock Holmes takes a lot of work. Creating a story about Sherlock Holmes after the character has been established is not nearly as time-consuming. According to the Kantian argument, if Conan Doyle knew that his creation was going to be copied by others, then he may well not have gone to the trouble of writing those stories.[10] Instead, he could have focused on his medical practice.

On its surface, the Kantian argument for intellectual property rights bears a resemblance to the one given by a consequentialist. The main difference might be that the Kantian is not interested in balancing the bad (and probably unintended) consequences of intellectual property rights against the good of free agency. The Kantian argument can go deeper than the consequentialist argument, though, because it is not just about deriving benefits from our creations. The Kantian perspective can also recognize that the act of authorship is a process in which we create a certain narrative for our character that we wish to share with the world. Conan Doyle's letter to his mother, Mary Doyle, as he was preparing to resurrect Holmes, reflects this attitude. He wrote, "I don't suppose any man has ever sacrificed so much money to preserve his ideal of art as I have done, witness my suppression of Girdlestone, my refusal to serialize 'A Duet' and my refusal to republish in a book the 'Round the Fire' series of stories. But I have done no short Sherlock Holmes stories for seven or eight years, and I don't see why I should not have another go at them and earn three times as much money as I can from any other form of work."[11] Conan Doyle's sense of himself as an artist depended on his ability to control his creations.

If Conan Doyle could not control the canonical depictions of Sherlock Holmes, then he would lose the ability to create Sherlock Holmes. Our idea of Sherlock Holmes is fleshed out in the course of Conan Doyle's stories. If other people wrote authoritative stories about Holmes without his permission, it could easily confuse the readership and even lead them to think Holmes had certain qualities that Conan Doyle did not intend to imbue him with. An unauthorized portrayal could even sour the audience on the character before he was done telling the story he wanted to tell. Imagine if someone had written *The Seven-Percent Solution* or *Without a Clue* (revisionist tales that portray Holmes as a drug-addled madman and as a bumbling fool) while Conan Doyle was still establishing the character in people's minds. It is true that Conan Doyle's estate licensed the use of Holmes in these stories, but that was at their discretion and almost a hundred years after the original stories were published (at which point it would be very hard to unseat the general impression of Sherlock Holmes as a great detective). Authorship entails the ability to create a narrative and determine its ending. Without such power, an author would be nothing more than a cog in a larger machine at the mercy of forces beyond their control, unable to act according to their desires.

The Many Lives (and Deaths) of Sherlock Holmes

The Kantian argument seems a promising defense of Conan Doyle's rights to do with Sherlock Holmes whatever he wishes. The problem with relying too much on this argument is that it is not clear we can continue to assign full ownership of Sherlock Holmes to Conan Doyle (or his estate) after a relatively short period. The Sherlock Holmes as we know him is not solely the product of Conan Doyle's labors. His original stories featuring Holmes and Watson are certainly at the core of our image of Sherlock Holmes today, but they are far from the only influence. Sherlock Holmes as an icon has certain attributes that are not to be found in anything that Conan Doyle wrote. This was true even during Conan Doyle's lifetime (at least as early as the Great Hiatus).

To begin with, Sidney Paget's illustrations helped shape the image of Sherlock Holmes in the mind of the audience. Actors like Basil Rathbone and Jeremy Brett were popular (at least in part) because they looked like Paget's illustrations of Holmes. When we see Holmes as a tall, lanky figure with slicked-back hair, it just seems right, but that's because of Paget's illustrations. Paget is also credited with adding some elements to the portrayal of Holmes that have become the costume by which most people recognize him, most notably his deerstalker cap and Inverness coat, with its cape. Nowhere in the writings of Conan Doyle are these specific details mentioned. As Paget's labors mixed with Conan Doyle's on thirty-seven stories and one novel, it would seem like Paget deserves at least some of the credit of being the author of the popular Sherlock Holmes. Paget's style was so definitive that after his death in 1908, other illustrators imitated it when depicting Holmes.

Paget's image of Holmes was further popularized by the actor William Gillette who, beginning in 1899, starred in seven different Broadway productions of Sherlock's adventures. Gillette wore the deerstalker cap and the Inverness coat as part of his costume, and he also smoked the distinctive large calabash pipe that most people associate with Holmes. In Conan

Doyle's stories, Holmes smokes several different kinds of pipes, but it is the question-mark-shaped calabash that sticks in people's minds as they imagine Holmes pondering a problem. In fact, that particular pipe goes against the portrayal of Holmes in Conan Doyle's stories because the kind of tobacco that Holmes is said to prefer would not have been well suited for a calabash pipe.

In many ways, Basil Rathbone's portrayal of Holmes in fourteen films just reinforces the elements of Paget's and Gillette's presentations of Holmes. However, those films also add well-known elements to the Sherlock Holmes mythos. The oft-repeated phrase, "Elementary, my dear Watson!" is one of the best-known movie quotes and is often included in any homage to Holmes. The closest that Holmes ever comes to saying something like that in Conan Doyle's stories is in "The Adventure of the Crooked Man," when he says, "Elementary!" in response to Watson's "Excellent!"[12] That is the only time it is ever said. The Rathbone films also gave us the popular image of Watson as a much older, retired gentleman who is a bit of a bumbler. Lestrade too suffers in those films, presumably to make Holmes seem all the more impressive in his deductive abilities. Those images of Watson and Lestrade have had a long legacy, though more recent portrayals of Watson (such as the Guy Ritchie movies with Jude Law and Stephen Moffatt's series for the BBC with Martin Freeman) have sought to restore the image of Watson as a much more vigorous companion to Holmes.

Most people know Sherlock Holmes as a character, and far more know of him from iconic popular images rather than from having read the stories. Show people a picture of a tall, thin man with a deerstalker cap, Inverness coat, and calabash pipe, holding a magnifying glass and shouting, "Elementary, my dear Watson!" and you can rest assured that most of them will identify him as Sherlock Holmes. This image of the world's greatest consulting detective is the product of many people's labors and has taken on a life that transcends the original works of Conan Doyle. Moreover, the numerous parodies and noncanonical explorations of Holmes (many produced with the permission of Conan Doyle's estate, which still owns the property) have further transformed this complex and well-loved character into an icon.

Looking at all of this, one might conclude that after more than 125 years, Holmes has become a communally held cultural property and should no longer be the limited possession of anyone. However, all of this happened much later and should not be a factor in judging Conan Doyle's rights to the character when he embarked on the Great Hiatus. Only Paget's contributions might undermine Conan Doyle's claim, and they undoubtedly depended on later portrayals to really make them iconic. There is one other creator of Sherlock Holmes who needs to be considered. By Conan Doyle's own admission, the character of Sherlock Holmes was inspired by Dr. Joseph Bell.[13] He even relates a story of Bell deducing someone's history that sounds strikingly similar to our first introduction to Sherlock's method when he identifies Watson as a recent veteran of Afghanistan.[14] That particular scene is one of a few of the more famous deductions that have been reproduced in a number of adaptations as a definitive example of Holmes's method. In light of how much Holmes is defined by the practice of the science of deduction, it seems that some credit for his creation should go to the real person who introduced Conan Doyle to it. Holmes's connection to Bell was clear to Robert Louis Stevenson, who wrote to Conan Doyle after the publication of *The Adventures of Sherlock Holmes,* "Can this be my old friend Joe Bell?"[15]

The reason for dwelling so much on the question of who created Holmes is because most people think of intellectual property in terms of the labor of creation, and the claim that Conan Doyle had a right to kill off Holmes often rests on the argument that he was free to do what he wanted with his intellectual property. Even if we do not like how he uses it, it was his to do with as he wished. We might be appalled if someone bought the Mona Lisa just so he could scrub the smug smile off her face, but there is no legal recourse to prevent him from exercising his property rights. The idea that Holmes might not really belong to Conan Doyle would go a long way to justifying the antipathy that greeted his decision to kill him off in "The Final Problem." If Holmes had ceased to be Conan Doyle's sole creation, then perhaps he would not have had the right to end the story in such a final manner.

Sherlock Holmes illustrates how difficult it is to ascribe authorship to a single individual, especially over time as a character or story is adapted into different media. Early in his career, Conan Doyle was the sole owner of Sherlock Holmes, and as time went on and others contributed to the popular images of Holmes and Watson, his claim of ownership became weaker until the character belonged to the public. The uncertainty in determining credit for Sherlock Holmes as we understand him today shows that it is impossible to own an idea, character, or story the way one owns a car or piece of jewelry.[16] There is no doubt that Conan Doyle is the author of the stories he wrote, but it is less clear that he is the sole author of the character of Sherlock Holmes. Without a clear sense of ownership, Conan Doyle's decision to kill off Holmes cannot be excused on the basis of intellectual property rights alone. Conan Doyle's sense of himself as an artist means that we cannot require him to write more Sherlock Holmes stories. Conan Doyle explained his reticence to write more Sherlock Holmes stories in a 1903 letter to his editor, in which he said, "You will appreciate more fully now my intense disinclination to continue these stories which has caused me to resist all entreaty for so many years. It is impossible to prevent a certain sameness and want of freshness."[17] Killing off Holmes in "The Final Problem" goes a step further than Conan Doyle's right not to write more short stories. What he did was to prevent anyone else who had contributed to the Sherlock Holmes character from being able to create adventures and mysteries for the public to enjoy. I would argue Conan Doyle's claim to ownership after the first two rounds of short stories was not strong enough to justify such a drastic action. If he was justified in killing off Holmes, it has to be for another reason than that he owned Holmes.

An Author's Moral Responsibility to His Audience

Not everyone will be convinced by the argument that intellectual property is a weak concept, but even those people might be persuaded by a secondary consideration concerning the morality of what Conan Doyle did. Let's grant that Holmes was the sole property of Conan Doyle during his lifetime, which gave him the legal right to do with it whatever he wanted and to prevent anyone else from supplying the public's demand for more adventures. Nevertheless, just because you can do something doesn't mean you should, or that you are a not a bad person for doing so. The hypothetical person who buys the Mona Lisa in order to deface it is displaying a lack of respect for the painting and the importance it has for so many people.

In the case of Conan Doyle, his concern for his audience should run even deeper than some random person who buys the Mona Lisa. The argument might go like this. Sherlock Holmes was a financial success for Conan Doyle because of the audience. The popularity of those stories also gave him a special status in society and literary prominence. Although I would not go so far as to say that he owed his audience for the success that he derived from Sherlock Holmes, he should have accorded them a certain level of gratitude. Out of respect for all that Sherlock Holmes had made possible for him (and later his family), he should, so this argument goes, have given greater thought to the impact of such a final act as killing off the character. Conan Doyle himself expressed surprise at the reaction to "The Final Problem." If he had been ignorant of how beloved the character was, he cannot be regarded as intentionally disrespectful his audience. Once he learned of how people reacted, maybe he morally should have considered how he might supply them with their regular Sherlock Holmes fix.

It's not surprising to think that Conan Doyle underestimated the value others placed on his creation, as he did not think too highly of it when compared to his other work. As he described it in "The Truth about Sherlock Holmes," he put Sherlock Holmes aside after *The Sign of Four* because he was

> encouraged by the kind reception which "Micah Clarke" had received from critics. . . . Hence came my two books, *The White Company,* written in 1889, and *Sir Nigel,* written fourteen years later. Of the two I consider the latter the better book, but I have no hesitation in saying that the two of them taken together did thoroughly achieve my purpose, that they made an accurate picture of that great age, and that, as a single piece of work, they form the most complete, satisfying, and ambitious thing that I have ever done. All things find their level, but I believe that if I had never touched Holmes, who has tended to obscure my higher work, my position in literature would at the present moment be a more commanding one.[18]

He could not have been more off base in assessing his literary status, but this just shows how he thought that Holmes was interfering with his true calling as an author. In light of the importance that Sherlock Holmes had for his audience, maybe it was indeed wrong, especially in retrospect, for Conan Doyle to kill Sherlock Holmes off merely because he wanted to do other things. Still, just because Conan Doyle shouldn't kill Holmes does not mean that he had to write more stories. Saying that Conan Doyle was in some measure obliged to produce more Holmes stories would be equivalent to saying that he should not be able to live his life in the manner he finds most fulfilling. It would mean treating him as a means to our aesthetic satisfaction and not respecting him as an end in himself.

The fear that Holmes was taking away from his real literary work was not the only reason Conan Doyle gave for doing away with the character. He also found writing Holmes to be a difficult and unfulfilling task. It was difficult because "every story really needed as clear-cut and original a plot as a longish book would do."[19] After a while, Conan Doyle grew tired of having to invent new plots. He even tired of the character. In his opinion, Holmes's character "admits of no light or shade. He is a calculating machine, and anything you add to that simply weakens the effect."[20] In the same essay, Conan Doyle even takes a dig at Watson as someone who never evidences a bit of humor in all his stories. Writing Holmes stories had ceased to be enjoyable to him. From a Kantian perspective, to insist that he continue to do something that he did not enjoy would be to endorse a form of enslavement.

Looking at Conan Doyle's reasons for wanting to do away with Holmes, it seems that the arguments rest on his desire to stop writing these stories. That is certainly a good reason why he should be allowed to stop. It is not as clear that this is a good reason for withdrawing Holmes from the public completely. He could have given permission to someone else to continue the stories, perhaps even commissioning a ghostwriter to publish them in Conan Doyle's name as so many mystery and thriller writers did in the twentieth century. At the very least, he could have ended his run with a triumphant story as opposed to foreclosing the possibility of his return by killing him off. The joy that his readers derived from the latest adventure in the *Strand* was a public good that he should not have taken away lightly.[21] However, his responsibility to his audience must be balanced against his free agency as an author. It would not have been morally right for him to kill Holmes simply because he was tired of the character or to spite his audience, or readers would be justified in regarding his actions as morally deficient for showing disrespect to his audience. At the same time, an author creates a narrative for some specific purpose. If Holmes's death in "The Final Problem" could be shown to fit with an admirable narrative, then we (the readers) do not have the right to condemn Conan Doyle for what happened at Reichenbach Falls and Conan Doyle wouldn't have been a brute after all. I will argue that "The Final Problem" was a fitting send-off for Holmes and Watson precisely because of its narrative power.

Death with Dignity

To see why "The Final Problem" was an ending that readers should have been content with, consider the character of Sherlock Holmes. He was defined early on by his desire to solve puzzles that befuddled an ordinary intellect. In *The Sign of Four,* an idle Holmes turns to drugs to relieve his boredom. He craves work and mental exaltation. Other than "*the* woman," Holmes did not seem to care much for the fairer sex. Nor did he seem very interested in cultivating family relationships or other sorts of social bonds. His work was nearly all-consuming; only his violin, his occasional drug use, and his friendship with Watson distracted him.

"The Final Problem" was the greatest problem Holmes had ever solved. Everything after that was bound to be anticlimactic for the detective. Holmes had discovered "the Napoleon of crime" after years of trying to decipher the malevolent force behind many of the crimes in London. The crimes were so varied that only Holmes's intellect could detect the existence of a pattern of influence. It is even implied that a number of his earlier cases were indirectly connected to Professor Moriarty. Discovering and then taking down this organized crime ring was the greatest of achievements. As he says to Watson, "If I could beat that man, if I could free society of him, I should feel that my own career had reached its summit."[22] When he finally confronts his nemesis, Holmes knows that ridding the world of Moriarty may mean his own death, but he accepts it: "My career had in any case reached its crisis. . . . No possible conclusion to it could be more congenial to me than this."[23] Solving such a difficult puzzle and triumphing over someone whose intellect matched his own made for a fitting climax to the stories. That Conan Doyle's instincts were right can be seen in the fact that most adaptations of the iconic Holmes (the ones that aren't trying to be faithful to a particular story) try to work Moriarty into the mix even though he only appeared in the one story and was mentioned in a few others. No other villain seems adequate to Holmes, but repeating their confrontation (or making Moriarty a constant presence in the mysteries) does not break new narrative ground.

Let's face it: the Holmes stories after the Great Hiatus are more of a mixed bag. Some of the stories seem to be retreads of older stories. A return to more traditional drawing room mysteries with cheating spouses, stolen items, and other bourgeoisie deceptions was a real letdown after defeating the Napoleon of crime. For example, the basic conceit of "The Adventure of the Six Napoleons" hearkens back to "The Adventure of the Blue Carbuncle." As a boatman once told Conan Doyle, "when Holmes fell over the cliff, he may not have killed himself, but all the same he was never quite the same man afterwards."[24]

I'm not claiming that there is nothing redeeming about the post-Reichenbach stories. A number of those stories show Conan Doyle developing as a writer, even helping to create the new genre of spy thriller with "The Adventure of the Bruce-Partington Plans" and *The Valley of Fear*. In fact, the second time that Conan Doyle appeared to bring an end to Holmes's adventures is a pretty interesting story too. "His Last Bow" is set during Holmes's retirement, so it is the latest chronologically of all the Conan Doyle stories. This story also has an important narrative as Holmes takes action to aid in the war effort. In "The Final Problem," Holmes was trying to bring an end to Moriarty's criminal empire. In "His Last Bow," he was trying to put a stop to the expansionist policies of Germany. Both stories feature eminently worthy causes. If Conan Doyle was going to end the series, then a spy story was the second-best ending after Reichenbach Falls.

Conan Doyle continued to supply the public's appetite for Sherlock Holmes after "His Last Bow," but he did so more sporadically. The final twelve stories that would be published as *The Case-Book of Sherlock Holmes* are arguably weaker in general. Undoubtedly there are people with favorite stories from the *Case-Book*, but many readers find most of them to be inferior to those that came before. The letter to his mother quoted earlier (as well as other letters that mention what he was being paid for each story) suggests that the amount of money he could get for each new Holmes story was driving his writing more than artistic inspiration, especially in his final set of short stories.

If Conan Doyle was writing more for the paycheck in the last ten years of his life, that is his right as well. His dignity as an author does not depend on purely artistic motives, nor does it depend on quality writing. It just depends on letting him craft his narratives as he sees fit. Conan Doyle was never obligated to write more Holmes stories (though perhaps he should have handed over the reins on the last dozen). The reason why he didn't have this obligation could be based on an appeal to intellectual property rights, but, as I have indicated above, I find much that is problematic with that argument because I don't think it can be said that Conan Doyle still owned his creation at the end of his life.[25] Instead, I am appealing to Conan Doyle's dignity to justify his decision to stop writing Sherlock Holmes stories, but his dignity alone is not enough to justify killing off Holmes. Even someone who thinks that Holmes is still the sole property of the Conan Doyle estate needs to recognize that ownership does not license all actions toward one's property, especially if it is something of great significance to the public.

To justify bringing an end to Holmes's career (and any stories that could have been written about him after Reichenbach Falls), Conan Doyle needed to do so in a way that it was necessary for the story and it should be a story that further developed Holmes beyond the stories that had already been written. "The Final Problem" was a well-crafted ending on both those counts. To show what a great nemesis Moriarty was, it was important that Holmes achieve victory at great cost. And "The Final Problem" was an important addition to the canon because it tied together many of Holmes's previous cases into one final expression of his superior deductive skills (as no one else had noticed this immense pattern). The story was even presented in a way that made the resurrection of Holmes possible. (Whether or not that was Conan Doyle's intention, it does show some respect for the idea that later writers should be able to produce more Sherlock Holmes stories to whet the public appetite.) "His Last Bow" was another great ending in this respect. It put Holmes in retirement as a beekeeper, but that also enabled Conan Doyle to emphasize how important the war effort was by bringing Holmes out of retirement to aid it. We were fortunate to see a series after the Great Hiatus with a number of strong stories, but that does not mean Conan Doyle was any less justified in his original decision to kill off Holmes. Had Holmes never returned from Reichenbach Falls, we still would have had such a strong ending to the Sherlock Holmes saga that we could not have demanded more from Conan Doyle.

Notes

1. It is true that "The Adventure of Wisteria Lodge" is dated to 1892, but many think this is an error.

2. Arthur Conan Doyle, "The Truth About Sherlock Holmes," in *The Complete Sherlock Holmes* (New York: Barnes and Noble Books, 2003), 2:684. Subsequent citations to Conan Doyle's work are from this text.

3. John Locke, *Second Treatise on Government* (1689; reprint, Indianapolis: Hackett, 1980).

4. Pierre-Joseph Proudhon, *What Is Property?*, trans. Donald R. Kelley and Bonnie G. Smith (New York: Cambridge University Press, 1994), 13.

5. Friedrich Engels and Karl Marx, *The Communist Manifesto* (1848; reprint, New York: International Publishers, 1948).

6. Immanuel Kant, *Grounding for the Metaphysics of Morals*, translated by James Ellington (1785; Indianapolis: Hackett, 1993).

7. Ibid., 37.

8. One might object that Ryder has good reason to think that most people would not violate his property rights and therefore he can feel secure in his possession of the blue carbuncle. However, Kant's philosophy is not based on such consequences. Kant would point out that even though Ryder is not likely to be the victim of theft, he is not treating people equally if he thinks that he has a right to violate other people's property rights, but they do not have the right to violate his.

9. Which is not to say that a proliferation of knockoffs cheapens the original product. The point is just that the usual reasons for writing something are to make money

or to become well known, and neither could happen in a world where people can easily copy an author's creation.

10. The Kantian argument is not interested in the actual consequences of our immoral actions (that is for the consequentialist to worry about). Conan Doyle seemed to enjoy the parodies of Sherlock Holmes, but that doesn't change the fact that someone was usurping his role as author and therefore taking away his freedom. That's what makes it an immoral action for Kant.

11. From Arthur Conan Doyle, *A Life in Letters*, ed. Jon Lellenberg, Daniel Stashower, and Charles Foley (Harmondsworth, UK: Penguin Press, 2007), 512.

12. "Crooked Man," 1:492.

13. "Truth," 679.

14. The anecdote can be found in "Truth," 679–80. Holmes's deduction about Watson is to be found in *A Study in Scarlet*, page 10, but the explanation, which bears striking similarities to the Bell anecdote's explanation, is found on page 18.

15. Kyle Freeman, introduction to vol. 2 of Conan Doyle, *Complete Sherlock Holmes*, 2:xv.

16. It's also worth bearing in mind that copyright started as a way to protect book publishers. Copyright literally meant the right to make copies of a book, not some special ownership over the ideas contained inside it. The copyright guaranteed that no one else could produce a cheaper copy that would compete with the inventory already in circulation, as unsold inventory would eat into the profit margin.

17. Conan Doyle, letter to *Strand* editor H. Greenhough Smith, in *Life in Letters*, 514.

18. "Truth," 682–83.

19. Ibid., 684.

20. Ibid., 688.

21. That Conan Doyle recognized this public good is evident by his statement that "from time to time I endeavored to supply" the public with a supply of new Holmes stories. Ibid., 684.

22. "Final Problem," 558.

23. Ibid., 569.

24. Freeman, introduction, 2:xxviii.

25. This is obviously a point on which I disagree with the law governing copyright, but moral philosophy is not beholden to what legislators decide (although they should consider moral arguments when constructing their laws and not just lobbyists from Disney). How long copyright should be extended is an arbitrary matter and varies from country to country, which is why Sherlock Holmes is completely in the public domain in the United Kingdom and completely not in the public domain in the United States.

Sherlock Holmes

Artist of Reason

D. Q. McInerny

Mr. Sherlock Holmes is the remarkably successful detective that all the world readily acknowledges him to be because he is a preeminent man of reason, which means, in more specific terms, that he is a man of method. The method, in turn, can be said to be the natural corollary to his complete dedication to logic. Holmes is capable of being languorously undisciplined while he is between clients, a time when boredom seems to set in quickly, engendering, according to the reports we receive from Dr. Watson, a type of melancholy that appears very much like clinical depression. Yet as soon as he is presented with a case to be solved he instantaneously emerges from the doldrums. It has to be the right kind of case, however, one with charm—that is, one he deems sufficiently interesting. This can be taken as a synonym for *difficult*. We have reason to believe that Holmes had no qualms about turning down cases that he did not think would offer the kind of challenge demanded by his lively and inquisitive intellect. Once the right kind of case is before him, he then sets himself to the task of solving it with near-obsessive concentration. His spirits soar, and the only stimulation he needs now is provided by the puzzles of the case, the more gnarled the better. He will cling to a case with bulldog tenacity, not letting go of it until it is satisfactorily solved, typically to the amazement and admiration of all parties involved.

Holmes himself would be the first to assure us that he is nothing if not a careful, systematic thinker, always proceeding in his reasoning step by calculated step until the envisioned end is attained. "They evidently failed to appreciate the fact, that I had begun to realize," the ever informative Watson tells us, "that Sherlock Holmes's smallest actions were all directed toward some definite and practical end."[1] In this we have the central characteristic of Holmes as a logical thinker, for what else is logical thinking but, as the logician Susan Stebbing so precisely put it, thinking to some purpose?[2] Holmes is always thinking to some purpose, his mind assiduously at work in the focused effort to gain a specific goal, such as the solution to a particular puzzle. It is difficult to imagine him, so long as he is on a case, giving much time to nondiscursive thought, much less to idle daydreaming.

Holmes may be regarded as a preeminent example of man thinking, a type principally defined by the fact that his mind is always engaged and running in high gear. For Watson, he is a "reasoning machine"—a rather forbidding description that he elaborates on when he tells us that Holmes is "the most perfect reasoning and observing machine that the world has ever seen."[3] Holmes, speaking for himself, tells his faithful companion: "I am a brain, Watson. The rest of me is a mere appendix."[4]

No Bloodless Automaton

Are we to conclude then that Holmes is nothing more than a consummate reasoner, whose whole life can be, if not entirely summed up, then at least chiefly identified by the intellectual athleticism he so energetically engages in? That would be rash. Granted, his role as a kind of mental Superman is what renders him especially fascinating to us, but we would not find him as interesting as we continuously do were he no more than a mechanistic problem solver. The thinking man we are dealing with here is not a bloodless automaton. Or, to put the whole matter in proper psychological context, thought—human thought—is never exercised, even by someone like Holmes, completely unaccompanied by emotion. The life of the intellect consists in considerably more than raw cogitation. Sherlock Holmes, in his methodical way of thinking, may properly be identified as a man of science, but the man of science, if he is to be successful in his endeavors, must rely on more than his pure reason. Imagination too, and importantly, must be actively at work. Intellect and imagination, far from being in conflict with one another, are comfortably complementary. Holmes, this peerless practitioner of the science of detection, while very much depending on his marvelously acute intellect, depends on his imagination as well, even though, in that canny way of his, he might be reluctant to make any public admission to this effect.

Aided by some of the more detailed descriptions of his modus operandi, which are sprinkled throughout the stories, we may be pardoned if we were to take Holmes's assertion that he is no more than a brain with a grain of salt. He does not in fact fit that description; furthermore, he knows that anyone who does fit it would not be a successful practitioner of his science. In "Silver Blaze," he makes the significant observation that a certain police detective with whom he is working, one Inspector Gregory, would have the wherewithal to "rise to great heights in his profession" if only he were "gifted with imagination."[5] Brains alone will not do the trick. In *The Hound of the Baskervilles,* we find Holmes stressing what he calls "the scientific use of imagination," by which we can take him to mean that scientific investigation, for all the emphasis it must give to reason, necessarily entails imagination. When in "The Problem of Thor Bridge" he berates himself for being too slow in putting together the pieces of a puzzle so as to bring the case to quick resolution, he explains by saying that he was "wanting in that mixture of imagination and reality which is the basis of my art."[6] Reality—the concrete circumstances of the case—presents him with the bare facts, but imagination must come into play in the interpretation of those facts.

Sherlock's Art—And Passion

We would do well to take special note of the reference he makes in that statement to his art. Clearly Holmes considers himself to be more than a staid scientist. He is an artist as well, and it is an open question as to which of the two he regards as the more precise way by which he should be identified. He speaks of the "touch of the artist"[7] that wells up at times, as if it were his more significant self spontaneously rising to the surface and asserting itself. In another place he refers to himself as a "true artist."[8] One might even want to say that he is an advocate and ardent practitioner of art for art's sake, for he takes delight in his detecting work just as such, simply for what he sees as its intrinsic value. He has no hesitancy in letting others, usually the official police, take credit for his accomplishments, nor does this bother him a bit. He works relentlessly to get results, but it is the process by which those results are achieved that sustains him and gives him the most satisfaction. Let others get the applause, even though they don't deserve it. The more Watson comes to know him, the less confident he is in the accuracy of his depiction of Holmes as a reasoning machine as a summary account of the man, for now he can see the "fiery soul behind the cold gray face."[9]

While duly acknowledging Holmes to be the scientific man of reason, it would be a mistake to fail to see that he is also a man of passion. If we do not immediately recognize him as such it is because we don't see how reason relates to passion in him—as the ruler to the ruled. Here is a man of passion who manages, through the exercise of reason, to keep his passions continuously under nearly perfect control, and this offers the best explanation for the man's amazing efficiency. Passion is tamed; it is trained to bolster, not bother, reason. He operates mainly within the realm of science and according to strict scientific principles, but his passional nature is called into service on those occasions when he intuits the need to move beyond the strict confines of science. His larger method involves occasional departures from method.

Guess or Hypothesis?

Is not this way of analyzing the man contradicted by Holmes himself when he tells us that he never guesses? Not really. The fact of the matter is that Holmes does guess. However, his guesses are not whimsical shots in the dark but rather studied surmises constructed on a solid scientific base. His guesses are of that educated variety otherwise known as hypotheses.

By taking note of the procedure Holmes regularly follows in solving his cases, we can see that his standard mode of operating has to it four distinct stages. There is first the fact-gathering stage, which consists of two steps: the interview and the on-the-scene investigations. The second stage is the one in which Holmes gives himself over to intense thought, analyzing the data that has been gathered and forming whatever conclusions the data will warrant. The third stage, representing the denouement of the story, is where he solves the mystery and closes the case. The fourth and final stage is the after-the-fact briefing in which Holmes ties up loose ends and answers any lingering questions concerning the case.

The first step of the fact-gathering stage, the interview, almost always takes place in his Baker Street quarters. The interviewee is either someone who is personally involved in the case or someone who is an outside observer but close enough to the case to be able to give a reliable account of all its pertinent particulars. There is a set ritual governing the interview. Holmes invites the person to sit down and to reveal all he knows ("You will kindly tell me what has happened, when it happened, how it happened. . . ."),[10] and then he becomes the complete listener, concentrating totally on what he is being told. His interruptions of the narrative are rare and brief, interjected only for the purpose of clarifying a point or two. To the interviewee, Holmes's queries sometimes seem to touch on trivial or irrelevant matters, but they invariably prove to be quite pertinent. Holmes attaches so much importance to the interview because of his need to get a holistic picture of the mystery to be solved. A loose aggregate of disjointed facts would be of no use to him. He is looking for a coherent narrative, a story line that moves in a certain direction and is therefore suggestive of a specific denouement. It is part of the artist in him that he sees human behavior as always story bound, and therefore interpretable in terms of the Aristotelian triad of beginning, middle, and end. If he can gain a good working sense of the first two, there is a fair chance that he can then figure out the third. "You have come to tell your story, have you not?" he asks a client in "The Adventure of the Beryl Coronet," and then, a few lines later: "Pray compose yourself, sir . . . and let me have a clear account of who you are and what it is that has befallen you."[11] With the knowledge provided to him by the interview, Holmes is now equipped with a structural framework, however incomplete, within which he can proceed with his investigation. It is unusual that Holmes should form any firm conclusions concerning a case at this stage of the proceedings, although he may have in mind a tentative hypothesis or two. If perchance he has formed a conclusion, it is very much part of his policy to keep it to himself. On rare occasions, he sees the solution to a case as soon as its general circumstances are known to him. In "The Adventure of the Noble Bachelor," he confidently informs Lord St. Simon: "I had formed my conclusions as to the case before our client came into the room."[12]

The second step of the fact-gathering stage is an active one. It commonly constitutes the heart of the adventure. It is the investigation proper, given over to collecting information firsthand, either at the principal scene of a crime or at another related location. Holmes sometimes performs this task on his own. In doing so, he will occasionally don a disguise. Sometimes he will instead commission Watson to do his legwork for him. To Watson's chagrin, this too often provides Holmes the opportunity of offering a prickly critique of his partner's investigative abilities. Most frequently, though, the two of them will do the investigating together—clearly the choice of preference for Holmes. He greatly depends on Watson's assistance, and the latter is always accommodating, often at the shortest possible notice. The reader might wonder if Holmes does not take advantage of his friend's boundless good nature in this respect, but there is no evidence that Watson himself ever thinks along those lines.

One-Man Think Tank

The second stage of Sherlock's standard mode of operating is dedicated to deep thought and analysis. Here the detective becomes a one-man think tank. Although Conan Doyle does not give us an account of the particulars of Holmes's cogitations, we can easily imagine that he is meticulously examining every bit of data available to him to date. He is attempting to discern in it intelligible patterns that will lead him to a solution of the case. Although this stage is distinct from the investigation stage in terms of the respective activities peculiar to each, in most cases the two are intermixed. This is seen in those instances where Holmes, in the thick of an investigation, will abruptly interrupt his fact-gathering activity and withdraw into himself, "entirely absorbed in his own thoughts."[13] Watson tells us that on one occasion Holmes "sat frequently, for half hour on end, with knitted brow and abstracted air."[14] This is by no means an unusual occurrence. When Holmes is in such a state, he may just as well be on the moon, so deeply plunged in thought is he, so completely cut off from everything and everyone around him. Here is the mastermind at work, and Watson, for one, knows better than to intrude on the private detective's privacy at so critical a time. At such moments, Holmes is engaged in framing his hypotheses, forging and testing "every link of the chain."[15] He is often prolific in generating viable hypotheses while in this state, and in "The Adventure of the Copper Beeches," he casually announces to Watson: "I have devised seven separate explanations, each of which would cover the facts as far as we know them."[16]

The duration of these deep-thought sessions can range anywhere from a half hour to many hours on end. In "The Man with the Twisted Lip," Holmes stays up all night, smoking pipe after pipe of strong tobacco, trying to put together the pieces of a particularly recalcitrant puzzle. Meanwhile, Dr. Watson enjoys a long and unperturbed sleep. If the reasoning goes well and feasible solutions are found, Holmes emerges from the session in an ebullient mood, raring to go. The end is now in sight—denouement—and he is full of nervous energy, anxious to take the necessary action without delay to clear up all the problems associated with the case and to ensure the triumph of justice.

Untangling the Web and Wrapping Up

In the third stage, Holmes deftly brings everything together, illumines what hitherto seemed irremediably obscure, untangles what had appeared to be hopelessly tangled, and neatly solves the case—but not always. There is that rare occasion, represented most famously in "A Scandal in Bohemia," when his best efforts go for naught and he is cleverly thwarted. Interestingly, he shows himself to be a good sport about it, perhaps because, in part at least, the case involved no murder or bloodshed and he can afford to take a more relaxed attitude toward it. In a magnanimous gesture on the part of someone whom some call a misogynist, he ever afterward respectfully refers to Irene Adler as "*the* woman."[17] I like to think, doubtless fancifully, that had Holmes met that remarkable lady a few years earlier, he would not have remained a bachelor.

The fourth stage is the *post factum* wrap-up, where Holmes will sometimes assume a decidedly professorial mien. With pedagogic earnestness, he provides Watson with a summary account of the case, explaining the conclusions he had arrived at and the rationale behind them. In "The Adventure of Abbey Grange," Holmes informs Watson that he proposes "to devote [his] declining years to the composition of a textbook, which shall focus the whole art of detection into one volume."[18] Perhaps its title could have been *The Scientific Art of Detection*?

In *The Valley of Fear,* Holmes explains to Mr. White Mason, the chief Sussex detective, a revealing aspect of his operational procedure: "I claim the right to work in my own way and give my results at my own time—complete rather than in stages."[19] This shows him to be a man who makes it a point never to act precipitously. He wants to be sure not just of his facts—though that goes without saying—but of the soundness of his analysis of those facts. He will not allow himself to be rushed in this regard. In one case he is asked if he has hit on something that might serve to unravel a particularly knotty mystery, to which he curtly replies, "Perhaps I have. But I do not care to discuss it until there is something more solid to discuss."[20] Unless he considers the case closed, he gives nothing away.

Holmes on Holmes

Throughout the stories, we can find any number of instances where Sherlock Holmes himself provides us with additional information concerning specific aspects of his standard mode of operating, sometimes in the form of a casual comment or two, sometimes by way of expanded explanations, and almost always addressed to Watson. Some of the more interesting cases are worth mentioning. By way of illustrating the ample use he makes of the logical faculty, note should be made of the reliance he places on what he calls "reasoning backward," which is simply the process whereby we reason from effect to cause, thus following the pattern of what is known in classical logic as *quia* argumentation. He often calls attention to his pet principle that theory should never get ahead of facts: "It is an error to argue in front of your data."[21] Nor should one ever neglect "to separate the essential from the accidental."[22] It would cripple the effectiveness of any investigation to allow oneself to become distracted by matters that do not have a direct bearing on the case at hand. As he puts it, "It is of the highest importance in the art of detection to be able to recognize, out of a number of facts, which are incidental and which are vital. Otherwise your energy and attention must be dissipated instead of being concentrated."[23]

Holmes is not against giving a friendly tip to a professional colleague on occasion, if the person shows promise and would benefit from the advice. "You'll get results," he tells Inspector MacKinnon in "The Adventure of the Retired Colourman," "by always putting yourself in the other fellow's place, and thinking what you would do yourself."[24] To ensure that the reasoning machine will operate at maximum efficiency, Holmes in certain cases takes to serious fasting, sometimes for a matter of days. Given the intensity of the man, it is not surprising that sometimes he carries this to extremes, to the point where Dr. Watson tells us that "[Holmes] fainted from pure inanition."[25]

Holmes considers himself to be a man without prejudices, one who does not allow his judgments "to be biased by personal qualities."[26] We can take this to be another of his guiding principles. There is no reason why we should question the sincerity of his commitment to this principle; however, there are some stories in which his faithfulness to it is not clear. Consider the case of "The Adventure of the Norwood Builder," in which a housekeeper is one of the key characters. Before he has any hard evidence that would suggest that she is not entirely trustworthy, he observes: "There was a sort of sulky defiance in her eyes, which only goes with guilty knowledge."[27] If that does not count as outright prejudice, it would seem at least to represent a rather chancy inference.

The devotee of logic would be pleased by the effective use Holmes makes of the venerable reductio ad absurdum argument, in which one tests a dubious hypothesis by first assuming it to be true, and then seeing what would follow from that assumption. If what follows is absurdity—a contradiction—then the hypothesis is shown to be false. In *The Valley of Fear,* Holmes points out to Watson that if a hypothesis that the doctor proposes is in fact true, as he takes it to be, then they will end up with a number of "nasty, angular, uncompromising bits which won't slip into their places."[28] In other words, they would find themselves in an unworkable situation, and that is enough to prove the hypothesis to be untenable.

If there is any character in modern fiction who can be said fairly to exude self-confidence at every pore, it is Mr. Sherlock Holmes of Baker Street. It would be difficult to imagine him ever having to seek counseling for problems relating to a lack of self-esteem. In the early months of the partnership between Holmes and Watson, Watson is not slow to discern in the detective a certain air of arrogant superiority that he finds disturbing. It is interesting to observe that in the later stories, two things happen: first, Watson no longer seems to interpret Holmes's air of superiority in negative ways, perhaps because he has come to see that it is, after all, quite justified in terms of what are his superior talents; and second, Holmes himself becomes noticeably less cocky in his attitude; he seems to acquire a degree of intellectual humility. Among other things, he is now willing to admit that logic, powerful though it be, is not without its limitations, and he even confesses that "the most logical mind may be at fault."[29] Putting things on a more personal level, he admits to having provided for Watson's files "an example of that temporary eclipse to which even the best balanced mind may be exposed."[30] In one of the last stories, "The Adventure of the Lion's Mane," Holmes roundly accuses himself of being "slow at the outset—culpably slow."[31] It is especially revealing that he is prepared to concede that his superior intellect itself may sometimes be the cause of his mistakes. We find this out in "The Adventure of the Abbey Grange," where he explains to Watson that "when a man has special knowledge and special powers like my own, it rather encourages him to seek complex explanation when a simpler one is at hand."[32]

Holmes the Metaphysician

Sherlock Holmes is the successful man of reason he is not simply because of his artful science and logic, but because, in the final analysis, he can qualify as a philosopher—a metaphysician. By this I mean that he is familiar with thinking in terms of the cosmic whole and of thus recognizing that the kind of order and intelligibility that he readily recognizes on the level of everyday experience is founded on and ultimately explained by the order and intelligibility to be found in the universe itself. "I am conscious of power and design," he tells Watson, thereby attesting to his conviction that he considered himself to be a resident of an ordered, intelligible universe.[33] "So all life is a great chain," he assures Watson in *A Study in Scarlet,* "the nature of which is known whenever we are shown a single link of it."[34] Even the actions of criminals have order to them and are thus intelligible; otherwise all of Holmes's feats of reasoning would be of no avail. Criminal actions, like all human actions, are necessarily structured and guided by finality, and that is what allows us to see the sense in them, although doing so is by no means an easy task.

Holmes acknowledges a recognizable order on the human scale, then, because he acknowledges it on the larger or cosmic scale. The cosmic order explains the microcosmic order. There is a telling paragraph in which Holmes shows himself to be in a particularly philosophic mood. "'What is the meaning of it, Watson?' said Holmes solemnly as he laid down his paper. 'What object is served by this circle of misery and violence and fear? It must tend to some end, or else the universe is ruled by chance, which is unthinkable. But what end? There is the great standing perennial problem to which human reason is as far from an answer as ever.'"[35]

That the universe should be ruled by chance is unthinkable for a man like Holmes; if this were allowed to be a possibility, then human reason would be totally impotent. By direct experience, he knows that not to be the case. If all were governed by chance, there would be no order, for chance is the very antithesis of order. If there were no order, not only would it be impossible to solve problems, which Holmes does so adeptly, but also problems would not even be recognizable as problems. If all were governed by chance, there would be nothing by which chance itself could be identified, for chance is not only the antithesis of order, it is defined in terms of order. For Holmes, we live in a meaningful universe because of the overriding reality of ends, the termini toward which all actions are directed. But how about *the* end, the grand purpose to which the universe as a whole is directed, which we might identify with Aristotle's Final End? There Holmes confesses agnosticism—but not complete agnosticism. He admits to his inability to pronounce on the exact nature of such an end, but he is nonetheless confident of its existence and essential goodness.

Sherlock Holmes is a professional problem solver, a dissipater of mysteries. The passionate intensity with which he throws himself into his work, however, cannot be explained only by the charm and interest his cases hold for him. To be sure, he is totally dedicated to finding the solution to the immediate mystery at hand, but beyond that mystery, there is always for him the haunting presence of a larger one—a mystery of cosmic dimensions, a mystery summed up in that needling question he put to his friend and confidant: "What is the meaning of it, Watson?"

Notes

1. Sir Arthur Conan Doyle, *A Study in Scarlet,* in *The Complete Sherlock Holmes* (New York: Barnes & Noble Classics, 2003), 1:27. All Holmes references in this chapter come from this edition.
2. L. Susan Stebbing, *Thinking to Some Purpose* (Harmondsworth, UK: Penguin Books, 1939).
3. "Scandal in Bohemia," 1:187.
4. "Mazarin Stone," 2:533.
5. "Silver Blaze," 1:403.
6. "Problem of Thor Bridge," 2:599.
7. *Valley of Fear,* 2:283.
8. "Dying Detective," 2:445.
9. "Disappearance of Lady Frances Carfax," 2:454.
10. "Priory School," 2:74.
11. "Beryl Coronet," 1:360.
12. "Noble Bachelor," 1:351.
13. "Silver Blaze," 1:406.
14. "Copper Beeches," 1:383.
15. "Golden Pince-Nez," 2:385.
16. "Copper Beeches," 1:385.
17. "Scandal in Bohemia," 1:187.
18. "Abbey Grange," 2:192.
19. *Valley of Fear,* 2:255–56.
20. "Lion's Mane," 2:626.
21. "Wisteria Lodge," 2:367.
22. "Priory School," 2:85.
23. "Reigate Puzzle," 1:487.
24. "Retired Colourman," 2:662.
25. "Norwood Builder," 2:32.
26. *Sign of Four,* 1:108.
27. "Norwood Builder," 1:31.
28. *Valley of Fear,* 2:274.
29. "Empty House," 2:20.
30. "Disappearance of Lady Frances Carfax," 2:460.
31. "Lion's Mane," 2:629.

32. "Abbey Grange," 2:198.
33. *Hound of the Baskervilles,* 1:601.
34. *Study in Scarlet,* 1:17.
35. "Cardboard Box," 2:396.

Sherlock Holmes and the Ethics of Hyperspecialization

Bridget McKenney Costello and Gregory Bassham

Sherlock Holmes is highly specialized in the art of criminal detection—hyperspecialized, in fact. He possesses highly trained powers of observation and reasoning, which he pairs with a deep knowledge of matters that bear directly on his profession, including chemistry, anatomy, the history of crime, footprints, bloodstains, mud splatters, and tobacco ashes. Yet Holmes—at least when we are first introduced to him—is almost totally ignorant of many areas of knowledge that virtually all educated Victorians took for granted. For instance, he knows "next to nothing"[1] about contemporary literature, philosophy, and politics, and he is so ignorant of modern astronomy that he doesn't even know that the earth revolves around the sun. When Watson asks why he only pursues knowledge relevant to his profession, Holmes responds by comparing the mind to an attic that must be kept clear of useless and obstructing lumber and that contains nothing "but the tools which may help him in doing his work."[2]

Sherlock's attic analogy is one that many of today's career-minded college students would cheer. Why waste so much time in college learning useless lumber like history, literature, and philosophy when they could be studying far more relevant things in their career-oriented major courses? Why bother to learn anything, in fact, that doesn't help one get a good job and make a good living?

Are these students—and Holmes—justified in placing so much emphasis on vocational education and career success? Is Holmes's attic metaphor an apt way of thinking about how we should furnish and organize the mind? Does the single-minded pursuit of career success or some particular form of human excellence (for example, athletic success) violate an ethical duty to be a well-rounded person, or an informed citizen, or some other duty of personal development or self-improvement? Here we'll explore these questions with the help of some leading philosophers, educators, and social theorists.

This Old Brain Attic

The clearest statement of Holmes's view of education and self-improvement is contained in Watson's famous introductory character sketch of Holmes in *A Study in Scarlet.* When Watson expresses astonishment at how little Holmes knows about literature, politics, and so forth, Holmes replies:

> I consider that a man's brain originally is like a little empty attic, and you have to stock it with such furniture as you choose. A fool takes in all the lumber of every sort that he comes across, so that the knowledge which might be useful to him gets crowded out, or at best jumbled up with a lot of other things, so that he has a difficulty in laying his hands upon it. Now the skilful workman is very careful indeed as to what he takes into his brain-attic. He will have nothing but the tools which may help him in doing his work, but of these he has a large assortment, and all in the most perfect order. It is a mistake to think that the little room has elastic walls and can distend to any extent. Depend upon it there comes a time when for every addition of knowledge you forget something you knew before. It is of the highest importance, therefore, not to have useless facts elbowing out the useful ones.[3]

Holmes here compares the human mind to a woodworker's attic. He notes three relevant similarities: limited storage capacity, the utility of stored items, and duties of proper stocking and organization. We address each of these in turn.

CAPACITY

The mind, says Holmes, is like a "little room," not a spacious warehouse. It can only store a limited amount of information. Fools who try to cram too much knowledge into their brains will inevitably end up either forgetting some useful bit of information or misplacing it in a jumble of useless facts.

UTILITY

A workman's attic should be well organized and include only tools and lumber that "may help him in doing his work."[4] Likewise, Holmes claims, a person's mind should be orderly and should include only knowledge that is of practical value.

DUTIES OF THE ATTIC'S OWNER

The workman is not merely able to distinguish between useful and useless tools; as a practitioner of a skilled craft, he has an ethical or professional duty to choose his tools well and maintain an uncluttered and well-stocked workroom. Holmes himself fulfills this obligation by ignoring useless information and focusing almost exclusively on matters that relate directly to his profession of crime detection.[5]

The Case of the Science of Memory

To some extent, Holmes's attic theory of the brain is supported by contemporary neuroscience and educational psychology, particularly his claim that the brain's tools must be kept "in the most perfect order." In cognitive psychology, interference theory seeks to show how some memories can block retrieval of other memories.[6] Research has shown, for instance, that interference can occur when a person tries to master two different areas of knowledge at the same time, such as two languages; the two subjects become jumbled together and are easily confused. Studies have also shown, however, that interference is rarely a problem when we use well-developed mental skills. So Holmes needn't be worried that learning a little basic astronomy will interfere with his ability to do bloodstain analysis, because he already knows that subject so thoroughly.

Moreover, cognitive science has shown that memories that are unrelated to other ideas are more likely to be lost than ideas that exist in a network of related thoughts and memories. According to prevailing theories of mental development, memories tend to fade or be forgotten quickly without a supporting context of intellectual or emotional associations.[7] The reason we tend to forget things is not because the memories are elbowed out by additional knowledge, but because the memories weren't securely anchored in a nexus of related thoughts and feelings.

Sherlock's solution to the problem of disorganization is to avoid clutter by attempting to acquire only useful information.[8] This stems from his view that the mind, like an early-generation computer, has a limited storage capacity. In fact, research has shown that the capacity of the brain to remember certain things becomes better developed—or, in brain attic terms, bigger—as our expertise in those areas develops. As we become more proficient in categorizing our memories, we retain more of them. This is one reason people remember so little from their early childhoods; at that age they lack sufficient life experience to know where to file those memories. So Holmes's worry about the capacity of his brain attic to store information is mostly groundless. The more we learn, the more our capacity to learn grows. In fact, current work in schema theory suggests that mental clutter may serve to enhance memory function by aiding the process of categorization. This theory likens the organization of memories to the arrangement of books in a cramped used bookstore. A musty pile of useless self-help books might bookend a fine collection of British detective fiction and keep them from becoming scattered and disorganized. The self-help books may have little value in themselves, but if they help patrons find the good books, they fulfill a useful purpose.[9]

The Usefulness of Useless Knowledge

There is an additional problem with Holmes's facile distinction between useless and useful information: people may be poor judges of which information is actually useful. Holmes himself invokes irrelevant knowledge on numerous occasions. After all, the ability to communicate with people in all walks of life is crucial to Holmes's profession, and often seemingly useless facts smooth this process of communication. In one instance, responding to Watson's ruminations about the beauty and power of nature, Holmes remarks, "Are you well up in your Jean Paul [Richter]?" When Watson replies that he has read a fair number of Richter's works, Holmes goes on to relate one of Richter's observations on the topic at hand.[10] It is unlikely that the works of Richter, a relatively obscure eighteenth-century German novelist, would qualify as "useful facts" for Holmes in theory.[11] Yet in practice, this knowledge serves as a handy conduit for Holmes's message.

The idea that people are not always good judges of what information will turn out to be useful is supported by the sociological literature on social and cultural capital.[12] Social capital is the value of our relationships with other people, through whom we gain access to goods and services.

Cultural capital is the value of knowledge of cultural practices—meaning everything from how to calculate a golf score to how to evaluate abstract mid-twentieth-century painting—through which we communicate with people in various social strata and so cultivate social capital. Both types of capital are resources that are interchangeable with other forms of capital to produce various advantages. For instance, in *The Sign of Four*, Holmes is able to gain entry to a building by trading on his knowledge of boxing (cultural capital) to exploit a weak relationship to the man guarding the entrance to a building who also happens to be a boxer (social capital), which ultimately allows him to pursue a lead (and possibly acquire some economic capital from a grateful client).[13] The value of social and cultural capital, and particularly cultural capital, lies in its superficially noneconomic nature combined with its relative exclusivity: not everyone knows the right people or would know what to say to the right people if suddenly put in their path, and this knowledge is neither easy to come by nor of explicit material value. Even those with substantial social or cultural capital holdings may not be aware of the extent to which they exchange it for material advantage. Moreover, cultural capital in particular is more potentially valuable as it becomes rarer and more obscure, and by the same token, the contexts in which one can meaningfully use rare and obscure cultural knowledge are much more limited. Consequently, those who work across a variety of social milieus—such as Holmes, who on a given day might need to wheedle information from both an archduke and a chimney sweep—are best served by cultivating multiple types of cultural literacy as a way to bridge the divisions of lifestyle and social class. Holmes, for example, can read the subtle cultural cues to uncover the identity of a disguised nobleman, as in "A Scandal in Bohemia," and he can also convincingly adopt the rakish demeanor of an inveterate gambler to establish common ground with a reluctant poultry merchant in "The Adventure of the Blue Carbuncle."[14] This is not merely a testament to Holmes's acting ability, but also of his mastery of the cultural mannerisms of a broad swath of late Victorian British society. In short, what Holmes derides as useless knowledge often proves critical to his success in solving crimes.

Holmes's distinction between useful and useless knowledge is even more problematic in our own day. In today's economy, workers who cultivate a narrow set of "practical" job skills may quickly find their knowledge obsolete because of technological innovations, restructured transnational labor forces, or the movement of entire industries offshore. Employer surveys consistently indicate a preference for workers who are broadly knowledgeable over those who are more narrowly trained. Among the most desired job skills today are critical thinking, good communication skills, ethical decision making, the ability to work well in teams, and global literacy.[15] Being able to distinguish useful and useless knowledge in today's economic climate may require a predictive power that not even the great Sherlock Holmes could claim.

Holmes and the Duty of Self-Improvement

We turn now to an even bigger problem with Holmes's attic analogy. The analogy assumes that no useless knowledge should be acquired—that the mind should be furnished only with tools relevant to one's career success. We shall argue, on the contrary, that there is a moral duty to acquire useless nonvocational knowledge, an obligation that follows from a more general duty of self-improvement. Talk of a duty of self-improvement smacks, perhaps, of Victorian moral earnestness, and this might explain why there has been so little systematic discussion of the idea in recent moral theory.[16] In fact, however, such a duty fits comfortably within many ethical frameworks.

Consider the three leading moral theories today: consequentialism, duty theory (aka deontological ethics), and virtue ethics. Consequentialists—ethicists who claim that acts are right or wrong depending on the consequences they have—could point to the public benefits that would result if people took seriously a duty to become more intelligent and responsible citizens, parents, students, teachers, workers, and public servants. Duty theorists—ethicists such as Immanuel Kant (1724–1804) and W. D. Ross (1877–1971), who believe that some acts, like promise breaking and torture, are wrong even if they do maximize good consequences—could appeal to the intrinsic value of developing one's moral and intellectual potential (Ross) or note that a rational being could not possibly will that a maxim such as "let your talents rust and go undeveloped" should become a universal law of human conduct (Kant). Virtue ethicists—theorists such as Aristotle, Aquinas, and Alasdair MacIntyre, who claim that ethics is centrally concerned with developing good character and fulfilling human potential—could note that inculcating a strong sense of personal responsibility for developing one's talents and capacities is crucial for human fulfillment.

In short, there appears to be a strong overlapping philosophical consensus for recognizing a general duty of self-improvement. There will, of course, be disagreements over specifics. Which should be given priority: intellectual, moral, physical, emotional, spiritual, or vocational improvement? Is there some single ideal pattern of human development that all humans should strive for, or does this vary from individual to individual and from culture to culture? Is it permissible for an individual to concentrate more or less exclusively on one area of improvement (say, physical improvement in an Olympic hopeful or wealth building in a young dot-commer), or is there some minimum level of intellectual, moral, or spiritual development that all persons should be expected to achieve? These are issues on which philosophers of different stripes would obviously disagree.[17]

However, there are certain fundamentals on which nearly all philosophers would concur. Any meaningful duty of self-improvement must include absolute or qualified bans on suicide, self-injury, and acts that rob one of one's autonomy, self-mastery, or capacity for rational reflection or responsible choice. Most philosophers would go further and say that persons who have the time, talent, and opportunity to become well-rounded, broadly educated individuals have an ethical responsibility to do so. We believe that there is such a duty for several reasons.

First, as we have seen, it is a mistake to sharply distinguish useless knowledge of things like literature and philosophy from practical knowledge relevant to career success. There's nothing more useful than being able to think. And that's what we get from a broad-based education. As philosopher Andrew P. Mills notes, thinking involves more than

> just knowing facts and figures and formulas. Being able to think means being able to write well and speak clearly. It means being able to organize your time, being able to offer creative solutions to intractable problems, and being able to deal with new and challenging situations. Above all, being able to think means being able to ask the right questions, make smart decisions, and teach yourself what you don't know.[18]

This, in fact, is why Conan Doyle's portrayal of Holmes is so unrealistic. Somebody who really knew next to nothing about literature, history, politics, and so forth would not possess either the background knowledge or the habits of disciplined thinking to make the accurate, lightning-quick logical inferences that are Holmes's stock in trade. Logical inference is only as reliable as the information contained in the premises. As Holmes himself admits, an ideal reasoner would have quickly solved the mystery in "The Crooked Man" by recognizing that the name David was an allusion to the biblical story of David and Bathsheba.[19] In fact, Holmes often solves mysteries by drawing on factual information that, in terms of his own attic metaphor, he should not possess.

Second, a broad knowledge base is important for civic literacy and the responsibilities of democratic citizenship. Being a good democratic citizen requires a basic understanding of democratic institutions, processes, and values. However, effective citizenship requires more than this. An effective citizen is a knowledgeable and informed citizen. Effective citizens must stay abreast of local, national, and international developments and intelligently appraise political office seekers' qualifications and views on the issues. This implies not only a willingness to acquire the intellectual skills and dispositions necessary for sound political judgment, but also a willingness to stay informed on political issues and events. Holmes, we're told, reads nothing in the newspapers except the criminal news and the "agony columns,"[20] and he knows next to nothing about politics. This means he is what philosophers call a free rider in Great Britain's democratic system of government. He benefits from the fact that others participate actively and knowledgeably in that system, making good governance possible, without doing his fair share to keep the process working. Not that Holmes is a useless citizen—far from it. He fights crime, and in one of his last adventures, he even helps Britain win the Great War by foiling a German spy network.[21] However, our point is that Holmes would have been a better crime fighter and a more useful citizen if he hadn't been totally uninterested in politics.[22]

Two reasons for recognizing at least a presumptive duty to become a well-rounded, culturally literate person are that by doing so, one can acquire skills and dispositions that will prove useful in one's career and in one's role as a responsible citizen. However, the deepest reason for recognizing such a duty is rooted in human nature itself. As Socrates said, care of the soul—leading an examined life and valuing virtue and wisdom over fickle and ultimately unfulfilling concerns such as fame, power, or wealth—should be our highest priority. As Aristotle noted, human beings have many capacities that other animals do not. In particular, he observed, humans have unique capacities for rational reflection, ethical decision making, and autonomous choice. Because of these unique capabilities, the richest forms of human fulfillment must consist in making the most of our potential—striving for excellence in all that we do, but particularly in those capacities of heart, mind, and spirit that make us distinctively human. This is precisely what a broad-based liberal education can help us to achieve. A liberal education broadens the mind, disciplines our rational powers, enlarges and sensitizes the imagination, and helps to free us from the biases and predigested dogmas of our upbringing, our culture, and our age. Through the liberal arts, we encounter the greatest minds of human history and can participate in the Great Conversation that stretches from the agoras of ancient Greece to the halls of top modern universities. As Allan Bloom remarks, people "may live more truly and fully in reading Plato and Shakespeare than at any other time, because then they are participating in essential being and forgetting their accidental lives."[23] By focusing single-mindedly on career success, as Holmes does, one fails to tap into the incredibly rich resources the Great Conversation provides for enjoyment, critical awareness, and the examined life.

Of course, Holmes's case isn't nearly so simple. For one who disdains useless facts, Holmes often proves to be an amazingly cultivated and well-rounded guy. As the stories unfold, we're surprised to find him quoting Goethe in German, discoursing learnedly on Buddhism in Ceylon, quoting the medieval Persian poet Hafiz, rhapsodizing over concert music, discussing the novelist George Meredith, writing a scholarly treatise on sixteenth-century choral music, and reading his pocket Plutarch. Eventually, we're told, Holmes becomes an "omnivorous reader,"[24] dividing his time in retirement "between philosophy and agriculture,"[25] and writing a learned monograph on beekeeping.[26] In short, Holmes doesn't practice what he preaches. He isn't at all the career-obsessed philistine one would expect from his own attic theory of the mind.

In the end, we don't want to be too hard on old Sherlock. As the German philosopher Hegel said, "Nothing great has been accomplished in the world without passion,"[27] and we can all admire the tremendous passion and dedication Holmes brings to his self-invented profession. Let's face it: Holmes became a great man and a great detective precisely because of his intense and single-minded devotion to his craft. Our point is simply that he took it too far.

Notes

1. Sir Arthur Conan Doyle, *A Study in Scarlet,* in *The Complete Sherlock Holmes* (Garden City, N.Y.: Doubleday, 1930), 21. All subsequent references to the Sherlock Holmes stories are to this edition. In later stories, as we shall see, this picture of Holmes as a single-minded, career-obsessed philistine is considerably softened.

2. Ibid. Compare "Five Orange Pips," 225, for a similar account.

3. *Study in Scarlet,* 21.

4. Although there is some sloppiness in his analogy here, he does make a distinction between knowledge and skills, and he privileges the latter over the former. Knowledge is clearly "lumber," which may clutter the brain attic rather considerably. Skills, however, exist outside the attic; they are vested in the "skilful workman" himself, who owns the attic but does not occupy it. The position of "tools" is less clearly specified, in that they are the necessary instruments for exercising the workman's skills, but they may also clutter the brain attic if the workman isn't careful.

5. "Red-Headed League," 177. See also *Sign of Four,* 91, when Holmes deploys his knowledge of "the influence of trade on the form of the hand" by remarking that "the fish that you have tattooed immediately above your right wrist could only have been done in China. I have made a small study of tattoo marks and have even contributed to the literature on the subject." Likewise, in "The Boscombe Valley Mystery" (214), Holmes employs his own cigar ash study, which was first noted in *Sign of Four,* 91.

6. This is why, among other reasons, the practice of cramming is inadvisable. See John W. Santrock, *Educational Psychology* (New York: McGraw-Hill, 2001), 288.

7. Ibid., 60, 288–89.

8. We can control what types of tools we put in our attics. We can't really control all the ideas that flow into the mind. As much as we'd like to forget that tragic car crash or annoying ear candy, we just can't. This is one of many major disanalogies between the brain and an attic.

9. Santrock, *Educational Psychology,* 284.

10. *Sign of Four,* 121.

11. Holmes also apparently counts steps on the off chance that this information might turn out to be useful. See "Scandal in Bohemia," 162.

12. Both terms are commonly used in sociological discussions of social class and other inequalities; the various properties of social and cultural capital were initially articulated in the works of Pierre Bourdieu, particularly in *Outline of a Theory of Practice* (New York: Cambridge University Press, 1977) and *Distinction: A Social Critique of the Judgment of Taste* (Cambridge, Mass.: Harvard University Press, 1987), both translated by Richard Nice.

13. *Sign of Four,* 106.

14. "Scandal in Bohemia," 165, and "Blue Carbuncle," 253.

15. See, for example, "Employers Seek More College-Educated Workers with Higher Levels of Learning and Broader Sets of Skills, New Survey Reveals," http://aacu.org/press_room/press_releases/2010/employersurvey.cfm.

16. See generally Gregory Bassham, "Lifelong Learning and the Duty of Self-Improvement," *Think* 6, no. 16 (December 2008): 101–5. The concept of a duty of self-improvement is found most prominently in deontological, self-realization, and natural law ethical traditions. For representative discussions, see David Ross, *The Right and the Good* (Oxford: Clarendon Press, 1930), 21; Immanuel Kant, *Lectures on Eth-*

ics, trans. Louis Infield (Indianapolis: Hackett, 1963), 116–26; V. J. McGill, *The Idea of Happiness* (New York: Praeger, 1967), chap. 7; and Samuel Pufendorf, *The Whole Duty of Man, According to the Law of Nature,* trans. David Saunders (Indianapolis: Liberty Fund, 2003), 69–80.

17. This and the preceding paragraph are adapted from Bassham, "Lifelong Learning," 101–2.

18. Andrew P. Mills, "Why Are You Here? College as a Health Club for the Mind," http://faculty.otterbein.edu/AMills/ConvocationSpeech.html. Arguments that colleges should just focus on relevant job skills are nonsensical when one considers the realities of the job market. Fewer than half of all college students graduate at all. Of those who do, considerably fewer than half are working in their major field within five years of graduation. In fact, in the first four months of 2009, less than half of all college graduates aged twenty-five or younger were even working in fields that require a college degree. Tony Pugh, "Recession's Toll: Most Recent College Grads Working Low-Skill Jobs," June 25, 2009, http://www.mcclatchydc.com/329/v-print/story/70788.html. Even more startlingly, none of the ten jobs most in demand in 2010 even existed six years ago. Nancy Gibbs, "Time Will Tell," *Time,* September 21, 2009, 92.

19. "Crooked Man," 422.

20. "Noble Bachelor," 288.

21. "His Last Bow," 970–80.

22. This paragraph is adapted from Bassham, "Lifelong Learning," 103.

23. Allan Bloom, *The Closing of the American Mind: How Higher Education Has Failed Democracy and Impoverished the Souls of Today's Students* (New York: Simon & Schuster, 1987), 380.

24. "Lion's Mane," 1094.

25. Preface to "His Last Bow," 869.

26. "His Last Bow," 978.

27. G. W. F. Hegel, *Introduction to the Philosophy of History,* trans. Leo Rauch (Indianapolis: Hackett, 1988), 26.

Passionate Objectivity in Sherlock Holmes

Charles Taliaferro and Michel Le Gall

The detective novel as we now know it has its origins in the nineteenth century. It was very much a phenomenon contemporary with the dissemination of Auguste Comte's (1758–1857) positivist philosophy, a rigorously scientific approach to problem solving.[1] Edgar Allan Poe (1809–49)—one of several authors heralded as the creator of the detective novel—was himself both taken with and skeptical of the powers of reason. In his short essay "Instinct vs. Reason—A Black Cat," Poe remarked, "The leading distinction between instinct and reason seems to be, that, while the one is infinitely more exact, the more certain, and the more far-seeing in its sphere of action—the sphere of action in the other is of the far wider extent."[2] Put simply, reason has its limits, while instinct is less limited in the range of its application.

This debate that Poe initiated—which carries on in the opening paragraphs of "The Murders in the Rue Morgue"—finds more than a counterpart or counterpoint in the stories of Sherlock Holmes. In fact, Conan Doyle both advances and elaborates this debate to encompass a broader ethical challenge. What is more important when making an ethical decision: to be analytical, impartial, cool, and dispassionate, or to be passionate and emotionally engaged with and committed to those about whom you care most?

In ethical theory today, there is a clear clash between those who maintain that resolving an ethical question or dilemma requires a vigorous impartial point of view (let's be detached and unbiased) and those who support particular loyalties (let's first support those we love and then think about others) while holding that such loyalties are not necessarily in conflict with ethical decision making. At first meeting, Sherlock Holmes with his devotion to logic seems to be in the first camp, as evidenced by a newspaper article he wrote and the conclusions of which Dr. Watson described in *A Study in Scarlet* as "infallible as so many propositions of Euclid."[3] Nevertheless, there are some hints that Holmes may have taken up a philosophically interesting and nonetheless rigorous and uncompromising middle ground in this debate.

The Objectivity of Mr. Holmes

In *The Sign of Four*, Holmes sets out his methodology of detection, which often starkly contrasts with Watson's accounts and analyses of Holmes's cases. Watson portrays detection in a way that is (for Holmes) too suffused with romance and emotion. Holmes's cool-headed approach to inquiry seems to go along with his narrowly chosen fields of interest and his solitary lifestyle. In social terms, too, Holmes seems to be just short of the perfect hermit who occasionally makes his way into society to procure the necessities of life and at his discretion to solve baffling crimes. As we know clearly from Watson's testimony, Holmes does not cultivate a wide scope of friends, nor does he seek out female companionship and courtship—though he does find some female clients interesting, in a somewhat detached fashion. Sir Conan Doyle once said, "Holmes is as inhuman as a Babbage calculating machine and just as likely to fall in love."[4]

Holmes is explicit about and conscious of the need to avoid particular commitments or relationships interfering with his reasoning. In *The Sign of Four*, Holmes maintains that it

> is of the first importance, not to allow your judgment to be biased by personal qualities. A client is to me a mere unit—a factor in a problem. The emotional qualities are antagonistic to clear reasoning. I assure you that the most winning woman I ever knew was hanged for poisoning three little children for their insurance-money, and the most repellant man of my acquaintance is a philanthropist who has spent nearly a quarter of a million upon the London poor.[5]

The context for Sherlock's analysis here is his denial of having observed the attractiveness of Miss Mary Morstan. Watson understandably thinks it's a bit inhuman of Sherlock to be so detached and impartial, perhaps especially because Holmes had just cast in such callous and cold, impersonal terms the woman Watson would end up marrying. Watson, in contrast with Holmes, wished to indulge his thoughts about "her smiles," "the deep rich tones of her voice," her sweet and amiable expression, and her large blue eyes, which were "singularly spiritual and sympathetic."[6]

By the end of *The Sign of Four,* Watson and Miss Morstan, mutually smitten, plan to marry, a prospect Holmes had "feared." For love and emotion are at odds, Holmes says, and he is unwilling to place anything above the "cold reason" that he prizes more than all else. This is why he denies that he will ever marry, "lest I bias my judgment."[7] The need for objectivity in his work had trained Holmes to aspire never to have prejudices, but rather always to follow "docilely wherever facts may lead me."[8] Close romantic attachments represented peculiar temptations for him to form a skewed perspective—biases and prejudices that compromise objectivity.

Holmes's position (thus far) seems to accord with the contemporary philosopher Simon Keller, who, in his book *The Limits of Loyalty,* argues against treating loyalty as a virtue. He and Holmes sound similar, but Keller pushes the point even further. Keller argues that loyalty to friends, nations (patriotism), and family tends to compromise our very integrity, given that the nature of loyalty in these domains requires that one side with the friend, nation, or family even when they are manifestly wrong. Keller goes so far as to suggest that friendships can be problematic to the extent that they lead us to assume exaggerated beliefs or false values. For Keller, friendship needs to be classified as a conditional (and not unconditional) good. Keller puts it this way:

> The achieving of distance from our friendships, and the weighing of the requirements of particular friendships against other considerations are quite familiar phenomena; in particular, we adopt strategies that help us to avoid and manage conflicts between our desires to be good friends and our desires to be good believers. The idea that we allow friendships to lead us wherever they may, that friendship is something that we embrace without hesitation, is a philosophical fantasy.[9]

It may seem odd for Keller to refer to being "good believers," but his thesis is not without support from common experience. Loyalty in friendship can manifest itself in such ways as believing in the innocence of a friend even when the evidence of his having committed the crime seems significant. We might be reluctant to think a friend was guilty of some crime unless the evidence was decisive, but look the other way when the evidence isn't clear.

Parents may be especially prone to disbelieving reports of their children's bad behavior (unless they have seen such behavior for themselves). If this is true, and loyalty not only affects our moral agency but also our ability to hold true beliefs, then clearly it could be an impediment to the kind of rationality and integrity that Holmes aims to cultivate. This common reality is compellingly captured in the predicament of the loving mother of the murderer Clyde Griffiths in Theodore Dreiser's *An American Tragedy.*

Contemporary philosopher Bruce Russell devises a thought experiment to gauge our intuitions on a moral matter involving loyalty that goes like this:

> Suppose your son has robbed a rich man of his jewels, the police are after him, and he asks you to help him escape to Brazil. You know you can arrange things so that neither of you will get caught. You also know that if he is caught he will be sent to prison and his life will be ruined, but if he escapes, he will have a good life in Brazil. It would be wrong of you to help him escape, but why isn't it true that what you have most reason to do is to help your son escape justice?[10]

Russell thinks the example shows that there can be a tension between what is moral to do (turn in his son) and what it is rational to do in the sense of what there is most reason to do (help his son escape). Surely much of the intuitive force to which Russell appeals here comes from considerations of loyalty, which is an instructive point even if Russell's analysis fails to exhaust the alternatives.[11]

Let's turn our attention to an example from the pages of Conan Doyle. Sherlock habitually tells Watson that Watson's stories aren't very good. According to Holmes, Watson's chronicles of their adventures are florid, suffused with romance, and preoccupied with needless narrative. They reverse the order of events, involve exaggeration, and underemphasize the role of logic in solving puzzles. Sherlock doesn't mince words, nor does he bother to bookend such critiques with affirmations to make the medicine go down more smoothly. He is honest to a fault—brutally so.

Watson, for his part, understandably tends to bristle a bit, though remaining long-suffering in putting up with Holmes. Such criticisms might be enough to put a strain on most any real-life friendships. In their case, perhaps Holmes's exceptional qualities make it a bit easier for Watson to put up with the critiques. But it still couldn't have been easy for Watson to hear. It's only much later, when Sherlock tries to write up some narratives himself, that he comes to appreciate some of the literary gifts of Watson. Early on there's not a hint of any appreciation at all. Sherlock does seem to appreciate Watson for a number of his qualities, including courage, loyalty, and trustworthiness—but not for his writing, at least for a while. What makes Sherlock's unwillingness to show any appreciation of his friend's writing perhaps a bit surprising is the depth to which Sherlock himself finds particularly gratifying the admiration and appreciation from a friend for his own gifts.

If, however, Holmes truly had a hard time appreciating Watson's gifts as a writer or method of chronicling their adventures, it would have been disingenuous for Holmes to act otherwise. His critiques, though harsh, at least had the virtue of honesty. It would seem that the primacy assigned by Sherlock to objectivity and truth obliged him not to sugarcoat or whitewash his reservations about Watson's writing.

Holmes, it could be argued, might agree with Keller that any impediments to reasoning and belief formation are not assets but rather liabilities, especially for a detective. On this analysis, Holmes seems to side unequivocally with Keller's notion that loyalty is well short of being a virtue. Or does he? More broadly, is Sherlock rightly thought to fall entirely into the category of reason over instinct, the discursive over the intuitive, the objective over the subjective, the head over the heart? Does he always privilege the analytical, impartial, and dispassionate over the emotionally engaged, personally involved, and affective? To answer such questions, let's look at some additional facts.

Passion in a Moment of Revelation

Against Keller and others who insist on the superiority of adopting a completely impartial point of view, philosophers such as Bernard Williams and Susan Wolf claim that our personal identities naturally (and rightfully) dispose us to sometimes give priority to those whom we love—our friends and family—even if that predisposition conflicts with our stated uncompromising and unconditional allegiance to morality. Put in another way, Williams and Wolf are suggesting that in certain circumstances where loyalty may be at stake, the morally right thing to do is not to reflect impartially on the circumstances of the case, but instead to act in ways that prefer and privilege those closest to us.

Williams makes this last point in an amusing quip offered in a response to Charles Fried. In an important essay, "Persons, Character, and Morality,"

Fried defends Williams's priority of loyalty.[12] Fried asks us to imagine an accident in which there is a man who can only rescue one of two drowning people, his wife or a stranger. Fried writes that "the occurrence of the accident may itself stand as a sufficient randomizing event to meet the dictates of fairness, so he may prefer his friend, or loved one."[13] Williams charged that Fried's proposal "provides the agent with one thought too many"![14] In other words, in that situation where the choice is between someone with whom you are connected and a complete stranger, of course you should choose the one you are connected to. The thought process shouldn't be, "Oh, I'm justified to save my wife over this stranger in a situation like this," but rather simply, "That's my wife in need of saving"![15]

If Holmes had to decide to support Keller on the one hand or Williams and Wolf on the other, whom would he choose? The evidence would suggest that Holmes holds his objectivity and his dedication to detached analysis in tension with his special friendship with and commitment to Dr. Watson. Probably the most revealing event and description of his loving friendship with Watson occurs in "The Adventure of the Three Garridebs," when Watson is shot and wounded. Here is the reaction that Watson provides to Holmes's outburst: "You're not hurt, Watson? For God's sake, say that you are not hurt!" Watson's response: "It was worth a wound; it was worth many wounds; to know the depth of loyalty and love which lay behind that cold mask. The clear, hard eyes were dimmed for a moment, and the firm lips were shaking. For the one and only time I caught a glimpse of a great heart as well as of a great brain. All my years of humble but single-minded service culminated in that moment of revelation."[16]

In this case, it does not seem that Holmes is guilty of "one thought too many"; his expression of care is instantaneous and affective. As we take a closer look at the loyalty that Holmes and Watson share, we have some reason to question Keller's thesis that loyalty in friendship tends to compromise our integrity as good believers.

Let's first consider Keller's definition of loyalty: "Loyalty is the attitude and associated pattern of conduct that is constituted by an individual's taking something's side, and doing so with a certain sort of motive: namely, a motive that is partly emotional in nature, involves a response to the thing itself, and makes essential reference to a special relationship that the individual takes to exist between herself and the thing to which she is loyal."[17]

What does "taking someone's side" mean? If it means believing almost unconditionally whatever the friend wants you to believe then, yes, Keller has a point: friendship can threaten or undermine your integrity in forming reliable beliefs. However, if "taking someone's side" means acting for their good and taking pleasure in their good, then there is no such abrogation of duty to clear thinking and reasonability on our part. In fact, one would naturally be led to think even more carefully and rationally about a friend than a stranger.

A modest thought experiment may serve to bring the point home. Imagine that your friend uses cocaine and morphine. He claims to be doing so only when he is not working on various projects and that this habit is under control. Are you bound—in the name of loyalty—to believe your friend? Not at all. You are, rather, bound to try to get the friend help. And this is precisely what Watson does for Holmes. Watson does not approve of Holmes's use of cocaine and morphine, and he eventually gets Holmes off addictive drugs altogether. Note that Watson returned Sherlock's favor of not mincing words. Watson, more concerned about what was genuinely good for Holmes rather than what Holmes wanted to hear, challenged him, stood up to him, chastised him. A failure to do have done so wouldn't have been the loving thing to do. Sometimes a friend says what needs to be said, and only a friend does. That's true loyalty and real love.

An occasionally recurring theme of the Conan Doyle stories, interestingly enough, is the way in which what goes by the name of love isn't love at all. The child's grasping, rapacious love for his father in "The Adventure of the Sussex Vampire" manifests in jealousy and cruel hatred, "distorted love," a "maniacal exaggerated love," which is of course not love at all.[18] C. S. Lewis once said that love, becoming a god, becomes a devil, and Augustine too wrote of the imperative to love ordinately rather than inordinately, lest the love become idolatrous and less than what it ought to be. Love that disguises cruelty or love that justifies wrongdoing isn't love at all. Carruthers's confusion of selfishness and love in "The Adventure of the Solitary Cyclist" is another example where dubbing something by the word *love* is not enough to identify the real thing. In "The Problem of Thor Bridge," Sherlock said of the woman who killed herself and tried framing the governess out of her love for her husband: "I do not think that in our adventures we have ever come across a stranger example of what perverted love can bring about."[19] Loving too much paradoxically results in not loving enough. Loyalty without truth, accountability, and a genuine regard for what's best for the beloved is no loyalty at all. Truth must be spoken, but preferably in love. Admittedly Watson may be more consistently good at this than Sherlock, but the reader, with Watson, can catch a glimpse of Sherlock's big heart, if only briefly.

Passionate Objectivity

Holmes leads us to make a few additional points about so-called objective and impartial inquiry. Holmes is content to think of himself as a kind of cold machine, but in understanding and solving crimes, he must in some fashion put himself in the place of—or empathize with—the murderer, thief, or victim. A mere machine cannot do this. In "The Adventure of the Devil's Foot," Holmes reflects on what drove Dr. Sterndale, an explorer, to kill the murderer of his wife. Holmes reports, "I have never loved, Watson, but if I did and if the woman I loved had met such an end, I might act as our lawless lion-hunter has done."[20]

From Holmes's consistent capacity to put himself into the shoes of others; to the single-minded passion with which he sought justice; to the way he privileged imagination, intuition, and instinct; from his artistic and aesthetic sensibilities to his dramatic and musical proclivities, Sherlock was a man with a dual nature. He was scientist and artist; logic and instinct; and even, more than he cared to admit, thought and feeling. Like all of us, it wasn't always easy for him to reconcile and integrate these disparate predilections, but he wouldn't have been human without feeling the tensions. His isn't a paradigm of how best to resolve such tensions, but his is a unique fictional example of their power. "In his singular character the dual nature alternately asserted itself, and his extreme exactness and astuteness represented, as I have often thought," Watson wrote, "the reaction against the poetic and contemplative mood which occasionally predominated in him."[21]

We conclude that Holmes offers us an intriguing model for objective reflection and inquiry, but that he is not entirely a man without passion—Watson's occasional sarcastic sidebars notwithstanding. In fact, as Holmes might well admit, some passion or acquaintance with passion is essential if one is to be objective and rigorously analytical. After all, passion is a variable with which every detective must contend. Finally, when the person he loved like a brother was in peril, Holmes was quick to react and did not demonstrate the aloofness of one who has "one thought too many." He did not reason that from an objective point of view it was permissible for him to care for Watson. He cared.

Notes

We thank Eric Erfanian for assistance in preparing this chapter, and we thank Kelsie Brust for a conversation about loyalty.

1. In time, Comte's ideas were popularized and touched many fields, notably history, where they were advanced by no less an authority than Lord Acton, who proclaimed with confidence, "If the past has been an obstacle and a burden, knowledge of the past is the safest and the surest emancipation" (John Emerich Edward Dalberg, Lord Acton, *Lectures on Modern History*, ed. John Neville Figgis and Reginald Vere Laurence [London: Macmillan, 1906], 4). To unlock the past, Acton and others—including the German historian Leopold von Ranke—preached the value of rigorous analysis and logic, intellectual virtues they believed had the power to unveil the full mysteries of the past. It followed, then, that the most effective historian was dispassionate, calm, and had a limited stake in the outcome or course of events she or he described.

2. Edgar Allan Poe, *Poetry and Tales*, ed. Patrick Francis Quinn (New York: Library of America, 1984), 371.

3. Sir Arthur Conan Doyle, *A Study in Scarlet*, in *The Complete Sherlock Holmes* (New York: Barnes & Noble, 2009), 11. All Holmes references in this chapter use this edition unless otherwise indicated.

4. Sir Arthur Conan Doyle, *The Adventures of Sherlock Holmes*, ed. Richard Lancelyn Green (London: Oxford World Classics, 1998), 299.

5. *Sign of Four*, 96.

6. Ibid., 80, 82.

7. Ibid., 140.

8. "Reigate Puzzle," 381.

9. Simon Keller, *The Limits of Loyalty* (Cambridge: Cambridge University Press, 2007), 22.

10. Bruce Russell, "Two Forms of Ethical Skepticism," in *Ethical Theory: Classical and Contemporary Readings*, ed. Louis Pojman (New York: Wadsworth, 1998), 595.

11. Surely another possible analysis is that the father's privileged knowledge of future events enables him to see that helping his son escape is morally justified after all to avoid the horrible consequences of going to jail. What is meant by a ruined life is all important. If, for example, the father knows that the son will be killed in the jail on his first night there, he's under no obligation, rational or moral, to refrain from helping his son escape such a fate.

12. Bernard Williams, *Moral Luck* (Cambridge: Cambridge University Press, 1981), 1–19.

13. Charles Fried, *An Anatomy of Values* (Cambridge, Mass.: Harvard University Press, 1970), 227.

14. Williams, *Moral Luck*, 18.

15. Ibid.

16. "Three Garridebs," 1010.
17. Keller, *Limits of Loyalty,* 21.
18. "Sussex Vampire," 1000.
19. "Thor Bridge," 1026.
20. "Devil's Foot," 929.
21. "Red-Headed League," 168.

The Industrious Sherlock Holmes

Gregory Bassham

Hard work was a prime Victorian virtue, and Sherlock Holmes, good Victorian that he was, was an exceptionally hardworking guy. Holmes was a person "who, when he had an unsolved problem upon his mind, would go for days, and even for a week, without rest, turning it over, rearranging his facts, looking at it from every point of view until he had either fathomed it or convinced himself that his data were insufficient."[1] True, Holmes didn't work all the time. When he had no interesting cases to absorb him, he frequently would fall into "fits of the blackest depression,"[2] "and for days on end he would lie upon the sofa in the sitting-room, hardly uttering a word or moving a muscle from morning to night."[3] At such times, Holmes was, by his own admission, "the most incurably lazy devil that ever stood in shoe leather."[4] All in all, though, Holmes was an extraordinarily industrious man.

Can we go further and say that Holmes was a workaholic? I think we can, but in Holmes's case, this wasn't such a bad thing. In fact, in exceptional cases like his, there is a kind of heroism and nobility in being a career-obsessed, intensely hardworking individual.

Was Holmes a Workaholic?

A workaholic is a person addicted to work—someone who works long hours, thinks about work all the time, and has little interest in other things. According to work therapist Bryan Johnson, there are several trouble signs of being a workaholic.[5] These include:

Thinking obsessively about work.
Having few friends and a troubled personal life.

Being obsessively perfectionist in one's work.
Having health concerns due to stress and poor care of one's physical and emotional health.

Holmes meets each of these four trouble signs.

First, as we've seen, when Holmes was working on an interesting mystery, he would go for days "without rest, turning it over . . . , looking at it from every point of view" until he had either solved it or decided he needed additional evidence. In his more intense moments, he wouldn't eat and would sometimes faint "from pure inanition."[6] These are signs of a work-obsessed individual.

Second, Holmes, sounding more than a little like Rousseau (if not Sartre), loathes "every form of society with his whole Bohemian soul," has "an aversion to women,"[7] has no friends other than Watson,[8] and is disinclined to make new friends.[9] All emotions, and particularly love, are "abhorrent to his cold, precise . . . mind."[10] He dismisses all "the softer passions" as "distracting factor[s] which might throw doubt upon all his mental results."[11] At one point Watson, newly smitten with the girl he would soon marry, is so shocked by Holmes's emotional coldness that he calls him "an automaton—a calculating machine."[12] Clearly Holmes cares nothing about a work/life balance.

Third, Holmes is a perfectionist, having "a passion for definite and exact knowledge"[13] and being "the neatest and most methodical of mankind"[14] in his professional work. Though untidy and eccentric in some of his personal habits,[15] Holmes fully agrees that—in detective work at least—"genius is an infinite capacity for taking pains."[16]

Finally, like many workaholics, Holmes often allows his passion for work to affect his health. Though capable of great muscular effort and an excellent amateur boxer, Holmes looks on all "aimless bodily exertion as a waste of energy, and seldom bestirred himself save where there was some professional object to be served."[17] "I am a brain," he once says to Watson. "The rest of me is a mere appendix."[18] "The state of his health," we're told, "was not a matter in which he himself took the faintest interest."[19] His failing health because of exhaustion led to a doctor-prescribed holiday in "The Devil's Foot": "It was, then, in the spring of 1897 that Holmes's iron constitution showed some symptoms of giving way in the face of constant hard work of a most exacting kind."[20] We have seen how Holmes would sometimes faint from hunger when he was absorbed in a knotty mystery. Far more serious is Sherlock's use of drugs such as cocaine and morphine when he had no interesting cases to work on. After a months-long drug binge, Holmes is warned by Watson that such chronic abuse might "leave a permanent weakness"[21] and impair the great powers with which he has been endowed. In light of Sherlock's aversion to romance because of its potential to blunt his cognitive apparatus, one might think that Watson's appeal would have been persuasive. To this Holmes replies, "Give me problems, give me work . . . and . . . I can dispense then with artificial stimulants. But I abhor the dull routine of existence. I crave for mental exaltation."[22] This is the very credo of the hardcore workaholic.

The Rise of the Protestant Work Ethic

When Watson speaks of Holmes as "the best and wisest man whom I have ever known"[23]—borrowing a line from Plato's *Phaedo*—he was clearly expecting his fellow Victorians to agree. The fact is that Holmes's supercharged work ethic was widely admired by Conan Doyle's Victorian readers. To see why, we need to take a brief look at how attitudes to work have evolved.

For most of Western civilization, work was seen more as a curse than as a fulfilling and dignified activity or vocation.[24] In the Old Testament, Adam is condemned to eat bread "in the sweat of [his] face" because of his disobedience to God.[25] Ancient Greeks like Xenophon and Aristotle dissed manual labor and working for money; they believed that such work, whenever possible, should be done by slaves. Early and medieval Christians rejected the pursuit of wealth and stressed the importance of contemplation over work. All of this changed with the Protestant Reformation and the rise of modern capitalism. Influential Protestant thinkers like John Calvin (1509–64) taught that work was a calling (*beruf*) and that worldly success was a sign of God's saving grace. Work was seen as a kind of worldly asceticism. It trains the soul in godly virtues such as diligence, competence, thrift, forethought, and responsibility. It promotes bodily health and mental sharpness. It protects us against the dangerous fruits of idleness, boredom, and pleasure seeking. ("The devil finds work for idle hands to do.") It enables humans to fulfill God's command to "fill the earth and subdue it."[26] It makes possible great achievements that redound to the glory of God. And it fuels economic prosperity and provides means for charitable giving and the support of one's family. This was the origin of what Max Weber famously labeled the Protestant work ethic.[27] Its most notable attitudinal and behavioral features include a high valuation of hard work, frugality, efficient use of time, shunning of leisure and ostentation, self-reliance, and delay of gratification.[28]

After the Reformation, the Protestant work ethic took hold throughout northern Europe, including England and the American colonies (particularly in the Puritan Northeast). In Conan Doyle's time, the religious motivations for an ethic of hard work had largely waned, and researchers today have found no correlation between religious affiliation and work-oriented values.[29] Nevertheless, paeans to hard work were common in Victorian novels and sermons, and many of Conan Doyle's contemporaries would have agreed with Thomas Carlyle, "the prophet of the religion of work,"[30] when he wrote, "There is a perpetual nobleness, and even sacredness, in work. . . . Know what thou can't work at; and work at it like a Hercules! . . . Blessed is he who has found his work; let him ask no other blessedness."[31]

The Decline of the Protestant Work Ethic

It is plain that the old Protestant work ethic is now declining in America and other industrialized nations. Business leaders increasingly complain about how hard it is to find employees with strong work values. So-called millennials—young people aged eighteen to twenty-nine—are the only generation of Americans in the twentieth century not to pick "work ethic" as an identifying characteristic of their cohort.[32] Since the 1980s, tens of millions of Americans have been inspired by the voluntary simplicity movement to work less and simplify their lifestyles. In England, it is estimated that 20 percent of employment disability benefits are fraudulently claimed by people who are able but unwilling to work.[33] In October 2010, a government proposal to raise the retirement age from sixty to sixty-two led to weeks of rioting in France. Nor is a declining work ethic limited to paid employment. Studies show that the amount of time American college students spend studying has fallen by over 40 percent since 1961[34] and that the average college student spends only 7 percent of his or her day studying (compared to 51 percent socializing).[35]

There are obvious downsides to an eroding work ethic. Who wants to live in a world with greater numbers of inattentive waitresses, lazy car mechanics, slacker students, welfare frauds, and slothful public servants? On the whole, though, it is good that people are rethinking older attitudes toward work and leisure and seeking a healthier work/life balance. As philosophers have pointed out, it's generally bad for the self, for society, and for the environment when individuals become obsessed with work and overvalue material success.

Henry David Thoreau's *Walden* (1854) offers a classic analysis of the toll a "living to work" attitude takes on the self. As Thoreau traveled about his native New England, most of its inhabitants appeared to be "doing penance in a thousand remarkable ways" and living lives of "quiet desperation":

> I see young men, my townsmen, whose misfortune it is to have inherited farms, houses, barns, cattle, and farming tools; for these are more easily acquired than got rid of. . . . Who made them serfs of the soil? . . . How many a poor immortal soul have I met well-nigh crushed and smothered under its load, creeping down the road of life, pushing before it a barn seventy-five feet by forty, its Augean stables never cleansed, and one hundred acres of land, tillage, mowing, pasture, and wood lot! . . . By a seeming fate, commonly called necessity, they are employed, as it says in an old book, laying up treasures which moth and rust will corrupt and thieves break through and steal. It is a fool's life, as they will find when they get to the end of it, if not before.[36]

The problem with such a work-obsessed lifestyle, Thoreau believed, is that it leaves us "with no time to be anything but a machine." We become "so occupied with the factitious cares and superfluously coarse labors of life that its finer fruits cannot be plucked."[37] Among these finer fruits, Thoreau thought, are the pleasures of friendship, the pursuit of knowledge, personal growth, and communion with nature—in short, to be "rich, if not in money, in sunny hours and summer days."[38]

Other philosophers have noted the high social costs that result from an overvaluation of work. In *Leisure, the Basis of Culture* (1952), Josef Pieper notes that the wise and creative use of leisure lies at the very basis of Western ideals of cultural excellence, educational attainment, and individual development. More recently, critics in the voluntary simplicity movement have argued that in modern consumer-driven capitalist economies an overvaluing of work has contributed to a condition of "affluenza," an oppressive social condition of stress, overwork, envy, waste, and dangerous levels of indebtedness that results from efforts to keep up with the Joneses.[39]

Finally, many philosophers have noted the serious environmental harms that result when people around the world are encouraged to work hard precisely in order to achieve Western standards of consumption and affluence.[40]

In short, bad things happen—to the self, to society, and to the environment—when huge numbers of people are convinced that they must work extremely hard to achieve prosperous, high-consumption lifestyles. Realizing this, more and more people around the globe are downsizing their career and lifestyle goals, choosing to work less and simplify their lives in exchange for greater freedom, less stress, more quality time with family and friends, and more leisure time to do the things they truly enjoy. This is all well and good. But how does all this apply to Holmes? Holmes worked incredibly hard—but not for the money or for a lavish lifestyle. He greatly enjoyed his work, he wasn't particularly stressed by it, he had no family to neglect, and he worked for a noble cause (righting wrongs and putting dangerous criminals behind bars). This raises the question: Is being a work-obsessed person always such a bad thing?

Why It's Sometimes Okay to Be a Workaholic

First, a personal disclaimer: By most definitions, I am a workaholic. I typically work fourteen- or sixteen-hour days doing the things college professors do: teaching, preparing for class, grading papers, serving on committees, doing research, and writing books and articles. I've written six books, and I generally publish five or six articles or book chapters a year. I work year round, including summer and Christmas vacations. (A good bit of this chapter, in fact, was written on Christmas Day.) I rarely watch TV or go to movies, I have no real hobbies, and I long ago gave up watching sports (which I enjoy) as a distraction from work. Aside from household chores, yard work, and chauffeuring my fifteen-year-old son around town, my one real break from work is running (I am a competitive long-distance runner). I work pretty much all the time, think about work all the time, and always look forward to getting back to work after some down time. Hearing this, most people probably would consider me a workaholic—though I hasten to add that I have good personal relationships, am in excellent health, and otherwise lack most of the warning signs of workaholism noted earlier.

The thing is, I'm happy and frankly rather proud to be a workaholic. I enjoy my work, place great importance on being a good teacher and mentor to my students, and take pleasure in contributing, through my scholarly work, to my discipline and the academic reputation of my college. I'm not terribly interested in making a lot of money or living an affluent lifestyle. Though I work hard, I don't neglect my family, my friends, or my obligations to my colleagues or my community. I am, in short, what I would consider a benign workaholic. And Holmes in certain respects was too.

What distinguishes a benign workaholic from a pathological one? There are two major differences.

WARNING SIGNS

We've seen that experts have identified a number of warning signs of workaholism. Often workaholics have poor personal relationships, suffer from stress or other work-related health problems, and are overly controlling or perfectionistic in their work habits. Pathological workaholics tend to suffer from these problems, but benign workaholics do not. Benign workaholics know when to say when. As Holmes said, the "supreme gift of the artist" is "the knowledge of when to stop."[41]

MOTIVATIONS

Some things are worth working hard for and some are not. If you work yourself to a frazzle because you want a gaudier Rolex than your neighbor, that's pathological. On the other hand, if you work assiduously to become a world-class violinist or cyclist, that's admirable. Benign workaholics are motivated by worthy ends, whereas pathological workaholics often are not.

How does Holmes measure up by these standards? We've seen that Holmes displays all the major trouble signs of workaholism. He works frenetically, thinks about work obsessively, lacks all but a few strong personal relationships, is very much a perfectionist in his craft, and suffers health effects due to overwork. In these respects, he is clearly a pathological workaholic. As I argue in my other chapter in this book, Holmes is too monomaniacal and sacrifices too much for the sake of his career.

On the other hand, Holmes's motivation for working hard was altogether good. Much like Batman, Holmes consecrated his life to a single, wholly admirable purpose: fighting crime and achieving justice. All his mind, heart, and training were devoted to this end. In this respect, Holmes was like Ignatius Loyola, Mother Teresa, and other great women and men of history who, at great personal sacrifice, consecrated their lives to achieve some single, great good. He was more motivated to fulfill his sense of destiny than merely to advance in a job. There is, I suggest, a kind of heroism and grandeur in such a life, however pathological it may be in some respects. To paraphrase Billy Joel: Holmes may be a little crazy, but he just may be the sort of lunatic we're looking for.

Notes

1. Conan Doyle, "Man with the Twisted Lip," 240. Elsewhere, Watson tells us that "nothing could exceed [Holmes's] energy when the working fit was upon him." *Study in Scarlet,* 20. All references to the Sherlock Holmes stories are to Arthur Conan Doyle, *The Complete Sherlock Holmes* (Garden City, N.Y.: Doubleday, 1930).
2. *Sign of Four,* 97.
3. *Study in Scarlet,* 20.
4. Ibid., 27.
5. Quoted in Tory Johnson, "You Might Be a Workaholic If . . . ," *Good Morning America,* June 14, 2007, http://abcnews.go.com/CleanPrint/cleanprintproxy.aspx?1290268761061.
6. "Norwood Builder," 505.
7. "Greek Interpreter," 435.
8. "Five Orange Pips," 218.
9. "Greek Interpreter," 435.
10. "Scandal in Bohemia," 161.
11. Ibid.
12. *Sign of Four,* 96.
13. *Study in Scarlet,* 17.
14. "Musgrave Ritual," 386.
15. Ibid.
16. *Study in Scarlet,* 31.
17. "Yellow Face," 351.
18. "Mazarin Stone," 1014.
19. "Devil's Foot," 955.
20. Ibid., 914.
21. *Sign of Four,* 89.
22. Ibid., 89–90.
23. "Final Problem," 480.
24. For a concise overview of Western attitudes toward work, see Joanne B. Ciulla, "From Curse to Calling: A Short History of the Meaning of Work," in *Honest Work: A Business Ethics Reader,* ed. Joanne B. Ciulla, Clancy Martin, and Robert C. Solomon (New York: Oxford University Press, 2007), 5–10.
25. Genesis 3:19.
26. Genesis 1:28.
27. Max Weber, *The Protestant Ethic and the Spirit of Capitalism,* trans. Talcott Parsons (New York: Charles Scriber's Sons, 1958).

28. Ibid., 48–52.

29. Michael J. Miller, David J. Woeehr, and Natasha Hudspeth, "The Meaning and Measurement of Work Ethic: Construction and Initial Validation of a Multidimensional Inventory," *Journal of Vocational Behavior* 59 (2001): 3.

30. Josef Pieper, *Leisure, the Basis of Culture* (1952; New York: Random House, 1963), 30.

31. Thomas Carlyle, *Past and Present* (1843; New York: Charles Scribner's Sons, 1918), 226, 228.

32. "The Millennials: Confident, Connected, Open to Change," Pew Research Center, February 24, 2010, http://pewresearch.org/pubs/1501/millennials-new-survey-generational-personality-upbeat-open-new-ideas-technology-bound.

33. Steve Doughty, "Benefits 'Wrecked the British Work Ethic,' New Study Finds," *Daily Mail,* October 8, 2009, http://www.dailymail.co.uk/news/article-1218873/Benefits-wrecked-British-work-ethic-new-study-claims.html.

34. Stephanie Findlay, "The Decline of Studying," Macleans.ca, September 5, 2010, http://www2.macleans.ca/2010/09/05/the-decline-of-studying/.

35. "Report: First Two Years of College Show Small Gains," *USA Today,* January 21, 2011, http://www.usatoday.com/news/education/2011-01-18-littlelearning18_ST_N.htm?loc=interstitialskip.

36. Henry David Thoreau, *Walden* (1854; Roslyn, N.Y.: Walter J. Black, 1942), 28–30.

37. Ibid., 30.

38. Ibid., 218.

39. See, for example, Clive Hamilton and Richard Denniss, *Affluenza: When Too Much Is Never Enough* (London: Allen & Unwin, 2006).

40. See, for example, Louis P. Pojman, *Global Environmental Ethics* (Mountain View, Calif.: Mayfield, 2000), 1–17.

41. "Norwood Builder," 510.

The Dog That Did Not Bark

Learning How to Read "The Book of Life"

Carrie-Ann Biondi

> It is fair to say that there exists in our era a tragic discrepancy between the staggering richness of the visible world and the extreme poverty of our capacity to perceive it.
>
> —Robert Pogue Harrison

Donning the Deerstalker Hat

A good detective asks himself the question, "Am I missing something?" One can miss something in at least three ways. The first and most obvious way is to overlook something that is in front of you, such as a book you are searching for when you misremember its being red rather than blue. A second and fairly common way is not to recognize the significance of what you do notice, discounting its relevance for the task at hand. For example, a police cadet might be baffled that all of the doors and windows of a robbed bank are locked, not realizing that this indicates an inside job. The third and least obvious way is to fail to note the significant absence of something. This last omission can take any number of forms: not realizing that something that once was there is now gone, not recognizing that what doesn't happen can provide important clues to what has, not seeing another option that would reveal the false alternatives in someone's argument. The failure to notice something's absence is easy to do; it takes a distinct set of skills, knowledge, and virtues to develop the ability to glean information from absence or silence.[1]

The disparity to which Harrison refers in the epigraph above—between the richness of the world and the poverty of perception—has been a perennial affliction. Sherlock Holmes notes the rarity of keen perceptual and mental faculties: "There are fifty who can reason synthetically for one who can reason analytically. . . . There are few people . . . who, if you told them a result, would be able to evolve from their own inner consciousness what the steps were that led up to that result."[2] Holmes is a fictional master of perceiving the "sounds of silence." A famous example of this comes from the Conan Doyle story "The Adventure of Silver Blaze," in which Holmes infers from the fact of a dog's *not* barking crucial details that put him on track to solve the case.

Called in to solve the apparent murder of a horse trainer, John Straker, and the disappearance of the prizewinning horse, Silver Blaze, Holmes collects evidence from the King's Pyland stable and the surrounding Dartmoor countryside. The terrain has already been examined by the police, who arrested the bookmaker Fitzroy Simpson, who had been lurking about the stable the night of the tragedy. Holmes, though, is able to perceive more than surface appearances. Is Simpson really the culprit? Many people had an incentive to keep Silver Blaze out of the upcoming race, but adding murder to theft seems unnecessary. Then there is the matter of the stable boy's being drugged with opium in his curried mutton dinner, allowing someone to enter the unguarded stable as the other stable boys slept soundly in the loft above. Holmes could see how the circumstantial evidence against Simpson could easily mislead.

After Sherlock offers an important lead to the police, Inspector Gregory (who fails to appreciate that lead) asks Holmes whether anything else is important:

> "Is there any point to which you would wish to draw my attention?"
> "To the curious incident of the dog in the night-time."
> "The dog did nothing in the night-time."
> "That was the curious incident," remarked Sherlock Holmes.[3]

In this story, Holmes, rather than Gregory, is the person who solves the mystery of the missing racehorse because, as Holmes notes, he possesses and understands "the value of imagination" that Gregory lacks.[4] Holmes soon explains his reasoning from silence: "I had grasped the significance of the silence of the dog, for one true inference invariably suggests others. The Simpson incident had shown me that a dog was kept in the stables, and yet, though someone had been in and had fetched out a horse, he had not barked enough to arouse the two lads in the loft. Obviously the midnight visitor was someone whom the dog knew well."[5] Gregory needed to be a much better student of Holmes's methods. How, then, can we avoid Gregory's mistake? And why should those who are not professional sleuths care?

Detectives are not the only ones who have lessons to learn from Holmes. It is important to unpack what is involved in his imaginative ability and to understand its value. Becoming a "philosophical detective" is essential in the pursuit of truth.[6] Logical analysis can help detect falsehoods, but moving toward truth takes creativity of a sort that requires us to drop our mental blinders. Theoretical breakthroughs often occur when someone notices an alternative that others have missed. More than this, though, imagination can benefit every person who cultivates the art of philosophical detection. This ability lies at the heart of the entrepreneurial spirit that employers look for in fields such as medicine, business, and science; and through attentiveness to detail and improved understanding, it secures greater efficacy in navigating personal relationships and life generally.

Contrary to popular opinion, imagination or genius is not some inexplicable flash of inspiration that a few lucky souls happen to possess. Rather, it is a creative ability that can be cultivated through due diligence; it is indeed 99 percent perspiration, as Thomas Edison famously remarked. The rapidity with which Holmes states his startling conclusions makes it seem as though he comes to them by magic, even to his longtime partner in crime detection, Dr. John Watson. Holmes explains, "From long habit the train of thoughts ran so swiftly through my mind that I arrived at the conclusion without being conscious of intermediate steps. There were such steps, however."[7] Holmes takes his associates and the reader through these intermediate steps on dozens of occasions, though to little avail for his associates, who never quite seem to replicate his methods. The imagination needed to become a philosophical detective, though, is within our reach and arises from the combination of "the three qualities necessary for the ideal detective," which Holmes identifies as observation, deduction, and background knowledge.[8] Constructing and evaluating arguments from silence require an understanding of these three qualities and their correlated virtues.

The Peerless Private Eye

Holmes's peculiar assortment of characteristics leaves him standing alone in his profession; he is the world's "only unofficial consulting detective."[9]

Watson insightfully remarks on Holmes's unusual method of inspecting a crime scene: "I had no doubt that he could see a great deal which was hidden from me."[10] A couple of remarkable instances when Holmes literally sees something that is right in front of everyone while others fail to notice it at all include Straker's wax vesta (which Inspector Gregory fails to notice) and a bullet hole in a window sash of the Cubitt's home (which Inspector Martin fails to notice).[11] He sees these things and appreciates their importance while others do not in part because his "long and patient study" of "the book of life" combined with "much practice has made [observation] second nature," and in part because he was looking for them.[12] Watson and others are repeatedly amazed by Sherlock's abilities and wonder how he does it.

Before turning to how Holmes develops this remarkable perceptual ability, one must understand why he does so, for all he does is directed toward an ultimate end. Describing Holmes, Watson notes that "his mind was so absolutely concentrated upon the matter before him that a question or remark fell unheeded upon his ears. . . . Every one of his actions was directed toward a definite end."[13] It is in virtue of this manner that Watson refers to Holmes as "the most perfect reasoning and observing machine that the world has seen."[14] Holmes, who "never remember[s] feeling tired by work," has a purposive energy, drive, and precision that Watson equates with an inhuman coldness and lack of passion.[15] Watson is mistaken, however, to call Holmes a dispassionate machine on account of these qualities; in fact, Holmes is a most passionate character, with a devotion to truth and justice rivaled by few. Stamford, an old acquaintance of Watson's who introduces him to Holmes, says that Holmes is "an *enthusiast* in some branches of science" and has "a *passion* for definite and exact knowledge." Watson himself recognizes this: "His *zeal* for certain studies was remarkable. . . . Surely no man would work so hard or attain such precise information unless he had some definite end in view."[16] Machines are hardly enthusiastic, passionate, or zealous; only humans are when they identify wholeheartedly with a purpose.

There are two aspects of Holmes's "definite end": first, detecting injustice for the public good, and second, his sense of self. In relation to the former, Holmes states that it is "our duty . . . to unravel ['the scarlet thread of murder'], and isolate it, and expose every inch of it"; "it's every man's business to see justice done." When preparing for the possibility of death at the hands of Professor Moriarty, Sherlock reflects that his life had not been "lived wholly in vain" because he had improved the lives of his fellow countrymen without ever knowingly using his "powers upon the wrong side."[17] In relation to the latter, his sense of self, Holmes swells with pride when his colleagues recognize his extraordinary talents in solving a difficult case, and he explains that he created his profession because he "crave[s] mental exaltation" and "the work itself, the pleasure of finding a field for [his] peculiar powers, is [his] highest reward."[18] These complementary goals are welded together in what can only be described as a love of the good and a desire to develop his capacities to their fullest potential in service to this noble end.

Holmes is not only uniquely purposive but also unofficial in ways that exemplify a certain virtue of independence. "The advantage of being unofficial," says Holmes, is that "I follow my own methods and tell as much or as little as I choose."[19] Being his own boss permits him to accept or reject any given request for assistance, to go as quickly or slowly as he needs, and to give free rein to whatever procedure he deems necessary in his own judgment to solve a case.

This independence is the backbone of his courage. He is not afraid to appear foolish because he is convinced of the effectiveness of his methods. If it takes lying on the floor to study footprints or lying on the ground to study trampled mud in search of a hypothesized wax vesta, then that is what Holmes does in order to solve a case.[20] Holmes's courage also takes the form of often placing himself in extreme physical discomfort and even life-threatening danger so as to trap desperate criminals, and he is bold at hypothesis formation.

Patience is another virtue that contributes to Holmes's perceptual acuity. He takes his time and does not settle for the obvious, for he knows that there are no shortcuts to the truth. He warns Lestrade that "there is nothing more deceptive than an obvious fact," and remarks that "it strikes me . . . as being just a trifle too obvious" for someone who has been alleged of murder to have committed the crime the day after being named in the missing person's will.[21] Other detectives often take the easy way out, falling for blinds that hamper their ability to see (deliberately planted red herrings intended to put investigators on the wrong trail). Investigators can fall for blinds for a wide variety of reasons: ignorance, impatience, conventionality, bias, peer pressure, jealous rivalry, lack of imagination. Conan Doyle offers readers many examples of Scotland Yard's best men faltering in their observations in some way or another on account of each of these causes.

Daydreams

We never get a firsthand narrative of Holmes's internal state when he is daydreaming, but we do get a report from Watson that it is a state of utterly inward-focused attention to matters of the highest order: "When I looked at him, he had finished reading the note, and his eyes had assumed the vacant, lackluster expression which showed mental abstraction."[22] Holmes either lapses into such a state out of a second nature created through deliberate habit, as when he remains in a carriage when all of the others disembark, or he enters such a state when he has hit a snag in his investigation, as when he prepares for an all-night meditation.[23] In either case, this daydreaming state results from focused attention so as to minimize distraction and maximize thought.

What is Holmes doing while daydreaming? He is practicing part of his famous art of deduction. Contrary to the meaning of this term familiar to beginning logic students, Holmes in fact employs something much more complex than a mechanical application of the argument forms of first-order logic. What he does is sift through the supposed facts of a case, distinguish relevant from irrelevant information, and generate a set of alternative explanations that might account for the case's mysterious elements. This is a process known as abduction, made famous by that name by Charles Sanders Peirce.[24] In abduction, one perceives a phenomenon in the world and then, in light of certain principles, conjectures a possible cause (or set of possible causes) of that effect. Unlike Peirce, Holmes most emphatically states that this method is not guesswork: "I never guess. It is a shocking habit—destructive to the logical faculty."[25] Rather, abduction is a process that involves observation, knowledge, good judgment, and imagination. One is first faced with a variety of facts obtained through testimony and careful observation, and one is then confronted with the need to render a judgment. When Holmes faces an especially bizarre case at which Watson expresses nothing but bewilderment, Holmes says that he has "devised seven separate explanations, each of which would cover the facts as far as we know them. But which of these is correct can only be determined by . . . fresh information."[26] The fact that the possible explanations pertain to the essential facts of a case and can be tested is part of what makes the procedure not mere guesswork. The other part involves drawing on relevant background knowledge.

We once again need to turn to a discussion of virtue to understand this particular skill. The virtue of impartiality is central for formulating abductive explanations. Holmes explains how partiality or bias can blind one from seeing certain competing hypotheses. A striking case where, for example, class bias stymies abductive reasoning arises when Inspector Forrester cannot solve burglaries and a murder. According to Holmes, "the inspector had overlooked [a simple point] because he had started with the supposition that these county magnates had nothing to do with the matter."[27] When it comes to crime, no one is beyond suspicion—not the wealthy, the respected, the elderly, women, children, clergy, or relatives.

How Holmes Found Silver Blaze

"The Adventure of Silver Blaze" features a superb example of Sherlock's methods. There are only three reasonable hypotheses that could account for the missing racehorse: the Gypsies on the moor stole him, he returned to his own stable at King's Pyland, or he trotted over to the stables at Mapleton. The horse is certainly not at King's Pyland. The Gypsies, who don't want to be harassed by the police, would run too high a risk in taking a famous horse that they would be unable to sell without detection. So Holmes is convinced that Silver Blaze must be at Mapleton where a rival horse is kept, even though previous searches failed to find him there. It is imagination that allows Holmes first to expand the set of possibilities beyond the false alternatives accepted by Inspector Gregory and then to narrow down the possibilities to this one improbable (but ultimately true) one.

Convinced that Silver Blaze is to be found at Mapleton, Holmes and Watson set off for a walk on the moor. They take one of Silver Blaze's horseshoes with them, realizing that Gregory has only "examined the ground very carefully for a hundred yards in each direction."[28] They do not go very far beyond that distance when they find horseshoe tracks leading in the direction of the Mapleton stables that match Silver Blaze's horseshoe. As the two men make their way to Mapleton, a set of distinctive, square-toed boot tracks soon accompanies those of the horse. After a discreet conversation with Silas Brown, the manager of Mapleton, who also happens to be wearing unusual square-toed boots, Holmes confirms that Brown has hidden Silver Blaze in plain sight in Mapleton stables with the intention of having the horse he manages win the upcoming race while Silver Blaze is missing.[29]

Possibility without Thought Experiments

Noticing omissions in disjunctive syllogisms and brainstorming alternative hypotheses, however, requires a "wide range of exact knowledge," which Holmes regards as "essential to the higher developments of [the] art [of detection]."[30] The abductive portion of Holmes's deduction thus depends on induction. This is where Holmes must rise from the consulting detective's armchair and consult "the book of life." It is this active engagement with the world that separates Holmes from his brother, Mycroft.[31]

The book of life that Holmes writes contains chapters not only on natural phenomena, but also on human history, psychology, and anthropology. He also has a vast storehouse of the history of crime, which helps him to see what many others cannot. Take the case where a wife has gone missing, which Holmes solves easily, whereas Inspector Lestrade and Watson are stumped. This sort of ignorance is excusable in Watson, but Lestrade is culpable for not having studied either the history of his profession or the areas of knowledge pertinent for his line of work.

Holmes's "trained eye" can recognize—not just see—uncommon things that others miss; for example, he understands the significance of a "singular knife" and a "singular epidemic [of lameness] among the sheep."[32] This is what allows him to solve the other half of the mystery in "Silver Blaze"—namely, who killed Straker. The answer is none other than Silver Blaze, acting in self-defense. The reasoning that leads up to this startling conclusion requires Holmes to consult several chapters in his book. The first significant clue was the curried mutton dinner containing the opium that drugged the stable boy. With his knowledge of poisons and drugs, Holmes knew that powdered opium has a discernible taste that would have only been masked by something as strongly seasoned as curry. But who else would have known that the curry was to be served for dinner other than Mr. and Mrs. Straker? This surmise highlighted the second main clue: the significance of the dog's silence, which would indicate a thief the dog knew well. But why Straker? The next set of clues could only reside in the contents of Straker's pockets, which contained a strange knife and a milliner's account for a woman's dress made out to one William Derbyshire. These two items led Holmes to question Mrs. Straker about a dress, a stable boy about the condition of the sheep, and a remote milliner about Derbyshire's appearance. The clues added up to Straker's motivation for wanting to render Silver Blaze lame: Straker was leading a double life with another woman who had expensive tastes in dresses, and he planned to bet against his own horse so that he could win enough money to get out of the debt into which this double life had led.[33]

Emersonian Advice on Evaluating Arguments from Silence

To apply and evaluate Sherlock's methods, it is crucial to appreciate not only the power of arguing from silence but also the limitations of the method and its practitioners. Here it behooves us to recall two of Ralph Waldo Emerson's aphorisms: "Study nature" and "Know thyself."[34]

"STUDY NATURE"

Holmes urges a rather Emersonian belief on Watson when he says, "Our ideas must be as broad as Nature if they are to interpret Nature."[35] Studying nature is a double-edged sword, though, albeit one that cuts much more one way than another in favor of scientific generalizations. We should bear in mind Aristotle's claim that substances have an internal principle that "holds always, *or for the most part.*"[36] There are patterns in nature that are helpful guides in numerous endeavors, including criminal investigation, but there are also occurrences that simply don't fit into anything we so far know. Singularities or irregularities both captivate and vex Holmes, which belie his claim that "there is nothing new under the sun."[37] There may, in one sense, be nothing new under the sun, but how much of that we know is another matter.

We also need to keep in mind that for all the similarities there are in human motivation, individuals have free will. Holmes's abductive method relies not only on scientific generalizations about, say, what a Trichinopoly cigar looks like when it burns into a pile of ash, but also on the softer social-scientific law of large numbers: "While the individual man is an insoluble puzzle, in the aggregate he becomes a mathematical certainty. You can, for example, never foretell what any one man will do, but you can say with precision what an average number will be up to."[38] Given the generalized range of human motivations for crime, such as power, money, fame, love, and jealousy, these possible causes of crime help Holmes abduct various possible explanations and to rule out others for particular crimes. The existence of free will, though, leaves open the possibility for cases that don't fit statistical generalizations, so we should remember not to equate an individual with an average individual when constructing and evaluating alternative hypotheses. When stuck, we should listen to what's missing and direct our attention toward new lines of thought.

"KNOW THYSELF"

Knowing oneself includes knowing one's own character, disposition, state of knowledge, and blind spots, which can be the most difficult to access, and no one—not even Holmes—is infallible when it comes to knowing oneself. He is much better than most people at self-knowledge, but he is not perfect. It is instructive to examine how Holmes slips up in at least two cases.

The first case involves Irene Adler (later Irene Adler Norton), referred to by Holmes as "*the* woman," who is a woman of uncommon intellect. According to Watson, Holmes "used to make merry over the cleverness of women" (he believed they were not clever at all), but he stopped doing so after being outsmarted by this particular one. Adler succeeds in slipping through the net that Holmes was drawing around her by dressing as a man and walking right past him—a feat she explains in a letter she leaves for him to find.[39] Holmes failed to consider this possibility and so was not on the lookout for it. His prejudice blinded him from seeing the alternative hypothesis.

The second case involves Effie Munro, formerly Mrs. Hebron, who lives with her second husband in Norbury. In this strange case, Mr. Munro is frantic because his wife has become secretive and distant, upsetting their previous marital bliss. A new, mysterious neighbor seems to lie at the heart of this problem. Holmes conjectures that the neighbor's disturbing presence signals that Effie's first husband from America is still alive and she is desperately trying to hide that shameful fact. When Effie's secret is about to be exposed, though, she reveals that her former husband died, but that they had a little girl who survived the illness that killed her father. Effie tried hiding her daughter's existence from her new husband because she feared she would lose him on account of the fact that her daughter looks like her father: "of African descent." Far from being a shameful secret, this incident reveals an unusually brave woman who "cut [her]self off from [her] race" in order to marry the man she loved. Shocked at his own inability to consider this possibility, Holmes says to Watson, "If it should ever strike you that I am getting a little overconfident in my powers, or giving less pains to a case than it deserves, kindly whisper 'Norbury' in my ear."[40]

We see very few cases where Holmes is outwitted or simply wrong, but we can glean from an occasional case or remark what the causes of perplexity are: daring assertions of free will and uncommon courage, unusual natural talent, or madness.[41] There is much we know and much that we have yet to know, and we need to keep in mind both of these facts if we are to develop our own reasoning skills. Being aware of and compensating for our ignorance and flaws is an essential step in this direction.

On Your Way Out, Mind the Gap

We've made a long foray into the qualities and virtues of an ideal sleuth. As we can now see as a result of this excursion, good philosophical detective work takes not just logical skills but also virtues of character and a rich understanding of the world. Whether it is to avoid falling yet again for a politician's gambit, or to pause and consider more charitable interpretations of the motives of others, we are better off by becoming a little more like Holmes. Adapting his words, if we are to evaluate arguments from silence, our ideas need to be as broad as the world in which we live. We could all use a descent from our armchairs and join Holmes in dwelling attentively in the realm of physical particulars that form the basis of abstract ideas. If we study and follow his methods, we too may be able to make out the whispering strains of the sounds of silence. Much truth is to be found in those gaps.

Notes

The epigraph is from Robert Pogue Harrison, *Gardens: An Essay on the Human Condition* (Chicago: University of Chicago Press, 2008), 114.

1. "Argument from silence" is sometimes used synonymously with, but ought not be confused with, the fallacious form of reasoning known as "argument from ignorance." An argument from ignorance, explains T. Edward Damer, "consists in arguing for the truth (or falsity) of a claim, because there is no evidence or proof to the contrary or because of the inability or refusal of an opponent to present convincing evidence to the contrary." *Attacking Faulty Reasoning: A Practical Guide to Fallacy-Free Arguments,* 5th ed. (Belmont, Calif.: Thomson Wadsworth, 2005), 146. Although an argument from ignorance is a fallacy on account of its creator fabricating a conclusion that is based on no evidence one way or the other, an argument from silence can legitimately be constructed from a constellation of background information bearing on the matter at hand. The latter point will be explained more fully below. Characters observing Holmes often accuse him of the wild conjecture involved in arguments from ignorance (or even of committing the fallacy of affirming the consequent), but only because they fail to appreciate or see the relevant background information that supports his conclusions.

2. *Study in Scarlet,* 115–16. All citations are to Arthur Conan Doyle, *Sherlock Holmes: The Complete Novels and Stories* (New York: Bantam Classics, 1986).

3. "Silver Blaze," 540.

4. Ibid., 544.

5. Ibid.

6. Thanks to Irfan Khawaja for drawing my attention to the fact that this phrase is also used (in a somewhat different way) by Ayn Rand in "Philosophical Detection," in *Philosophy: Who Needs It* (New York: New American Library, 1982), 12–22.

7. *Study in Scarlet,* 18.

8. *Sign of Four,* 126.

9. Ibid., 124.

10. *Study in Scarlet,* 24.
11. "Silver Blaze," 534, and "Dancing Men," 820.
12. *Study in Scarlet,* 16, 116.
13. "Boscombe Valley Mystery," 321.
14. "Scandal in Bohemia," 239.
15. *Sign of Four,* 185.
16. *Study in Scarlet,* 4, 6, and 12 (emphases mine).
17. Ibid., 37; "Crooked Man," 658; "Final Problem," 750.
18. *Sign of Four,* 124.
19. "Silver Blaze," 538.
20. See *Study in Scarlet,* 29, and "Silver Blaze," 533–34.
21. "Boscombe Valley Mystery," 310, and "Norwood Builder," 790.
22. *Study in Scarlet,* 20. We get a description from Watson of an even more extreme version of this when he meets Holmes's brother, Mycroft: "His eyes . . . seemed to always retain that far-away, introspective look which I had only observed in Sherlock's when he was exerting his full powers." "Greek Interpreter," 685.
23. "Silver Blaze," 531, and "Man with the Twisted Lip," 368.
24. Peirce began developing this method of analysis as distinct from deduction and induction in the 1870s, and he continued to refine and amend it after the turn of the twentieth century. See especially his 1877–78 series of lectures "The Illustrations of the Logic of Science," in *Writings of Charles S. Peirce: A Chronological Edition,* vol. 3, ed. Peirce Edition Project (Bloomington: Indiana University Press, 1986), and "A Theory of Probable Inference" (1883) in his *Studies in Logic,* in *Writings of Charles S. Peirce: A Chronological Edition,* vol. 4, ed. Peirce Edition Project (Bloomington: Indiana University Press, 1989). The literature on abduction—both Peircian and Holmesian—is vast. Significant works from that literature include Jaakko Hintikka, "The Role of Logic in Argumentation," in *Inquiry as Inquiry: A Logic of Scientific Discovery* (Dordrecht: Kluwer Academic Publishers, 1999), 25–46; Thomas Sebeok and Jean Umiker-Sebeok, "'You Know My Method': A Juxtaposition of Charles S. Peirce and Sherlock Holmes," in *The Play of Musement,* ed. Thomas Sebeok (Bloomington: Indiana University Press, 1982), 17–52; Jerold J. Abrams, "From Sherlock Holmes to the Hard-Boiled Detective in Film Noir," in *The Philosophy of Film Noir,* ed. Mark T. Conard (Lexington: University Press of Kentucky, 2006), 69–88; and Ilkka Niiniluoto, "Defending Abduction," *Philosophy of Science,* Proceedings, 66 (1999): S436–51.
25. *Sign of Four,* 129.
26. "Copper Beeches," 503.
27. "Reigate Puzzle," 638.
28. "Silver Blaze," 534.
29. Ibid., 535–37, 542.
30. *Sign of Four,* 125.
31. *Study in Scarlet,* 12–18. Watson is surprised that Mycroft, whose reasoning

skills surpass those of Holmes, is not known in the detective world. Holmes explains that Mycroft would be the best detective "if the art of the detective began and ended in reasoning from an armchair," but since it doesn't and Mycroft is lazy and "incapable of working out the practical points which must be gone into," he works as a government auditor. "Greek Interpreter," 684. For an excellent discussion of why philosophers should rouse themselves from Mycroft's armchair and avoid outlandish thought experiments, see Kathleen Wilkes, *Real People: Personal Identity without Thought Experiments* (Oxford: Clarendon Press, 1988), esp. chap. 1.

32. *Study in Scarlet,* 116, and "Silver Blaze," 532, 540.

33. "Silver Blaze," 543–46.

34. Ralph Waldo Emerson, "The American Scholar," in *Anthology of American Literature: I: Colonial through Romantic,* 3rd ed., ed. George McMichael (London: Collier Macmillan, 1985), 1040. It should not be surprising that Emerson is relevant to arguments from silence. Conan Doyle was influenced not only by the "dark Romantic" Edgar Allan Poe's detective Dupin (who is mentioned by name in *Study in Scarlet,* 18), but was also familiar with other figures of the mid-nineteenth-century American Renaissance, even mentioning Emerson's close friend Henry David Thoreau in "Noble Bachelor," 456.

35. *Study in Scarlet,* 39.

36. Aristotle, *Physics,* II.5.196b10–11 (emphasis mine). Author's translation.

37. *Study in Scarlet,* 26.

38. *Sign of Four,* 202.

39. "Scandal in Bohemia," 261–63. Perhaps this is where Holmes's ignorance of literature, as well as his prejudice against female intellect, blinded him. Anyone familiar with Shakespeare's *The Merchant of Venice* recalls the vivid example of Portia, who disguises herself as a man to win a case in court in favor of her husband's friend, Antonio, thus relying on and subverting male stereotypes of female incompetence.

40. "Yellow Face," 564–65.

41. Given the lack of knowledge about mental illness in Conan Doyle's time, he has Holmes quickly reject any cases as inherently unsolvable when he thinks that there is madness involved; see his initial rejection of the case in "Six Napoleons," 924–25.

Aristotle on Detective Fiction

Dorothy L. Sayers

Some twenty-five years ago, it was rather the fashion among commentators to deplore that Aristotle should have so much inclined to admire a kind of tragedy that was not, in their opinion, "the best." All this stress laid upon the plot, all this hankering after melodrama and surprise—was it not rather unbecoming? rather inartistic? Psychology for its own sake was just then coming to the fore, and it seemed almost blasphemous to assert that "they do not act in order to portray the characters; they include the characters for the sake of the action." Indeed, we are not yet free from the influence of that school of thought for which the best kind of play or story is that in which nothing particular happens from beginning to end.

Now, to anyone who reads the *Poetics* with an unbiased mind, it is evident that Aristotle was not so much a student of his own literature as a prophet of the future. He criticized the contemporary Greek theatre because it was, at that time, the most readily available, widespread, and democratic form of popular entertainment presented for his attention. But what, in his heart of hearts, he desired was a Good Detective Story; and it was not his fault, poor man, that he lived some twenty centuries too early to revel in the Peripeties of *Trent's Last Case* or the Discoveries of *The Hound of the Baskervilles.* He had a stout appetite for the gruesome. "Though the objects themselves may be painful," says he, "we delight to view the most realistic representations of them in art, the forms, for example, of the lowest animals and of dead bodies." The crawling horror of *The Speckled Band* would, we infer, have pleased him no less than *The Corpse in the Car, The Corpse in Cold Storage,* or *The Body in the Silo.* Yet he was no Thriller-Fan. "Of simple plots and actions," he rightly observes, "the episodic are the worst. I call a plot episodic when there is neither probability nor necessity in the sequence of the episodes." He would not have approved of a certain recent book which included among its incidents a machine-gun attack in Park Lane, an airplane dropping bombs on Barnes Common, a gas attack by the C.I.D. on a West End flat, and a pitched battle with assorted artillery on a yacht in the Solent. He maintained that dreadful and alarming events produced their best effect when they occurred "unexpectedly," indeed, but also "in consequence of one another." In one phrase he sums up the whole essence of the Detective Story proper. Speaking of the denouement of the work, he says: "It is also possible to discover whether some one has done or not done something." Yes, indeed.

It is well known that a man of transcendent genius, though working under difficulties and with inadequate tools, will do more useful and inspiring work than a man of mediocre intellect with all the resources of the laboratory at his disposal. And so Aristotle, with no better mysteries for his study than the sordid complications of the Agamemnon family, no more scientific murder-methods than the poisoned arrow of Philoctetes or the somewhat improbable medical properties of Medea's cauldron, above all, with detective-heroes so painfully stereotyped and unsympathetic as the inhuman array of gods from the machine, yet contrived to hammer out from these unpromising elements a theory of detective fiction so shrewd, all-embracing, and practical that the *Poetics* remains the finest guide to the writing of such fiction that could be put, at this day, into the hands of an aspiring author.

In what, then, does this guidance consist? From the start Aristotle accepts the detective story as a worthy subject for serious treatment. "Tragedy," he observes (tragedy being the literary form which the detective story took in his day), "also acquired magnitude"—that is, it became important both in form and substance. "Discarding short stories and a ludicrous diction, it assumed, though only at a late point in its progress, a tone of dignity." I am afraid that "short stories and a ludicrous diction" have characterized some varieties of the *genre* up to a very late point indeed; it is true, however, that there have recently been great efforts at reform. Aristotle then goes on to define Tragedy in terms excellently applicable to our subject: "The imitation" (or presentment, or representation—we will not quarrel over the word) "of an action that is serious"—it will be admitted that murder is an action of a tolerably serious nature—"and also complete in itself"—that is highly important, since a detective story that leaves any loose ends is no proper detective story at all—"with incidents arousing pity and fear, wherewith to accomplish its catharsis of such emotions."

Too much has already been said and written on the vexed subject of the catharsis. Is it true, as magistrates sometimes assert, that little boys go to the bad through reading detective stories? Or is it, as detective writers prefer to think with Aristotle, that in a nerve-ridden age the study of crime stories provides a safety valve for the bloodthirsty passions that might otherwise lead us to murder our spouses? Of all forms of modern fiction, the detective story alone makes virtue *ex hypothesi* more interesting than vice, the detective more beloved than the criminal. But there is a dangerous error going about, namely that "if . . . detective fiction leads to an increase in crime, then the greater the literary merit, the greater will be the corresponding increase in crime."[1] Now, this is simply not true: few people can have been inspired to murder their uncles by the literary merits of *Hamlet.* On the contrary, where there is no beauty there can be no catharsis; an ill-written book, like an ill-compounded drug, only irritates the system without purging. Let us then see to it that, if we excite evil passions, it is so done as to sublimate them at the same time by the contemplation of emotional or intellectual beauty. Thus far, then, concerning the catharsis.

Aristotle next discusses Plot and Character. "A detective story," we gather, "is impossible without action, but there may be one without character." A few years ago, the tendency was for all detective stories to be of the characterless or "draught-board" variety; today, we get many examples exhibiting a rather slender plot and a good deal of morbid psychology. Aristotle's warning, however, still holds good:

> One may string together a series of characteristic speeches of the utmost finish as regards Diction and Thought, and yet fail to produce the true dramatic effect; but one will have much better success with a story which, however inferior in these respects, has a Plot.

And again:

> The first essential, the life and soul, so to speak, of the detective story, is the Plot, and the Characters come second.

As regards the makeup of the plot, Aristotle is again very helpful. He says firmly that it should have a beginning, a middle, and an end. Herein the detective story is sharply distinguished from that kind of modern novel which, beginning at the end, rambles backwards and forwards without particular direction and ends on an indeterminate note, and for no ascertainable reason except the publisher's refusal to provide more printing and paper for *7s. 6d.* The detective story commonly begins with the murder; the middle is occupied with the detection of the crime and the various peripeties or reversals of fortune arising out of this; the end is the discovery and execution of the murderer—than which nothing can very well be more final. Our critic adds that the work should be of a convenient length. If it is too short, he says, our perception of it becomes indistinct. (This is meiosis; he might have said that it will not be perceived at all, since the library subscriber will flatly refuse to take it out, on the ground that "there isn't enough reading in it.") He objects, still more strongly, to the work that is of vast size or "one thousand miles long." "A story or plot," he reminds us, "must be of some length, but of a length to be taken in by the memory." A man *might* write a detective story of the length of *Ulysses,* but, if he did, the reader would not be able to bear all the scattered clues in mind from the first chapter to the last, and the effect of the final discovery would be lost. In practice, a length of from 80,000 to 120,000 words is desirable, if the book is to sell, and this is enough to allow, in Aristotle's general formula, of "the hero's passing by a series of probable or necessary stages from misfortune to happiness or from happiness to misfortune." Later, however, he conveys a very necessary warning: "A writer often stretches out a plot beyond its capabilities, and is thus obliged to twist the sequence of incident." It is unwise to "write-up" a short story type of plot to novel length, even to fulfill a publisher's contract.

The next section of the *Poetics* gives advice about the Unity of the Plot. It is not necessary to tell us everything that ever befell the hero. For example, says Aristotle, "in writing about Sherlock Holmes" (I have slightly adapted the instance he gives):

> the author does not trouble to say where the hero was born, or whether he was educated at Oxford or Cambridge, nor does he enter into details about incidents which—though we know they occurred—are not relevant to the matter in hand, such as the cases of Vamberry, the Wine-Merchant, the Aluminium Crutch, Wilson the Notorious Canary-Trainer, or Isadora Persano and the Remarkable Worm.

The story, he says:

> must represent one action, a complete whole, with its several incidents so closely connected that the transposal or withdrawal of any one of them will disjoin and dislocate the whole.

In other words, "murder your darlings"—or, if you must write a purple passage, take care to include in it some vital clue to the solution, which cannot be omitted or transposed to any other part of the story. Thus, in *Trent's Last Case*, the description of Marlowe's room conveys the necessary clue that he has been a member of the O.U.D.S. and is therefore to be presumed capable of acting a part; the poker game in *The Canary Murder Case* throws needful light on the murderer's character; the picture of the shivering sands in *The Moonstone* prepares us for the discovery of the paint-stained nightgown in that spot; and so forth.

But now comes the important question: What kind of Plot are we to choose? And this raises the great central opposition of the Probable and the Possible. It is *possible* that two negroes should coexist, so much alike as not only to deceive the eye, but to possess the same Bertillon measurements; that they should both bear the same Christian and surnames; and that they should both be confined in the same prison at the same time: it is possible, since it actually occurred.[2] But if we are to found a plot upon such a series of coincidences it will have an improbable appearance.

It is open to us to contrive stories based upon such incidents in real life, either giving the characters their real names, or otherwise calling upon the witness of history. Thus there have been books founded on the Bravo Case, the Crippen Murder, the Penge Tragedy, the Case of W. H. Wallace, and so on. When the facts are well known, the reader will accept the events as narrated. But it often turns out that the stories so written appear less convincing than those that are wholly invented; and it is frequently necessary to add inventions to the known facts, in order to make these true events appear probable. "So that," says Aristotle, "one must not aim at a rigid adherence to the traditional stories," particularly as "even the known stories are known only to a few." Thus, even where the Possibility cannot be challenged, Probability should be studied.

But where both names and incidents are invented, then, "a likely impossibility is always preferable to an unconvincing possibility." It may be impossible that the leaden bullet buried in a man's body should be chemically recovered from his ashes after cremation; but by skillful use of scientific language, Dr. Austin Freeman persuades us that it is probable, and indeed inevitable. Whereas, when an author seeks to persuade us that a pleasant young Cambridge man of gentle birth is affronted by being asked to take his place in a queue behind a taxi driver or some such person, the incident, though physically possible, offends by its improbability, being contrary to the English character, whose eternal patience in arranging itself in orderly queues is well known to amount to genius. "The story," says Aristotle, "should never be made up of improbable incidents; there *should* be nothing of the sort in it." Lest this seem too severe, he suggests as a practical compromise that "if such incidents are unavoidable, they should be kept outside the action." Thus, in the story of *The Gloria Scott,* while the previous history of Old Trevor is not merely improbable but, according to the dates given, impossible, we do not notice this in reading, because the episode stands outside the action of the plot. Similarly, as regards the Characters, the impossible-probable is better than the improbable-possible; for (says Aristotle again) "if a detective such as Conan Doyle described be impossible, the answer is that it is better he should be like that, since the artist ought to improve on his model."

In the matter of scientific detail, Aristotle is all for accuracy. If, he says in effect, you cannot attain your artistic end without some impossible device (such as the instantaneously fatal and undiscoverable poison), then, at a pinch, you may be justified in using it.

> If, however, the poetic end might have been as well or better attained without sacrifice of technical correctness in such matters, the impossibility is not to be justified, since the description should be, if it can, entirely free from error.

Thus, in Mr. John Rhode's *The Corpse in the Car,* the undetectable gas emitted from the wireless set is more justifiable, because scientifically correct, than the same author's release of hydrocyanic acid gas from a rubber hot-water bottle in *Poison for One,* a method which (I am told) would not be effective in practice.

Concerning the three necessary parts of a detective plot—Peripety, or Reversal of Fortune; Discovery; and Suffering—Aristotle has many very just observations. On Suffering, we need not dwell long. Aristotle defines it as "action of a destructive or painful nature, such as murders, tortures, woundings, and the like." These are common enough in the detective story, and the only remark to be made is that they ought always to help on the action in some way, and not be put in merely to harrow the feelings, still less to distract attention from a weakness in the plot.

A Reversal of Fortune may happen to all or any of the characters: the victim—who is frequently a man of vast wealth—may be reduced to the status of a mere dead body; or may again turn out not to be dead after all, as we had supposed. The wrongly suspected person, after undergoing great misfortunes, may be saved from the condemned cell and restored to the arms of his betrothed. The detective, after several errors of reasoning, may hit upon the right solution. Such Peripeties keep the story moving and arouse alternating emotions of terror, compassion, and so forth, in the reader. These events are best brought about—not fortuitously, but—by some *Hamartia* or defect in the sufferer. The defect may be of various kinds. The victim may suffer on account of his unamiable character or through the error of marrying a wicked person, or through foolishly engaging in dubious finance, or through the mistake of possessing too much money. The innocent suspect may have been fool enough to quarrel with the victim, or to bring suspicion on himself by suppressing evidence with intent to shield somebody. The detective suffers his worries and difficulties through some failure of observation or logic. All these kinds of defect are fruitful in the production of Peripety.

Aristotle mentions many varieties of the Discovery which forms the denouement. This is usually the discovery, either of the identity of the murderer, or of the means by which the crime was committed.

1. The worst kind are *Discoveries made by the Author himself.* These are, indeed, so inartistic as to be scarcely permissible in the true detective story: they belong to the Thriller. It is, however, possible, where the villain's identity is known, to make an agreeable story by showing the moves and countermoves made successively by villain and detective (Wilkie Collins in *No Name*; Austin Freeman in *The Singing Bone*).

2. *The Discovery by Material Signs and Tokens* is very common: in *The Trial of Mary Dugan* the discovery that a person is left-handed leads to his conviction; in *The Eye of Osiris* the identity of the (supposed) Egyptian mummy with the missing corpse is proved by the discovery of identical tooth-stoppings and a Potts fracture in both.

3. *Discovery through Memory* is also used: thus, in *Unnatural Death* the murder-method—the production of an air lock in a main artery—is discovered to the detective by his memory of a similar air lock in the petrolfeed of a motorcycle.

4. *Discovery through Reasoning* is perhaps most common of all: the murderer was in the house at such a time, he is an electrician, he is tall and smokes Sobranie cigarettes; only X corresponds to all these indications, therefore X is the murderer.

5. Aristotle's fifth type of Discovery is particularly interesting. He calls it, *Discovery through Bad Reasoning by the Other Party.* The instance he adduces is obscure, the text being apparently mutilated and referring to a play unknown. But I think he really means to describe the *Discovery by Bluff.* Thus, the detective shows the suspect a weapon, saying, "If you are not the murderer, how do you come to be in possession of this weapon?" The suspect replies: "But that is not the weapon with which the crime was committed." "Indeed," says the detective; "*and how do you know?*"

This brings us to the very remarkable passage in which Aristotle, by one of those blinding flashes of insight which display to the critic of genius the very core and centre of the writer's problem, puts the whole craft of the detective writer into one master-word: PARALOGISMOS. That word should be written up in letters of gold on the walls of every mystery-monger's study—at once the guiding star by which he sets his compass and the jack-o'-lantern by which he leads his readers into the bog. Paralogism—the art of the false syllogism—for which Aristotle himself has a blunter and more candid phrase. Let us examine the whole paragraph, for it is of the utmost importance.

"Homer," says he—if he had lived in our own day he might have chosen some more apposite example, such as Father Knox or Mrs. Agatha Christie, but, thinking no doubt of Odysseus, he says Homer—"Homer more than any other has taught the rest of us the art of *framing lies in the right way.* I mean the use of paralogism. Whenever, if A is or happens, a consequent, B, is or happens, men's notion is that, if the B is, the A also is—but that is a false conclusion. Accordingly, if A is untrue, but there is something else, B, that on the assumption of its truth follows as its consequent, then the right thing is to present us with the B. Just because we know the truth of the consequent, we are in our own minds led on to the erroneous inference of the truth of the antecedent."

There you are, then; there is your recipe for detective fiction: the Art of Framing Lies. From beginning to end of your book, it is your whole aim and object to lead the reader up the garden; to induce him to believe a lie. To believe the real murderer to be innocent, to believe some harmless person to be guilty; to believe the detective to be right where he is wrong and mistaken where he is right; to believe the false alibi sound, the present absent, the dead alive, and the living dead; to believe, in short, anything and everything but the truth.

The art of framing lies—but mark! of framing lies in *the right way.* There is the crux. Any fool can tell a lie, and any fool can believe it; but the right method is to tell the *truth* in such a way that the *intelligent* reader is seduced into telling the lie for himself. That the writer himself should tell a flat lie is contrary to all the canons of detective art. Is it not amazing that Aristotle, twenty centuries ahead of his time, should thus have struck out at a blow the great modern theory of fair play to the reader? A is falsehood; B is truth. The writer must not give us A upon his own authority, for what he says upon his own authority we must be able to believe. But he may tell us B—which *is* true—and leave us to draw the false conclusion that A is true also.

Thus, at the opening of a story, the servant Jones is heard to say to his master, Lord Smith, "Very good, my lord, I will attend to the matter at once." The inference is that, if Jones was speaking to Smith, Smith was also speaking to Jones; and that, therefore, Smith was alive and present at the time. But that is a false conclusion; the author has made no such assertion. Lord Smith may be absent; he may be already dead; Jones may have been addressing the empty air, or some other person. Nor can we draw any safe conclusion about the attitude of Jones. If Jones is indeed present in the flesh, and not represented merely by his voice in the form of a gramophone record or similar device (as may well be the case), then he may be addressing some other party in the belief that he is addressing Smith; he may have murdered Smith and be establishing his own alibi; or Smith may be the murderer and Jones his accomplice engaged in establishing an alibi for Smith. Nor, on the other hand, is it safe to conclude (as some experienced readers will) that *because* Smith is not heard to reply he is *not* therefore present. For this may very well be the Double Bluff, in which the reader's own cunning is exploited to his downfall. The reader may argue thus:

> Jones spoke to Smith, but Smith did not speak to Jones;
> Many authors employ this device so as to establish the false inference that Smith was alive and present;
> I therefore conclude that Smith is absent or dead.

But this syllogism is as false as the other. "Many authors" is not the same thing as "all authors at all times." It does not exclude the possibility that an author may at some time imply the truth in such a manner that it looks like a lie.

A fine example of this Double Bluff is found in Father Knox's *The Viaduct Murder.* A man is found dead, with his face beaten into unrecognizable pulp. Circumstantial evidence suggests that the dead man was X. The detectives and the reader are invited to reason after the following manner:

> The dead man is thought to be X;
> But he is unrecognizable;
> Therefore he is not X;
> Therefore he is someone else, namely Y;
> And, since X is undoubtedly missing, X is probably the murderer.

But the disfigured corpse turns out to be X after all; so that all the ingenious conclusions founded upon the false premise are false also.

Another variety of the Paralogism is found in a syllogism built upon the following lines:

> A is the obvious suspect;
> But in a detective story, the obvious suspect is always innocent;
> Therefore A is innocent.

But for the middle term of this proposition there is no warrant whatever. The statement is neither universally true nor logically necessary. The obvious suspect is innocent more frequently than not, but nothing compels the author to make him so.

Nothing in a detective story need be held to be true unless the author has vouched for it *in his own person.* Thus, if the author says:

> Jones came home at 10 o'clock,

then we are entitled to assume that Jones did indeed come home at that time and no other. But if the author says:

> The grandfather clock was striking ten when Jones reached home,

then we can feel no certainty as to the time of Jones's arrival, for nothing compels us to accept the testimony of the clock. Nor need we believe the testimony of any character in the story, unless the author himself vouches for that character's integrity.

Thus, let us suppose that the butler gives evidence that Jones returned at 10:00. The butler's employer asserts that he has always found the butler scrupulously truthful. Are we, therefore, to believe the butler? By no means; for the employer may be deceived, or may have deceived the butler, or may be backing up the butler's testimony for reasons of his own.

But if the author himself says: "No one could possibly doubt that the butler was speaking the truth," then, I think, we must believe that the butler is a truthful witness, for the author himself has stated, on his own authority, that doubt was impossible.

Remember, however, that the person telling the story is not necessarily the author. Thus, in *The Murder of Roger Ackroyd,* the story is told by the detective's *fidus Achates* or (to use the modern term) his Watson. Arguing from the particular to the general, we may be seduced into concluding that, because the original Dr. Watson was a good man, all Watsons are good in virtue of their Watsonity. But this is false reasoning, for moral worth and Watsonity are by no means inseparable. Thus, the first man sinned and laid the blame upon his wife; but it would be an error to conclude that all men, when they sin, blame their wives—though in fact they frequently do. There may yet be found rare men who, having wives, yet refrain from blaming them and are nonetheless men on that account. So, despite the existence of a first innocent Watson, we may yet admit the possibility of a guilty one; nor, when the Watson in *Roger Ackroyd* turns out to be the murderer, has the reader any right to feel aggrieved against the author—for she has vouched only for the man's Watsonity and not for his moral worth.

This brings us, however, to the consideration of the Characters, concerning whom Aristotle takes a very twentieth-century point of view. He says that they must be *good.* This, I suppose, must be taken relatively, to mean that they should, even the meanest and wickedest of them, be not merely monsters and caricatures, like the personages in a low farce, but endowed with some sort of human dignity, so that we are enabled to take them seriously. They must also be *appropriate*: a female, he says, must not be represented as clever. This is a delicate point—would he, or would he not, have approved of Miss Gladys Mitchell's diabolically clever Mrs. Bradley? We may take it, however, that the cleverness should only be such as is appropriate to the sex and circumstances of the character—it would be inappropriate that the elderly maiden sister of a country parson should carry out or detect a murder by means of an intricate and lever method knowable only to advanced chemical experts; and so with the other characters. Thirdly, the characters must be *like the reality.* Scholars differ about what Aristotle means by this word. Some think it means, "conformable to tradition": that the villain should be easily recognizable as villainous by his green eyes, his moustache, and his manner of ejaculating "Ha!," and the detective by his eccentricities, his pipe, and his dressing-gown, after the more ancient models. But I do not agree with them, and believe that the word means, as we say today, "realistic"—i.e. with some moderate approximation in speech and behavior to such men and women as we see about us. For, elsewhere, Aristotle takes the modern, realistic view, as when he says, for instance, that the plot ought not to turn on the detection and punishment of a hopelessly bad man who is villainous in all directions at once—forger, murderer, adulterer, thief—like the bad baron in an Adelphi melodrama; but rather on that of an intermediate kind of person—a decent man with a bad kink in him—which is the type of villain most approved by the best modern writers in this kind. For the more the villain resembles an ordinary man, the more shall we feel pity and horror at his crime and the greater will be our surprise at his detection. So, too, as regards the innocent suspects and the police; in treating all such characters a certain resemblance to real life is on the whole to be desired. Lastly, and most important and difficult of all, the characters must be *consistent* from first to last. Even though at the end we are to feel surprise on discovering the identity of the criminal, we ought not to feel incredulity; we should rather be able to say to ourselves: "Yes, I can see *now* that from the beginning this man had it in him to commit murder, had I only had the wits to interpret the indications furnished by the author." Thus, the villainy of the apparently amiable father in *The Copper Beeches* betrayed by his participation in his offspring's cruel enjoyment in the slaughter of flies, and the character is seen to be consistent. Inconsistency in the characters destroys the probability of the action, and, indeed, amounts to a breach of the rule of fair play, since we are entitled to believe that a character remains the same person from beginning to end of the story and *nemo repente fuit turpissimus.*

This discourse is already too long. Let me remind myself of Aristotle's own warning: "There are many writers who, after a good Complication, fail to bring off the Denouement." This is painfully true of detective stories; it has also some application to lectures and speeches upon whatever occasion. But indeed, everything that Aristotle says about writing and composition is pregnant with a fundamental truth, an inner rightness, that makes it applicable to all forms of literary art, from the most trivial to the most exalted. He had, as we say, the root of the matter in him; and any writer who tries to make a detective story a work of art at all will do well if he writes it in such a way that Aristotle could have enjoyed and approved it.

Notes

The following headnote appeared at the beginning of the original essay: The translation of *The Poetics* used throughout this lecture, delivered at Oxford March 5, 1935, in London June 21, 1935, is that of Professor Ingram Bywater, published by the Clarendon Press.

1. Editorial in *The Author,* Spring 1935.
2. The case of the two Will Wests, U.S. Penitentiary, Leavenworth, Kansas, 1903.

The Grim Reaper on Baker Street

Elizabeth Glass-Turner

Long before *CSI: Crime Scene Investigation* and other murder mystery shows, people gathered around—and under—the guillotine to watch the bloody spectacle of death, and even, as *The Scarlet Pimpernel* describes, to collect hair from the fallen heads. Centuries before that, crowds roared around the ultimate reality series at the Coliseum, watching contestants literally fight to the death. Most of the denizens of history have had close contact with mortality. Disease, battle, and starvation used to be the norm around the world. Longer life expectancy and low mortality rates haven't diminished interest in death. If anything, as the specter of death has left our day-to-day lives, our need to encounter it through the arts has only grown. From the burgeoning vampire genre to television comedies and drama, the dead—and undead—have never been so popular.

Death is certainly on display front and center in the works of Sir Arthur Conan Doyle. He introduces his readers to the forensics of detective work through his colorful creation of Sherlock Holmes (and his loyal Watson). What insights might we glean from them about this biggest mystery of all, the puzzle of death itself?

The Metaphysics of Death in Fiction

Death in fiction is not something that is confined to mystery novels. Trace the morbid and macabre back far enough, and you find it littering Greek tragedies with abandon. *Beowulf* continues to entertain high school students with a thirst for blood. More recently on the human scene, Shakespeare probed the mysteries of life and death with Hamlet's famous "To be or not to be" soliloquy. Flannery O'Connor autopsied the function of violence in fiction in terms of acceptance of death. And it is easy to find examples of a character's death revealing a philosophy of life, meaning, and dying. Rarely is a corpse ever just a corpse.

In Sir Arthur Conan Doyle's tales about Sherlock Holmes, there are robberies, conspiracies, suspense—and sometimes death, though not always murder. The great Danish philosopher Søren Kierkegaard (1813–55) once wrote that death has no need of an explanation and certainly has never requested any thinker to be of assistance. But the living need the explanation—and why? In order to live accordingly. Death does not need the explanation, Kierkegaard concludes, because death remains inexplicable. Death might as a matter of fact be incomprehensible because it represents a certain otherness, a certain unknowing. Any explanation of death is necessarily indirect in the sense that it returns to the reader as a question, as a challenge, as a fundamental otherness questioning the being and acting of the explainer. "The earnestness lies in just this, that the explanation does not explain death but discloses the state of the explainer's own innermost being."[1]

One may ask whether Sherlock Holmes ever moves from unraveling evidence and explaining the cause of death to "disclosing his own innermost being." Certainly the character is known more for his strict reasoning than his midnight confessionals, but we might begin by asking why Sherlock Holmes engaged in his assiduous detective work. Why did Holmes hunt the Reaper?

House and Holmes

It is perhaps little surprising that one of the most memorable television characters in recent memory is based, at least in part, on one of the most memorable fictional characters ever conceived. Dr. Gregory House, the protagonist of David Shore's critically acclaimed medical TV show *House,* is a misanthropic curmudgeon, a sardonic genius often insufferably bored by life and the niceties it habitually imposes. He's a doctor who, like Holmes, is unconventional, brilliant at solving puzzles (medical ones, in House's case), and adept at formulating accurate diagnoses with remarkable rapidity. The parallels between House and Holmes (including their names) don't stop there. By Shore's own admission, the similarities were intentional; both play music, live at 221B Baker Street, experience ennui, have few friends, and are only engaged by sufficiently interesting cases. The prosaic and commonplace aren't enough to capture their imaginations.

After Watson gave Holmes high praise for solving a perplexing case, Sherlock answered, "It saved me from ennui," yawning. "Alas! I already feel it closing in upon me. My life is spent in one long effort to escape from the commonplaces of existence. These little problems help me to do so."[2]

In part, then, Holmes's chase of the Grim Reaper was due to his need for intellectual stimulation. Impossibly difficult cases gave him cause for activity. His examinations of dead bodies and their surroundings would occasion strange facts and circumstances that befuddled others while bringing him the thrill of the chase—a reason to get off the couch. Surely death is among the greatest of all mysteries. If anything were to constitute a big enough challenge for an intellect like Sherlock's, this was it.

Both House and Holmes largely represent a materialistic bias as they go about their lives. House is an atheist, mocking colleagues and patients who display a religious bent. Holmes, though far less vociferously negative toward a religious worldview, does demonstrate at least a naturalistic tendency when he goes about his work unearthing explanations. At the prospect of vampires explaining a particular mystery, he said to Watson, "But are we to give serious attention to such things? This agency stands flat-footed upon the ground, and there it must remain. The world is big enough for us. No ghosts need apply."[3] In "The Adventure of The Devil's Foot," he reasoned to Watson like this: "I take it, in the first place, that neither of us is prepared to admit diabolical intrusions into the affairs of men. Let us begin by ruling that entirely out of our minds."[4]

Sherlock always began his inquiries with the physical evidence, as he asserts in *The Hound of the Baskervilles:* "But we are bound to exhaust all other hypotheses before falling back upon this [supernatural] one."[5] In that particular investigation, he pursued all possible lines of questioning in the material world before considering any supernatural explanation of the ghoulish, haunting hound. In contrast to the uneducated villagers in the story, Holmes is seen to scoff at superstition—while acknowledging that a very real danger exists to the Baskervilles. It is the source of the danger that he questions. In fact, at the beginning of the story, Conan Doyle sets the stage for the dilemma in a comical conversation between Sherlock and the town doctor.

> "I have hitherto confined my investigations to this world," said [Holmes]. "In a modest way I have combated evil, but to take on the Father of Evil himself would, perhaps, be too ambitious a task. Yet you must admit that the footmark is material."
>
> "The original hound was material enough to tug a man's throat out, and yet he was diabolical [demonic] as well."
>
> "I see that you have quite gone over to the supernaturalists."[6]

Here Conan Doyle's characters emerge puzzling over the state of the victims—tangible and real—and what that reveals about the perpetrator—a supernatural, curse-driven hound, or a flesh-and-blood enemy? In one instance, a corpse was found with its throat ripped out. In another, the body showed no wound or distress save for the horrified expression on the victim's face. Holmes insists on solving the puzzle from hard evidence, refusing to consider the supernatural as the cause of death, at least until every naturalistic explanation of the evidence has been exhausted.

I See Dead People

What did Holmes see, then, when he saw a corpse? Conan Doyle's hero never crafted lengthy psychological profiles. Unlike Agatha Christie's detective Hercule Poirot, Holmes did not claim to solve murders from the comfort of his armchair. Rather, he scouted out empirical evidence, studying the condition of the corpse and its physical surroundings, compiling data for the puzzle to be solved.

One author explains the historical background for Holmes's preoccupation with the material:

> The rationale for what is known as "orthodox," "Western," or, more accurately, "biomedical" medicine, is very materialistic. It's focused on the physical, and has been since the morbid anatomists of the 15th and 17th century Parisian hospitals began conducting postmortem dissections and claimed that disease was what you could see, touch, and measure. This reduction of human suffering to physical components was a new phenomenon which was dramatically captured by Rembrandt in "The Anatomy Lesson of Dr Tulp."[7]

The famous painting depicts an autopsy being performed on a pallid corpse with curious medical students surrounding the body, displaying wonder and disgust.

In Conan Doyle's world, an early exchange between Watson and a friend reveals the following of Holmes, whom Watson had not yet met: "He appears to have a passion for definite and exact knowledge . . . but it may be pushed to excess. When it comes to beating the subjects in the dissecting-room with a stick, it is certainly taking rather a bizarre shape . . . to verify how far bruises may be produced after death. I saw him at it with my own eyes."[8]

But Holmes's early CSI techniques extended beyond his experiments on cadavers in the morgue:

> If you could have looked into Allardyce's back shop, you would have seen a dead pig swung from a hook in the ceiling, and a gentleman in his shirt sleeves furiously stabbing at it with this weapon. I was that energetic person, and I have satisfied myself that by no exertion of my strength can I transfix the pig with a single blow.[9]

The purpose of the seemingly bizarre pig experiment was revealed later in the tale:

> Have you tried to drive a harpoon through a body? No? You must really pay attention to these details. My friend Watson could tell you that I spent a whole morning in that exercise. It is no easy matter, and requires a strong and practiced arm. But this blow was delivered with such violence that the head of the weapon sank deep into the wall.[10]

More than chasing away boredom, Holmes's treatment of a corpse showed detailed attention to the mode of death, to the scientific evidence at hand, and to the careful reasoning that constructed an explanation of the evidence. Holmes, like House, cultivated the ability to remain objective, treating corpses and cadavers as one more item in the inventory of crime scene details, manipulable means to the end of solving the crime. In so doing, he exhibited part of what he represents: the emergence of a scientific, dispassionate examination of the physical facts at the disposal of investigators. His aversion to extrascientific hypotheses, diabolical forces of evil, or spiritual or supernatural explanations seems to put him, in a real sense, on the side of the materialists over that of the spiritualists. Perhaps why House inhabits so clear a role as an atheist owes to this aspect of the model Sherlock provides.

Dead Philosophers' Society

Did Holmes's value of the empirical lead him to conclude that it was impossible to harm the dead—that "dust can be neither wronged nor harmed"?[11] Or did his scientific conclusions simply serve his desire to right the harm that death inherently is? That is to say, did Holmes's experiments with corpses show a disregard for the dead, or did they show respect for the dead by helping him to accumulate knowledge that would assist in avenging murder victims? Is it possible that "the dead, then, can be wronged: they can be the victims of injustice, slander, betrayal. They can also be honored, justice rendered to them"?[12]

Most arguments about death as a harm inevitably invoke the specter of Epicurus. When it came to death as harm, Epicurus argued that death itself could not be harm to oneself because "death is nothing to us, for good and evil imply sentience, and death is the privation of all sentience. . . . It is nothing, then, either to the living or to the dead, for with the living it is not and the dead exist no longer."[13] Epicurus did not suggest that dying cannot be harmful to a person; certainly, dying can cause suffering and constitute a lack of good. Although one can argue that death can withhold future unknown pleasure, thus being harmful, the problem in this speculation is that death may also prevent future unknown pain, thus being beneficial.

Epicurus's argument that death is not a harm to a person depends on the assumption that consciousness ends at death—that not only the body but the very person expires. However, here murder enters the picture, because "there are many connections between the metaphysical issues . . . and the moral issues pertaining to death. If the Epicurean position is correct, then it might lead to very implausible results concerning the moral status of killing. Presumably, killing another person might be considered wrong to the extent that *others* suffer as a result of the death, but it could not be considered morally objectionable to the person who is killed (insofar as the death is quick and painless)."[14]

Epicurean arguments, in other words, might make it easier to justify murder—something that Holmes would most definitely object to. It is plausible that Sherlock Holmes would object to Epicurus's claims that death is not a harm. For although Epicurus—and modern philosophers sympathetic to him—might contend that consciousness ends with death, many instances in Conan Doyle's tales suggest that the detective would disagree. Sherlock would not assume that consciousness ends with death. It would seem that Holmes's methods and typical privileging of naturalistic explanations did not exclude a belief in the afterlife. Was he a dualist, then, who believed in the coexistence of material and spiritual, body and soul?

This is an interesting question, and an important one if we're to grasp anything like the philosophy of Sherlock Holmes. The question of what constitutes the ultimate constituent makeup of human beings—atoms and molecules, matter and energy on the one hand, or some sort of composite of body and soul, matter and spirit on the other—is one of the most important questions of philosophy generally and metaphysics specifically. Questions of paramount and ultimate importance rest on its proper analysis. Who and what we are as human beings make a great deal of difference to how we understand a great number of vital aspects of the human condition.[15]

Here it's important that we augment our earlier account of Sherlock's philosophy of death. For the evidence already adduced fails to do justice to aspects of his belief system hard to square with a thoroughgoing materialism. To begin with, a recognition of the reality of our corporeal selves and the importance of something like brain activity in explicating human behavior does not rule out something nonmaterial. In contrasting spiritualists with "associationists," William James (1842–1910) once wrote that they must both be "cerebralists" to the extent at least of "admitting that certain peculiarities in the way of working of their favorite principles are explicable only by the fact that the brain laws are a codeterminant of the result."[16]

Although Sherlock represented in one respect the emerging scientific mentality according to which naturalistic explanations are assigned primacy, in other respects, he retained convictions about aspects of reality that transcended the physical. Various other chapters in this book accentuate some of these aspects of his thought, so for present purposes it will suffice to but tip our hat in their direction. Sherlock's consistent commitment to empirical investigation and the primacy of observable facts didn't preclude his openness to aspects of reality that weren't reducible to the material, aspects of reality whose significance was wider than a purely physicalist account could explain. Like William James, again, Sherlock would have been averse to a reductionist analysis that would rule out deeper meanings and realities. He likely would have resonated with James when the latter once wrote that the reductionists feared superstition whereas he himself more greatly feared desiccation, an emaciated worldview stripped of its profounder meanings and deeper realities. As evidence for this claim, consider the following words of Sherlock at the end of "The Veiled Lodger": "'Poor girl!' he said. 'Poor girl! The ways of Fate are indeed hard to understand. If there is not some compensation hereafter, then the world is a cruel jest.'" Note his hope for "compensation hereafter"—hardly the words of a committed naturalist.

Knowing the plight of the horribly disfigured woman to whom he was speaking, and recognizing a sort of resignation in her words "the case is closed," Sherlock turned swiftly back to her before leaving.

> "Your life is not your own," he said. "Keep your hands off of it."
> "What use is it to anyone?" she answered.
> "How can you tell?" Holmes replied. "The example of patient suffering is in itself the most precious of all lessons to an impatient world."[17]

His simple but profound words of encouragement led the woman to send to him, two days later, the prussic acid that had been her temptation—presumably her temptation to take her own life out of desperation and despair, experiences of which Sherlock himself was existentially aware. It's been said that suicide is the only real philosophical question, and Sherlock's answer to it was clear. Her life was not her own. Patient endurance is among life's most important lessons, even if we can't see who might benefit from our example. There's hope for afterworldly compensation. Once more, these are hardly the words of a hardened physicalist or myopic empiricist.

Something else reveals Sherlock as something other than a consummately dispassionate empiricist. Several accounts reveal that Holmes does not merely appreciate the evidential value of the corpses, but actually demonstrates care for the remains he has examined. In one situation, he asks what shall be done with a body to avoid leaving it to the foxes and the ravens. Another of Watson's accounts describes Holmes minutely surveying a room before finally laying the body reverently under a sheet. This poses an apparent contrast to his cadaver-beating habits.

Both instances are reconciled, though, by Holmes's recognition of the value of human life and justice—a trait that occasionally leads him to execute justice both inside and outside the law. Some narratives detail his satisfaction in handing over killers to the police, while others show him righting wrongs—but not necessarily turning in criminals, as this Christmastime discussion reveals: "I suppose that I am commuting a felony, but it is just possible that I am saving a soul. This fellow will not go wrong again; he is too terribly frightened. Send him to jail now, and you make him a jail-bird for life. Besides, it is the season of forgiveness."[18]

Sentiments like these echo the value Holmes put on persons, living or dead. Interpreted literally, they would also provide evidence for his acceptance of dualism—the belief in both body and soul. Even if those particular words were meant more figuratively, enough other evidence suggests his openness to more than just the reality of the physical. It seems likely, then, that Holmes's perspectives on the dead are informed both by scientific inquiry into their demise and by a basic acceptance of existence beyond the material.

It is not a negative view of the body or even a lack of belief in the afterlife that fuels Holmes's experiments on the dead or his coldly analytical assessments of them. Instead, his intellectual curiosity and his commitment to achieving justice for the dead—and the living—motivate his otherwise inexplicable behavior.

Dr. Watson: The Jarhead of Baker Street

While Holmes was beating cadavers to study postmortem bruising, Dr. Watson was serving as a medic in Afghanistan—a surprisingly relevant battle region to the modern reader. Where Holmes's knowledge was gained in the benign confines of school in England, Watson returned shell-shocked from battle, injured, and suffering frequent nervous bouts. Conan Doyle's early short stories expose a weakened, easily tired doctor facing a long recovery—both physical and psychological. Later adventures feature a healthier, recovered colleague able to withstand more strain.

Watson's trauma from battle and injury provided an emotional rendering of events, while his vivid narratives served Conan Doyle well as a vehicle for suspense. What Watson saw when he encountered the dead was filtered through his lens as a physician—yet his firsthand knowledge of war often made for imaginatively vivid impressions. Especially gruesome injuries occasionally stopped Watson in his tracks: "It gave even my hardened nerves a shudder to look at it. There were four protruding fingers and a horrid red, spongy surface where the thumb should have been. It had been hacked or torn right out from the roots."[19] Although his professionalism allowed him to care for the wound, the first response as an emotional one was not uncommon in the short stories and novels. While Conan Doyle spared no gory detail in his physical descriptions of the dearly departed, it was through Watson's voice that he interjected horror at the evils of human suffering.

> On his rigid face there stood an expression of horror, and, as it seemed to me, of hatred, such as I have never seen upon human features. This malignant and terrible contortion . . . was increased by his writhing, unnatural posture. I have seen death in many forms, but never has it appeared to me in a more fearsome aspect than in that dark, grimy apartment.[20]

The intensely personal nature of the narratives fused both the sense of the transcendent horror felt at brutality with the concrete personhood of the victims—Watson embodied both the recoiling instincts of self-preservation and respect for the person who had been. It was not inconsistent for Watson to display both horror and respect because the horror in witnessing evil stemmed from respect for personhood and life. Dr. Watson could relate that he followed Holmes with that subdued feeling at his heart that the presence of death inspires.

While frequently Watson's troubled perceptions were linked to the facial expressions on the faces of the dead—images of fear, panic, terror, and shock—occasionally his colorful accounts dealt with the entire corpse.

> It was a dreadful sight which met us as we entered the bedroom door. I have spoken of the impression of flabbiness which this man Blessington conveyed. As he dangled from the hook it was exaggerated and intensified until he was scarce human in his appearance. The neck was drawn out like a plucked chicken's, making the rest of him seem the more obese and unnatural by the contrast. He was clad only in his long night-dress, and his swollen ankles and ungainly feet protruded starkly from beneath it.[21]

Clearly victims were often beyond the reaches of a doctor's help by the time Holmes and Watson arrived on the scene to investigate. But Watson was not just a sidekick, there to aid and abet Holmes's detective efforts. Occasionally Watson's brushes with death turned out better: "Mr. Melas, however, still lived, and in less than an hour, with the aid of ammonia and brandy, I had the satisfaction of seeing him open his eyes, and of knowing that my hand had drawn him back from that dark valley in which all paths meet."[22] In these instances, Watson's work as a doctor helped to save people—innocent or not—from shuffling off their mortal coils prematurely.

Holmes frequently criticized Watson's poor attempts at emulating Sherlock's reasoning, and even went so far as to rant about Watson's published accounts of their adventures for being focused too much on narrative and excitement and not enough on technique and method. Holmes critiqued Watson for being vulnerable enough to get engaged, citing emotion as being destructive to clear thinking. It could be that Watson's poetic interpretation of death could be seen simply as an extension of his subjective, emotional responses—a wish for an afterlife fueled by the suffering he had witnessed.

However, despite Sherlock's enjoyment of his own logical superiority, there are regular allusions to Watson's quality as a doctor—because he was, in fact, a man of science, with an ability to analyze medically: "Might not the nature of the injuries reveal something to my medical instincts? In the surgeon's deposition it was stated that the posterior third of the left parietal bone and the left half of the occipital bone had been shattered by a heavy blow from a blunt weapon. I marked the spot upon my own head. Clearly such a blow must have been struck from behind."[23] Watson's vivid narratives did not negate critical thinking, but rather went beyond it to capture not only fact but also mood. His emotional response in the presence of the dead did not trump his reason, even if he did frequently fail to follow Holmes's reasoning. Watson writes,

> A higher Judge had taken the matter in hand, and Jefferson Hope had been summoned before a tribunal where strict justice would be meted out to him. On the very night after his capture the aneurism burst, and he was found in the morning stretched upon the floor of the cell, with a placid smile upon his face, as though he had been able in his dying moments to look back upon a useful life, and on work well done.[24]

Watson combined a philosophical belief in the afterlife with the medical cause of death and a subjective interpretation of the scene enabled by his knowledge of Jefferson Hope's story. These are all held in balance rather than tension.

The Death of Sherlock Holmes

> It was not a pleasant business, Watson. The fall roared beneath me. I am not a fanciful person, but I give you my word that I seemed to hear Moriarty's voice screaming at me out of the abyss. . . . There I was stretched, when you, my dear Watson, and all your following were investigating in the most sympathetic and inefficient manner the circumstances of my death.[25]

The most famous death in all the tales, the shocking demise of Conan Doyle's hero rocked not only Watson but also readers around the world. The telltale indicator that perhaps all was not as it seemed should have been the absence of a corpse. But the circumstances seemed undeniable: Professor Moriarty had brought about Sherlock Holmes's death. Not only did the immediate circumstances indicate struggle, peril, and death—the danger in which the detective found himself had repeatedly led him to refer to the possibility of his own demise. Holmes's attitude toward his own possible death was one of quiet acceptance. As Watson recounted, "Again and again [Holmes] recurred to the fact that if he could be assured that society was freed from Professor Moriarty he would cheerfully bring his own career to a conclusion."[26]

Sherlock's willingness to die in order to stop his nemesis from continuing his violent reign as a criminal mastermind did not stem from a conviction that there is no harm in death. It could, however, be argued that Holmes, as a rational man, did not fear death because he saw his own as inevitable. That is to say, it was clear that Holmes was the only person able to stop Moriarty. It was clear that Moriarty would challenge Holmes to the death, and it was clear that Holmes would be willing to sacrifice his life in order to prevent Moriarty's victims from further suffering. Dying to stop Moriarty would be fraught with value and significance. Having faced death, Sherlock was willing to live accordingly. Having endured angst and torpor, he had found meaning.

The threat of Moriarty was not the first time that Holmes startled Watson with his seemingly casual attitude toward his own death:

> "See here," said Holmes, pointing to the wooden hatchway. "We were hardly quick enough with our pistols." There, sure enough, just behind where we had been standing, stuck one of those murderous darts which we knew so well. It must have whizzed between us at the instant we fired. Holmes smiled at it and shrugged his shoulders in his easy fashion, but I confess that it turned me sick to think of the horrible death which had passed so close to us that night.[27]

Holmes and Watson regularly found themselves in danger, with Holmes urging Watson to bring his revolver or stand watch with him throughout the night. Frequently the pair ran considerable risk. Although Watson was both accustomed to and weakened by the suspense of war, Holmes had not had his mettle tested in central Asia. Holmes craved activity—mental and physical—and while he endured infamous fits of depression, he was not cavalier with his own life.

Perhaps the most revealing look at Holmes's perspective on his own mortality is not found in his struggle with Moriarty, but in his reflections on those with darker fates than his own:

> "Farewell, then," said the old man solemnly. "Your own deathbeds, when they come, will be easier for the thought of the peace which you have given to mine."
>
> "God help us!" said Holmes after a long silence. "Why does fate play such tricks with poor, helpless worms? I never hear of such a case as this that I do not think of Baxter's words, and say, 'There, but for the grace of God, goes Sherlock Holmes.'"[28]

Conan Doyle's War on the Grim Reaper

It is reasonable to assume that the words of the characters resemble some attitudes of the author himself. But authors change, and Sir Arthur Conan Doyle was no different. If his early career resembled Dr. Watson's—he was a physician practicing medicine—his later propensities stretched beyond the bounds of the good doctor's imaginative impressions and explicitly engaged what can only be termed the paranormal. With the death of his wife, Conan Doyle shifted his focus from x-rays to an *X-Files*-like preoccupation with the afterlife. From crafting a famous empiricist to seeking out spiritualists, the man who invented Sherlock Holmes ended his life ridiculed for pursuing psychics in his desperation to contact his dead wife—though truth be told, his attitudes toward the paranormal ranged from credulity to skepticism.

Once more a parallel with the great philosopher and psychologist William James emerges. Conan Doyle eventually joined Britain's Society for Psychical Research, founded in 1882 by three members of Cambridge University. The American society followed in 1885 with founders that included William James of Harvard.[29] It would seem that Conan Doyle, like James, was willing enough to suspend skepticism and endure criticism long enough to at least consider the evidence for spiritual realities. Is it really that surprising that the creator of Sherlock Holmes might care enough about evidence to follow it wherever he thought it might lead?

> Of the final spiritualist phase only those who have made careful study of those problems can profitably speak. But there was no stage of the life, from the poor student doing without lunch to buy

> books to the famous author enduring painful hostility for his psychic faith, which did not reflect the courage, the chivalry, the sagacity we would have expected from the creator of Holmes. Certainly it was characteristic of that student of mysteries to attack the greatest one we know.[30]

"To philosophize is to learn to die," Montaigne said. Sherlock Holmes certainly learned of human nature, life, and death in his studies of the dead—and in his confrontation with his own death. Over the years, Holmes's creator had deconstructed the horror of the corpse repeatedly through the detective's unraveling of the surrounding mysteries. In the end, however, Conan Doyle was not spared the grief that death brings any more than Watson was spared the loss of his own wife. It is unsurprising for "that student of mysteries to attack the greatest one we know," no matter where the chase took him. Holmes and Watson would gladly have tagged along.

Notes

1. Marius Timmann Mjaaland, *Autopsia: Self, Death, and God after Kierkegaard and Derrida* (Berlin: Walter de Gruyter, 2008), 131–32.

2. "Red-Headed League," 173. All the Sherlock Holmes references come from Arthur Conan Doyle, *The Complete Sherlock Holmes* (New York: Barnes & Noble, 2009).

3. "Sussex Vampire," 992.

4. "Devil's Foot," 919.

5. *Hound of the Baskervilles,* 649.

6. Ibid., 647.

7. Dr. Bob Leckridge, "Person Sized Medicine vs. Molecule Sized Medicine," *Heroes Not Zombies,* April 18, 2008, http://heroesnotzombies.com/2008/04/18/person-sized-medicine-vs-molecule-sized-medicine/.

8. *Study in Scarlet,* 5.

9. "Black Peter," 528.

10. Ibid., 536–37.

11. George Pitcher, "The Misfortunes of the Dead," in *The Metaphysics of Death,* ed. John Martin Fischer (Stanford, Calif.: Stanford University Press, 1993), 162.

12. Ibid., 160.

13. Stephen E. Rosenbaum, "How to Be Dead and Not Care," in Fischer, *Metaphysics of Death,* 121.

14. Fischer, introduction to *Metaphysics of Death,* 27.

15. As a brief aside, some might suggest that dualism, more so than Epicureanism,

might be taken as an excuse for murder. For if killing someone involves only killing his body, the person lives on. Strictly speaking, then, murder would be impossible. We could only kill bodies, not persons. That most of us think it eminently reasonable to speak of persons being killed, however—even those of us who may believe that we aren't reducible to our bodies alone—might be related to the concern that some versions of dualism trivialize the metaphysical connection between persons and bodies, treating such a connection as more easily severable than it actually is. Even traditional Christian teachings, for example, aren't Platonic accounts that suggest the soul is destined to be freed from its body; rather, teachings about bodily resurrection make it clear that personal identity in some ultimate sense is inextricably linked not just to a soulless body, but to some version of our corporeal self.

16. William James, *The Principles of Psychology* (New York: Dover, 1918), 1:4.

17. "Veiled Lodger," 1057.

18. "Blue Carbuncle," 238.

19. "Engineer's Thumb," 255.

20. *Study in Scarlet*, 16.

21. "Resident Patient," 403.

22. "Greek Interpreter," 416.

23. "Boscombe Valley Mystery," 192.

24. *Study in Scarlet*, 68.

25. "Empty House," 457.

26. "Final Problem," 447.

27. *Sign of Four*, 123.

28. "Boscombe Valley Mystery," 199.

29. Sir Arthur Conan Doyle, *A Life in Letters*, ed. Jon Lellenberg, Daniel Stashower, and Charles Foley (New York: Penguin, 2007), 268–69.

30. Christopher Morley, preface to Arthur Conan Doyle, *Complete Works of Sherlock Holmes* (New York: Barnes & Noble Books, 1992), 8.

Acknowledgments

We would like to say a few words of thanks to the many people who helped bring this project to the light of day.

Many thanks to Anne Dean Watkins, Bailey Johnson, Amy Harris, Karen Hellekson, Ila McEntire, and Steve Wrinn at the University Press of Kentucky for all your help. Thanks also to Mark Conard, the series editor, for having faith in the project. Our thanks to Georgia Glover at David Higham Associates, for arranging permission to reprint Dorothy Sayers's essay "Aristotle on Detective Fiction." Thanks to Allie Osterloh, artist extraordinaire, for providing some strategic help with the cover design. And special thanks are due to the excellent contributors, without whom this book would literally not exist.

I (Phil) would like to thank my patient wife, who let me hide away on a large number of Saturdays, when I should have been helping with the kids, to work on this book. She is a true partner and a lovely woman—John Watson and Irene Adler rolled into one. And I would especially like to thank my coeditor, David Baggett, for his support and assistance in editing this book. Without him, this work would have never seen print, much like Holmes's unchronicled encounter with the giant rat of Sumatra.

Contributors

David Baggett is professor of philosophy at Liberty University in Lynchburg, Virginia. His most recent book is *Good God: The Theistic Foundations of Morality* (2011), with Jerry L. Walls. He has seen too much not to know that the impression of a woman may be more valuable than the conclusion of an analytical reasoner.

Gregory Bassham teaches at King's College (Pennsylvania), where he specializes in philosophy of law and critical thinking. He wrote *Original Intent and the Constitution: A Philosophical Study* (1992), coauthored *Critical Thinking: A Student's Introduction* (4th ed., 2010), and has edited or coedited several volumes on pop culture and philosophy, including *"The Lord of the Rings" and Philosophy* (2003), *The Ultimate Harry Potter and Philosophy* (2010), and *"The Hobbit" and Philosophy* (forthcoming). Greg thinks it's highly significant that his cat has never barked in the night.

Carrie-Ann Biondi is associate professor of philosophy at Marymount Manhattan College in New York. She has published articles on Aristotle's moral and political philosophy, contemporary political philosophy, and philosophy of education. Students often remark on her uncanny ability to know who is approaching her office simply by the sound of their footsteps.

Kyle Blanchette holds a master's degree in theology from Asbury Theological Seminary. He is currently pursuing a master's degree in philosophy at Western Michigan University, leaving conspicuous traces on his path toward doctoral work in philosophy.

Bridget McKenney Costello is an assistant professor of sociology at King's College in Wilkes Barre, Pennsylvania. Her work examines the strategic exercise of alternative scientific beliefs (astrology, folk medicine) among socially marginalized groups, a line of inquiry guaranteed to keep her brain attic marvelously cluttered.

Elizabeth Glass-Turner is a freelance writer with a diverse collection of published articles, interviews, and essays covering topics ranging from drug cartel violence in Juárez, Mexico, to *Narnia* producer Douglas Gresham; aging and dementia; and Liberian president Ellen Johnson Sirleaf. Though her nickname from college is Bitty, she prefers to go by "the woman."

Kevin Kinghorn is associate professor of philosophy of religion at Asbury Theological Seminary in Wilmore, Kentucky. He has published in the fields of ethical theory, religious philosophy, and philosophy of mind. He has also written on evidential reasoning, though his own powers of deduction are not exactly Holmesian, given that Holmes didn't have daily battles to locate his keys.

Michel Le Gall, former associate professor of Middle Eastern and Islamic history at St. Olaf College, is a senior speechwriter at a large New York–based global consultancy. His interest in Holmes was sparked at the age of eleven when he first read *The Hound of the Baskervilles* and roamed Montreal's Mount Royal Park armed with a toy revolver, in pursuit of an imaginary Stapleton. At the top of his bucket list is bog hopping in the great Grimpen mire of Dartmoor.

D. Q. McInerny is a professor at Our Lady of Guadalupe Seminary, where he teaches philosophy. He is the author of *Being Logical: A Guide to Good Thinking, A Course in Thomistic Ethics,* and *Philosophical Psychology.* Like Sherlock Holmes, he does not have an e-mail address.

Massimo Pigliucci is professor of philosophy at the Graduate Center of the City University of New York. His most recent book is *Nonsense on Stilts: How to Tell Science from Bunk*, and he is currently working on a book on what science and philosophy can tell us about the meaning of life. He has religiously read all the Sherlock Holmes stories, in chronological order of appearance.

David Rozema is professor of philosophy at the University of Nebraska at Kearney. He is coauthor of *Platonic Errors, or, Plato, a Kind of Poet* (1998), and has published numerous articles on the works of Plato, C. S. Lewis, Ludwig Wittgenstein, Søren Kierkegaard, Joseph Conrad, and Alexander Solzhenitsyn. He is currently ascertaining all the facts necessary for formulating a theory about why it is a fundamental mistake to theorize before one has ascertained all the facts.

Dorothy L. Sayers (1893–1957) was a playwright and novelist, most famous for her Lord Peter Wimsey mysteries, including *Strong Poison, Gaudy Night,* and *The Five Red Herrings.*

Charles Taliaferro is professor of philosophy at St. Olaf College and the author or editor of fifteen books, including *The Image in Mind,* coauthored with Jil Evans. When Charles was a teenager, he thought it was normal to smoke a pipe and wear a cape and deerstalker hat. At fifty-something, he has resumed this practice and has taken up the violin.

Philip Tallon teaches at Asbury Theological Seminary in Wilmore, Kentucky. He has published widely on philosophy and popular culture, including essays in *Star Trek and Philosophy, Superheroes and Philosophy, Hitchcock and Philosophy,* and *The Philosophy of Horror.* His first monograph, *The Poetics of Evil,* was published in 2011. His next monograph will be on the distinction between the ashes of various tobaccos.

Andrew Terjesen received his Ph.D. in philosophy from Duke University and is currently pursuing a J.D. at the University of Virginia School of Law. He has been a visiting assistant professor of philosophy at Rhodes College, Washington and Lee University, and Austin College. His interests in ethics and the law and love of popular culture have led him to write several essays for volumes like this one, including *Supervillains and Philosophy, "The Onion" and Philosophy,* and *Serial Killers and Philosophy.* He's always thought "The Great Hiatus" would make a good name for a band.

INDEX

The Philosophy of Popular Culture

The books published in the Philosophy of Popular Culture series will illuminate and explore philosophical themes and ideas that occur in popular culture. The goal of this series is to demonstrate how philosophical inquiry has been reinvigorated by increased scholarly interest in the intersection of popular culturc and philosophy, as well as to explore through philosophical analysis beloved modes of entertainment, such as movies, TV shows, and music. Philosophical concepts will be made accessible to the general reader through examples in popular culture. This series seeks to publish both established and emerging scholars who will engage a major area of popular culture for philosophical interpretation and examine the philosophical underpinnings of its themes. Eschewing ephemeral trends of philosophical and cultural theory, authors will establish and elaborate on connections between traditional philosophical ideas from important thinkers and the ever-expanding world of popular culture.

Series Editor
Mark T. Conard, Marymount Manhattan College, NY

Books in the Series
The Philosophy of Stanley Kubrick, edited by Jerold J. Abrams
Football and Philosophy, edited by Michael W. Austin
Tennis and Philosophy, edited by David Baggett
The Philosophy of Film Noir, edited by Mark T. Conard
The Philosophy of Martin Scorsese, edited by Mark T. Conard
The Philosophy of Neo-Noir, edited by Mark T. Conard
The Philosophy of Spike Lee, edited by Mark T. Conard
The Philosophy of the Coen Brothers, edited by Mark T. Conard
The Philosophy of David Lynch, edited by William J. Devlin and Shai Biderman
The Philosophy of the Beats, edited by Sharin N. Elkholy
The Philosophy of Horror, edited by Thomas Fahy
The Philosophy of The X-Files, edited by Dean A. Kowalski
Steven Spielberg and Philosophy, edited by Dean A. Kowalski
The Philosophy of Joss Whedon, edited by Dean A. Kowalski and S. Evan Kreider
The Philosophy of Charlie Kaufman, edited by David LaRocca
The Philosophy of the Western, edited by Jennifer L. McMahon and B. Steve Csaki
The Philosopy of Steven Soderbergh, edited by R. Barton Palmer and Steven M. Sanders

The Olympics and Philosophy, edited by Heather L. Reid and Michael W. Austin
The Philosophy of David Cronenberg, edited by Simon Riches
The Philosophy of Science Fiction Film, edited by Steven M. Sanders
The Philosophy of TV Noir, edited by Steven M. Sanders and Aeon J. Skoble
Basketball and Philosophy, edited by Jerry L. Walls and Gregory Bassham
Golf and Philosophy, edited by Andy Wible

www.ingramcontent.com/pod-product-compliance
Lightning Source LLC
Chambersburg PA
CBHW030811310726
48980CB00006B/463/J

* 9 7 8 0 8 1 3 1 3 6 7 1 4 *